The Remnant

Laura Liddell Nolen grew up in Hattiesburg, Mississippi. She has a degree in French and a license to practice law, but both are frozen in carbonite at present. She lives in Texas with her husband and two young children. The Ark was made possible in part by a SCBWI Work-In-Progress Award. Laura can be found on Twitter @ LauraLLNolen.

Also by Laura Liddell Nolen

The Ark Trilogy
The Ark

The Remnant

LAURA LIDDELL NOLEN

Book Two of The Ark Trilogy

HARPER
Voyager

Harper*Voyager*
an imprint of HarperCollins*Publishers Ltd*
1 London Bridge Street
London SE1 9GF

ISBN: 9780008181475

This novel is entirely a work of fiction.
The names, characters and incidents portrayed in it are
the work of the author's imagination. Any resemblance to
actual persons, living or dead, events or localities is
entirely coincidental.

Typeset in Sabon by Palimpsest Book Production Limited,
Falkirk, Stirlingshire

Automatically produced by Atomik ePublisher from Easypress

Printed and bound in Great Britain

For Ava and Liam

I must walk without the sun, darkness must cover the path of my feet.

—*The Pilgrim's Progress*

One

They came for me at dawn, and all I could think was, *it is way too early for this.*

And actually, it might have been. Adam's programming tended to be erratic at the best of times, and downright scary at the worst. Looking back, I guess we should have been grateful. Surely any dawn at all, however cruel, is better than the endless night of space.

Hindsight, and all that.

"Charlotte Turner." The judge glanced at me over the top of her delicate, silver-rimmed glasses. The crowd quieted down, just for a moment, in spite of itself, but when rough hands shoved me up onto the platform, giving the Remnant its first good look at me, the shouting cranked right back up again. *Death to the traitor!* and *She's a terrorist! Worse than the Commander!* echoed through my mind. I stopped trying to make sense of the words, letting them roll over me like pebbles on a riverbed, until I heard one I couldn't ignore: *Throw her out the airlock.*

Something like fear, or horror, made me tilt up my chin and square my shoulders. My tongue was nearly numb, so I turned up the corners of my mouth to keep from crying.

"I'm glad to see that we amuse you, Prisoner." Her voice was warm and sure, like a kindly librarian, and sounded older than her face appeared. "You got any last words before we vote?"

"Vote?" I twisted around to look at her. Gray hair. Wrong side of forty, especially up here. Slightly heavy in her chair, but thin to the point of frailty around the shoulders. Nothing about her qualified her for a spot on the Ark. But then, this was the Remnant: the Earth's last rebels. So she fit right in.

She returned the favor, sizing me up before responding. "On your sentence." She raised her eyebrows, anticipating my reaction. "Life or death."

From my new vantage point, I could see the upturned faces of the crowd, and I scanned them as fast as I could, a growing sense of desperation gnawing at my lungs.

No Isaiah, which stung. No Adam, thank goodness. There was the gardener, a withered old man who'd taught me how to grow potatoes, and maybe a couple hundred strangers, including a large group of feral-looking children whose faces I searched more thoroughly.

No West.

The thought of his face, his wide brown eyes, flared through my mind, and I felt a weird sense of disconnect, like trying to laugh and gasping for air all at once. It had been years since I'd seen my brother, and I was so close. I searched and searched, but the room grew smaller as my panic expanded, and I ran out of places to look before I found him.

I pressed my lips together. In my experience, these things tended to go a lot better if you dropped the act and showed a little vulnerability, but again, there was my brother's face in my mind, so my ribs were like steel around my lungs.

The crowd shouted louder, and the sounds merged together in my mind, until all I heard was a single accusatory voice. I tried to imagine what that voice would sound like when it sentenced me to die.

I didn't have to wonder long.

"Nothing at all?" The judge regarded me dispassionately. "Then I'm afraid it's time for the sentence."

"Your Honor, I never meant to betray the Remnant."

"She speaks," said the judge, and the other voice quieted to a low buzz. "Is it your position that your actions on the day of the Battle for Sector Seven were undertaken with the interest of the Remnant at heart?"

"I—no. But I wasn't trying to hurt anyone. I only wanted to save my family. I'd just started to belong here, and my family, my blood family, was still living in Central Command. When I found out what the Noah Board was capable of I—"

"Was? Where are they now?"

It was a good question. "I'm not sure, Your Honor. My brother joined the Remnant, but I haven't seen him since…" my voice caught, and I stopped talking for the space of several heartbeats. When I spoke, it was in a low, even tone, my face carefully composed. "I haven't been out of my cell for six weeks. And my father is… somewhere in Central Command, I think."

"And your mother?"

My throat tightened again, and my volume was reduced further. "She died. On Earth."

It was a common story, but her voice softened. "Charlotte Turner. You placed every life in our sector in peril when you betrayed us to the High Commander. You've been found guilty of high treason."

"Wait. Please."

"Please what, Prisoner?"

"Please don't... throw me out the airlock."

"I've been a judge for over a decade. In that time I have never found any particular pleasure in ruining the lives of the young people who come before me. But in your case, Miss Turner, I fail to see what you gained from ruining *us* so thoroughly." She shook her head. "In any event, that's not how we'd execute someone, surely. Airlocks. Honestly."

"I did bring you the Noah Board," I said, hopefully.

"You brought us a strike team straight from the Commander himself," she said, referring to Eren's failed mission to retrieve the program I'd stolen. I had the sense not to point out that Isaiah, the blind King of the Remnant, hadn't given me much of a choice about whether to steal it, or that Eren's father, the High Commander, had known about the theft way before I confessed. "If I were a different kind of judge, and this were a different kind of courtroom, this is the moment where I'd tell you that you're young."

She paused, seeing my expression.

"You are. And if things were only a little different, I would remind you that there is still time for you to consider what kind of girl you want to be. What kind of woman."

Back on Earth, I'd gotten the same speech at more than one sentencing, albeit for lesser crimes than treason. It was the juvy defendant's cue to appear remorseful. At least, in my case it was. I had no idea what kind of speech they gave the kids whose parents weren't doctors and senators.

But the judge was right. Things were different now. Besides, I already knew what kind of girl I was. It was hardly the first time the issue had come up.

"Unfortunately, things work a little differently up here.

Look around, Turner. These are the lives you tried to destroy."

I saw no softness in the faces of those gathered. I read the judgment in their eyes. I was as much to blame as the five governments who'd left them to die when the meteor destroyed the Earth. If the Commander had won the Battle for Sector Seven, what would he have done with them? With their children? Only Isaiah, their so-called King, had saved them, and he wasn't here to speak for me.

"Citizens of the Remnant. Survivors of the Earth. How do you find the defendant?"

The voice of the Remnant grew terrible and loud, so loud that my ears could no longer bear the pain. But the judge maintained her stature, allowing the noise to swell through the room and settle deep in my brain before she spoke.

"Charlotte Turner. You knowingly betrayed your people to our enemy and actively sought to effect the downfall of the Remnant. You have been found guilty of treason and are hereby sentenced to death."

Two

I'm sitting in the kitchen, watching my mom ice a cake. Her knife slides up and down the straight edges, creating a series of perfectly even waves of blue frosting. Her other hand is spinning the base of the stand with surgical precision.

It's mesmerizing.

West thinks so, too, and joins me at the counter. I'm mad at him for some reason or another, but I'm thirteen now, and turning over a new leaf, so I choose to ignore him. Even though he shouldn't be here.

The cake is for him, for his birthday, and it's a complete violation of family rules for him to see it before we light the candles, but apparently I'm the only one who cares about tradition around here.

Mom offers him a little smile, just enough to show the first hints of recently formed wrinkles at the corners of her eyes, and he returns it in full force, his stupid teeth gapping in my face.

West loves birthdays. I guess all nine-year-olds do.

"Can I lick the spoon?" he asks.

Mom purses out her bottom lip, pretending to consider

the request for maybe half a millisecond, and hands over the entire bowl of sugary, leftover goo.

I am given the knife.

My icing is gone in two licks, one for each side of the blade, and I shouldn't care that West's far more enthusiastic efforts have barely made a dent in his supply.

New leaf. I'll focus on my mom instead. She's arranging the piping tip over a plastic sandwich bag full of red frosting, and her face takes on a calm, easy focus as she pipes a series of perfect tiny stars around the top.

It's going to be a beautiful cake.

"Want some of mine?" West asks.

I turn, mimicking my mom's lower lip-pursing, and pretend not to care. "Sure, if you're not going to eat it all." I shrug a little, making the point. "Whatever."

"Open up," he says, and I can't help but match his goofy grin. He shoves an enormous glob directly in my mouth, and I bite down. It's more icing than I can hold at once, and I'm starting to giggle in spite of my newfound maturity.

"You're getting it everywhere," I say, or try to say, and reach for a dishcloth.

West only laughs.

I'm scrubbing away a tiny speck of blue from the countertop when a thick splat hits the side of my neck. I swat at it in confusion, and my fingers come away covered in icing.

I'm glaring up at West, about to make sure Mom saw what happened, when I realize that he's as shocked as I am. We turn to Mom, who's suppressing a snort.

I'm still trying to wrap my mind around the idea of my mom voluntarily creating a mess of any kind when West fires back.

The glob catches half on her cheek and half in her hair, just below the ear.

She gives a little snicker. "You're asking for it, buddy."

Suddenly, West is covered in a thin stream of sticky red buttercream, straight from the piping tip. It's simultaneously the strangest and the funniest thing I've ever seen. Without thinking, I reach into his bowl and launch the contents at my mother, who spares maybe one second to glance at her ruined blouse before reaching for the flour.

"Get down!" I shout, and we duck behind the bar together. The flour whispers by overhead, dusting us in a silent arc that ends on the floor far behind us, inches from the living room rug.

She has missed! We nearly choke with giddy laughter.

"We're outta ammo," I say, as soon as we catch our breath, and West nods seriously. "She's got total access to the fridge, everything."

"But we have the pantry," he says.

"You sure about that?" our mother taunts us.

"Cover me," I say, and roll toward the pantry.

I'm too slow. A blast of water catches me square in the back, and I'm completely soaked before I reach the door. I grab the first thing I can find, Cheerios, and rip open the bag in a frenzy. I toss it back to West, reserving a few handfuls for myself, and we begin pelting her in unison.

Some of the water has caught the cake, and for a moment, I regret everything. It was such a beautiful cake.

But then West goes flying over the top of the counter and jumps to land on the island, next to the cake.

"West, no!" I scream, but it's too late. He shoves a fist way down into the delicate icing and lobs his sugary grenade

8

straight at Mom. I follow him, grabbing for the flour at the same time as her.

The bag rips open, and the kitchen explodes into a feathery cloud of white.

Thin wisps of flour rain down onto the brawl beneath for several seconds. We are all grabbing at the cake, gasping with laughter.

Our mother is strong. Stronger than I expected, and I feel my face being shoved into the fractured remains of the lowest layer of cake. I'm powerless to stop it. My defeat is complete.

West is next. He emerges from the forced faceplant covered in cake and wonder.

She has won, she has won. There can be no question. We dissolve into helpless laughter, and the pain of the year lessens its vice around my heart, and the horror of my first stint in juvy shrinks and retreats into the darkest corner of my thoughts. For the moment, it is harmless. I breathe, finally. I smile even though I'm not laughing anymore. The sensation feels foreign.

My arm is around my brother for the first time in far too long. My mother is holding us both. I find that my skinny legs can still fold in far enough so that I fit entirely on her lap, and I am warm. West and I regard each other from twin positions under her chin.

No one speaks for a while, but my mother finally breaks the silence. "Things have been too tense around here lately. We had a rough year. I know that. But you'll never stop being each other's family. You can't ever stop loving each other." And she is squeezing us both, gently at first, and then more and more tightly, until it is too much, too tight, and I have to hold my breath, and still I do not try to stop her.

Three

The thing about war is that everyone knows where you stand. Lines are drawn; everybody picks a side, and boom. You're fighting.

Except that for me, things were more confusing than ever. That morning, the morning of my sentencing, the four walls of my cell pressed in harder than usual. I was a prisoner of the Remnant, but only because I'd traded my freedom for Eren's by turning myself over to the Commander, with the bright idea that he then hand me over to the Remnant to get his son back.

In my defense, it seemed like a good idea at the time. I'd needed to get back into the Remnant so I could find my brother, West, like I promised my father. Of course, I spent the next six weeks locked in a cell, and now, I was probably about to be executed. So my mission wasn't exactly a rousing success so far.

On the other hand, it's not like I had anywhere better to be. Because of my illegal status on the ship and my ties to the Remnant, I was a fugitive from Central Command. And although I'd saved his son in the hostage exchange, I was pretty sure the High Commander still wanted me dead in all possible haste.

I couldn't judge him for that. The feeling was mutual.

The silver lining was obvious: he'd have a heck of a time trying to kill me in here, and I doubted the Remnant would give him the satisfaction anyway. The Remnant controlled its sliver of a sector with an iron fist, guarding the dark space that separated Sector Seven from Central Command as though their lives depended on it.

Which was absolutely the case.

I made myself focus on the slow, even breathing of Helen, my cellmate, until the time passed more easily.

Helen was a lifer, and over the course of several decades, prison had made her in its image. Convicted of one thing after another back on Earth, she'd had the criminal connections to find her way to the Remnant without the difficulty the rest of us had suffered. You'd think illicit organizations dedicated to saving the dregs of Earth would have higher standards, but no. The Remnant left the sorting of humanity to Central Command, which had dedicated itself to the task with an admirable fervor, which is how Command ended up with all the young, straight-and-narrow scientists and doctors.

By contrast, if you were alive, the Remnant believed you should have a shot at survival. All you had to do was find them.

Which is how the Remnant ended up with all the criminals.

Suffice it to say, no one around cared how Helen had gotten here, let alone whether she'd done hard time. The Remnant were way past that line of thinking. They'd been willing to overlook every mistake she ever made in her life, right up until they found out that she was fencing meds from the sickbay. I suppose everyone has to draw the line somewhere.

11

The dawn broke bright and cold, as though Adam, Isaiah's pet computer prodigy, had designed it just for this occasion. I shook out my arms, imagining a thin film of dew clinging to the sheets. At least, I thought I'd imagined it. Erratic or not, these climate programs were getting more advanced every day.

The thought was not comforting.

I fiddled absently with my hair before tying it into a knot just above my neck. There's only so much a girl can do without a hairbrush.

"So today's the big day, huh? You want me to work on it?" Helen's voice was sharp and clear, and in the short weeks I'd known her, that had been the case at all hours of the day and night. I struggled out of sleep, and into it. But Helen was like a light that switched on and off as needed. I envied her that.

"No, it's fine. No one cares what it looks like, anyway."

The door to my cell opened, and I stood. What else could I do? The guards' hands were rough, and I understood, then, that I was their enemy. I was naïve enough to feel a new kind of pain, something akin to betrayal, like this moment was the death of the strangeness in my heart that had, until now, kept me from rushing the nearest guard and turning his gun on myself.

Instead, I let him force me into the wall.

Helen let out a string of pain and bitterness disguised as profanity and rage, and I was reminded of another woman, just as hard, who'd had enough hurt for ten lifetimes and hadn't let it break her. But I tried never to think too long about Meghan.

"I'm fine, Helen. Wish me luck." I tugged at my yellow prison scrubs, trying to make them lie straight, before finally feeling the cuffs lock into place.

Helen's voice faded into the stark corridor as the cell door slammed shut behind me. "Girls like us make our own luck, sweetheart."

The guards didn't speak. Their silence throttled the intervals between clanging locks and scuffing boots.

Guns. They were everywhere. I figured my old friend Isaiah had distributed them to every guard in the Remnant. I wished I could feel sick over it, the end of all our hopes for peace, but instead, I felt relieved. Central Command would be fully armed by now, too. There was too much at stake for the Remnant to retain its innocence.

So maybe I was hard like Helen. There was a time I'd wanted to be like Meghan, a woman who'd saved my life back on Earth. She was strong, in her way, because she was able to love a stranger, to die for one, but I didn't think I could be like her anymore.

Rough hands made dents in my upper arms. I let them. *You betrayed us,* they seemed to say. I was guided around a corner so hard my feet left the ground. The pain felt right. *We took you in. You didn't have to become one of us, but you were.*

One of us.

The guards halted their even pace abruptly before the door to the Commons, a room where once I'd danced a long tango on the arm of a king. I tripped, righted myself unsteadily, and offered a glare to the guard on my right. He returned it without flinching.

You betrayed us.

The massive doors swung open, instead of sucking into the wall, and the effect was a pale flash of nerves, which I silenced without much effort. The time for fear had long passed.

They were right, after all. I had been one of them. I had betrayed them. I looked all around, craning my head over the shoulders of the men who forced me forward into the cold, crowded Commons, but Isaiah wasn't there. To be fair, a king would have better places to be than his ex-almost-girlfriend's latest trial, but it still stung.

That was when I realized that I was his enemy, too.

The last time we spoke had ended badly, to say the least. He'd forced me to steal something from Central Command— the life support program for the entire ship, called the Noah Board—and I'd taken it pretty hard. I didn't want to be a thief anymore.

I didn't want to be a prisoner anymore, either, but here we were.

The Commons was my favorite thing about the Remnant, other than the greenhouse. It was their gathering-place, where huge crowds gave full vent to their fears and frustrations, and life to their memories of Earth. But it was more than that. This was where they *lived*, and spoke, and created and danced and thought together.

It was the beating heart of everything we might have lost when the Earth died.

Right now, it was a courtroom.

I heard only silence in the moments that followed the death sentence. I was not a leader, like Isaiah. Even if I were, I no longer had a people to belong to. No one's fate aligned with mine. I wasn't a soldier, like Eren, nor a budding scientist, like my brother. I would never be a decision-maker, like my father.

My fate was sealed: I would simply cease to be anything. Maybe that was how it should be. A lifetime of prison, endless and white, made me think of drowning. Couldn't these people see that I was dying either way? Hadn't they known that I had loved them? A cold certainty swept through me.

The Remnant knew exactly what kind of girl I was.

A pair of enormous hazel eyes peered up at me, and I froze, found out. This kid was maybe seven or eight years old. Too young to understand so much, to know me at a glance. Too young for anything.

A moment passed before I recognized her: Amiel. Adam's sister.

She was dirty. Not with actual dirt, as she might have been on Earth. But unwashed. Greasy.

Unwanted.

There was nothing surprising about any of that. I read her life in her eyes, and it was a familiar story. Children were abandoned back on Earth every day. In juvy, I had lived among them. By far, the majority of us had mothers at home who traded sleep for endless worry, then worry for resignation, and, at last, for some, resignation for rejection. But there were those the world had failed so completely that they did not cry at night, even on their first night. Why would they? No one cried for them. What home could they mourn, they who belonged to no one? I knew them, to the extent that anybody could know them, and I knew what it did to their souls. To their eyes.

No, it wasn't shocking.

And yet, my breath caught in my throat.

The guard nearest me reached for my arm, but he was distracted by the spectacle. It was all too much: the Remnant's mortal enemy, sentenced to die before those she'd betrayed. He was as entranced as the rest of the crowd. I couldn't blame him.

I disarmed him easily, flipping the small weight of his gun directly from his holster and into my fist.

I reached the podium in the next instant, before the shock extinguished from his face. The judge's shoulders were frail underneath her black robe, in spite of the thickness of her lower body, and they bent backwards with my weight. The gun—*my* gun, now—was cold against her neck, and she tried to shrug it away with her shoulder even as her hands splayed before her. Instinct told me to shelter myself behind the wooden platform, but I ignored it and forced her body to cover me instead.

I was not a healer, like my mother.

"Everyone stay back." I locked eyes with the now-unarmed guard and nodded toward the door behind us. "You, open this door. No one else move." I wrenched the judge from the platform, and she made a little sound when we hit the floor behind it, like she was afraid.

She didn't speak at all. I did not think of Amiel, whose eyes followed my every move, or even of West. I closed my mind to the coldness that stabbed through my heart. I'd never wanted to hurt anyone. I was trapped. I needed out, and this was the only plan I could think of. The judge stumbled, and I pulled her up, helping her to balance before pressing her through the door and into the hallway. I knew exactly what kind of girl I was.

I was a criminal.

Four

There was only one place I could go: the dark, unplanned space that separated the sectors of the Ark at the outermost level, which people had started calling the Rift. Its construction had been unexpected and was thought to be the result of a misplaced wall, so the Rift wasn't on the official maps.

The Rift was technically controlled by the Remnant, but I was fresh out of other options, what with the kidnapping and hostage-taking and all. When we reached the entrance, I shoved the judge into the darkness as gently as possible, then threw myself in after, never losing my grip on her arm.

"Just go straight," I muttered after her. "Fast as you can."

She complied, haltingly at first, then with increasing steadiness. I had to be impressed. Not everyone could move that fast in pitch-black, although the gun may have had something to do with it. We'd gone maybe a hundred paces before she started talking. "Look, you've got your whole life ahead of you."

A door opened somewhere behind us, and I gave her a frank look in the brief splash of pale light from the hallway. "Do I?"

She pursed her lips. We kept moving.

The sound of footsteps along the path urged me forward. It felt like ages before we got to the end of the Rift, where the entrance to the cargo hold was located, but the twisted knot in my stomach made me pause before forcing open the door.

"You decide people's fates. Have you ever had to accept one?"

She gave me an appraising glance and tightened her mouth even further. "You could leave me here. I'm only going to slow you down."

It was tempting. I would never shoot her, after all, and sooner or later, someone was bound to call my bluff.

But the sounds of the guards shuffling through the Rift made me tighten my grip on the gun. "I'm afraid not. Let's go."

She looked from my face to the pistol, and I realized that I'd been careful not to point the barrel at her ever since we'd gotten out of sight of the guards. Not even when I waved her through the doorway. Judging by her expression, Judge Hawthorne had already figured me out. She knew I wasn't going to hurt her if I could possibly help it.

On the other hand, I wasn't too fired up about being executed, either. It was like we were caught in an impromptu game of charades. I made a mental note not to take another hostage again, ever.

But I did have a gun, and a hostage, and a death sentence, courtesy of my hostage, so my options were limited. Charades it was. I made my face stern and forced her through the door. "Chop chop, Your Honor."

She maintained an admirable inscrutability even as the door latched, locking us out of the darkness of the Rift.

* * *

After six weeks in my cell, the vastness of the cargo hold was overwhelming, and I gaped up at the bins that held North America's final exports: the physical remains of the civilizations we had created, then left behind to be swept away by the meteor.

High ceilings, endless rows of brightly colored bins, and an excess of gravity added to the effect. At the other end of the hold, maybe a thousand yards away, was the stairwell that led up to the main decks of Central Command.

When I cleared my mind, the first thing I noticed was that the locks on the bins had changed. The new ones looked a lot more techy and far less blastable than they used to. My plan—the only one that made any sense at all—was to try to break into a bin. Hopefully, one that had some food. From there, I could regroup and try to think through my priorities, maybe figure out a plan that didn't involve going back to prison and my certain death at the hands of either government.

Priorities. *West.* Six final weeks in the Remnant, and I was no closer to keeping my promise to my father that we would be a family again. The thought made my feet heavy, but I kept our pace as near a sprint as I could manage, hoping we'd eventually pass a lock I had a shot at cracking.

The second thing I noticed was the lack of guards. That made no sense. Here were the physical remains of North America. Untold treasure lay behind the thin walls of the bins, not to mention supplies. More importantly, Central Command knew the location of the entrance to the Remnant's dark space, so it only made sense that they'd want to guard it. But I was alone among the aisles. Blue faded into red, then yellow, and back again, with no sign of Command personnel. At some point, the locks changed abruptly. I stopped, skidded back a couple of bins, and took another look. Judge Hawthorne made a face, as though my change of pace inconvenienced her.

"Well?" she said impatiently.

How was she not out of breath? I was fairly gasping. "Hang on. I'm trying to plan."

"It doesn't strike me as your strong suit."

It was official: I didn't care much for Judge Hawthorne. "Oh, I don't know, Your Honor. I'd say I'm doing better now than I was twenty minutes ago. Now move."

From where we stood, maybe a fifth of the way into the area, it appeared that the hold was divided into two kinds of locks. It's the kind of thing you might not notice if you weren't trying to break into something, but everything near the Remnant was one kind of tech, and this part of the hold had a wave of older-looking locks.

"What's going on here?" I waved an arm back toward the new locks.

"Lockies," she said. "Command sends out a team every day. So do we. The cargo hold is demilitarized as part of the ceasefire agreement between Central Command and the Remnant, but they still try to keep us out of as many bins as possible. We do the same."

"By... what, changing the locks?"

She nodded. "They're children, mostly. The governments make the locks, of course."

That meant that I had a significantly reduced set of options. I couldn't possibly get past the newer mechanisms from either government. Older locks it was.

By some miracle, we'd stayed a few aisles ahead of the advancing guards, who made no attempt at staying quiet.

Why would they? The hold was huge, but the aisles were straight. It wouldn't take long to clear them. Our lead was draining gradually away, like sand.

We waited in silence for the row of soldiers to pass the aisle with the door, then slipped around the corner and doubled back. Judge Hawthorne made a fair companion. She kept quiet and moved fast in spite of her age.

I fumbled the return to the door, hitting the aisle slightly too soon. But the pair of guards I'd been avoiding didn't look back once they'd cleared the space, and I was granted a few short seconds with the lock.

There was no possible way to break it.

I had a gun, but its bullets only penetrated flesh, not the components of the bins, as I'd learned too well during a previous excursion to the area.

Good thing I had a Guardian Level access card. Being a criminal had its benefits on occasion, not least of which was that I had yet to miss an opportunity to pick the pockets of whichever guardian was escorting me at the time, assuming they were slow enough to let me. Normally, Jorin Malkin, the Commander's lieutenant, would be out of my talent range, but someone had knocked him unconscious during the prisoner exchange, and I'm not the kind of girl who lets an advantage like that go to waste. Besides, I liked to think it caused him at least a little inconvenience when he noticed it was missing.

If the Commander were smart, the card would be monitored instead of deactivated. I yanked the front of my shirt out and slid the card from the band of my undergarments. The judge gave me a dirty look, which I ignored. The lock popped open on the first swipe, and I threw open the door, marked "North America/Sector 7/Cargo Level/Bin 23/Generators." We were greeted by metal boxes stacked floor-to-ceiling, with only a few inches between stacks. We didn't fit.

I grunted in frustration, pressing Hawthorne down the aisle to the next bin. The heavy footsteps halted, then resumed at a fast pace, looming closer. They'd heard me.

The judge chewed the side of her face, looking nearly as nervous as I felt. It hit me that the sound of boots was as clear as glass, and I turned around.

They'd found me.

Four men at my six, with ten yards to spare. My heart thumped almost hard enough to make my hands shake with the mere force of its pressure, but I had years of practice with adrenaline like this. Experience won out, and my first swipe was good. The flimsy door sucked open. I swung Judge Hawthorne through by the arm and slammed my fist into the doorpad, then the keypad, in a single, frantic motion. There was a heavy *wham* as the lead guard hit the door an instant too late.

I touched the lightpad and tried to take stock of the bin, but my nerves were getting to me. I couldn't afford to keep breathing so hard. It showed weakness, and I had to stay in control.

Breathe, Char, Breathe. Just not so hard.

This bin was a sight better than the last and might even prove useful. Smaller crates lined a series of built-ins, and irregular wooden boxes were strewn around the floor. I wasn't beaten yet.

I turned to the judge, who was cradling her arm pointedly, an accusatory look on her face. From what I knew of her, she had nerves like boiled leather, and a brain to boot. If she were twenty years younger, I'd have had a problem on my hands. "Hide in the back," I told her.

"Oh, hiding? In the back?" she said. "What an impressive plan."

I smiled in spite of myself. Maybe I liked her a little.

"You can't shoot them all," she said, clambering past the crates.

"I'm not going to shoot any of them," I muttered back. "And keep your voice down."

"It's over, honey. They're just gathering the rest of the troops."

"This card is monitored. Central Command will send a team now, too."

"So you are one of them."

I looked at her. The suggestion was absurd, but I couldn't prove it now. It was probably better to bluff, anyway. So I raised an eyebrow and motioned for her to get down behind a crate. I didn't know if the Remnant would try to blast their way in or something. She complied, but not before shooting me a look so disapproving it could churn butter.

The lock on the door clicked softly a few times, but the door didn't open, a process I found unnerving. Why didn't they try to break the lock? Or the door?

It didn't even matter. It wasn't like I could go anywhere.

"Okay, we got her," the guard in the aisle said finally. "Call it in." Then he raised his voice to a shout, so that it was unmistakable through the thin tin and plastic walls of the bin. "Hope you're comfortable in there. Might be a while."

A while until what?

"I got nothing but time," I shouted back. I thought I heard a snicker, but the door stayed shut, and Hawthorne stayed mercifully quiet, having made her mind up about me before we'd even left the courtroom. I settled down in the bin to wait.

Five

Time flies when you're spending your last moments of relative freedom locked in a stuffy cargo bin with an equally stuffy elderly judge who's looking forward to your execution for high treason, but has mercifully decided to stop berating you over your questionable life choices in the meantime.

Before I knew it, there was a rustle in the aisle outside the bin, then another click on the lock.

I considered threatening to shoot the judge, but to be honest, I didn't have much of an endgame in mind, and I was a little sick of having her as a hostage anyway. Maybe I'd just threaten the next person to enter the bin and call it even.

"Don't shoot." I knew the voice before he spoke the second word. It was low and confident and laced with some emotion I couldn't place. "I'm coming in, Charlotte. I'm unarmed." Wait. Was he *smiling*?

I lowered the gun. "I'm not going to shoot you, Isaiah."

He stepped fully into the bin, taking care to hold the door ajar behind him. As was his habit these days, he didn't carry his white-tipped cane. In the Remnant, I'd assumed he simply hadn't needed it, since he'd memorized the layout of the rooms he frequented. But now, I thought there must have been some other reason to avoid it. To avoid letting me see it.

"That's a start, then." He turned to the judge, still holding the door open behind him. "You may go," he said.

She did, sparing me a final, judgy glare on her way out.

I returned it with my brightest smile, in spite of the darkness in Isaiah's tone. "I think it's a little late to talk about beginnings," I said.

He tilted his head slightly, as though considering me. "Once, you let me show you the way out. I told you then you'd only find a bigger cage."

I glanced at the upper corners of the bin. They were close enough that, if I stood on two crates, I could dust them for cobwebs. "Yeah, well, we've said a lot of things to each other, Ise. I'm never sure which ones still count."

His smile faded in the silence that followed. The last time we spoke, he begged me to return to the Remnant with him, to be protected by him, and he'd called me his enemy when I refused. To be fair, the conversation before that one hadn't gone much better. We'd been dancing around the idea of each other for a while now, but we could never nail down exactly what we both wanted. He'd once told me that he loved me. I still believed that was true.

But I had absolutely no idea what it meant.

I gestured around the bin. "At least this cage is mine. And it beats the hole you've kept me in for the last six weeks."

He unclenched his jaw and gave me something like a patient sigh. "I had to make you see reason, Charlotte. Had to get my ducks in a row, too. You're not in there anymore. You're not dead, yet. I don't have much to apologize for."

I had nothing to say to that.

He continued. "So what's next? You like it out here? You want to stay?"

"I don't have too many options."

"You don't have any options at all. You can't stay in my jail. Not after that nonsense with the judge. You'll never make it through the appeal. You don't belong with my people."

"I'll manage."

"Like you are right now? I found you in less than an hour. How long do you think it will take the Commander? How long until you starve?"

"I'll *manage*. Just because I picked the wrong—"

"Let me be more to the point." He gestured to the bin. "I have you surrounded."

"Ah. The perils of lock-picking in an enclosed space. I could write a book."

"Let's write that book, then, Charlotte. Jail. Not for you, though." He ticked the words off on long, outstretched fingers. "So you fight. You're looking at a stab wound, maybe a gunshot. The fight won't last long. Then you'll come quietly. You'll be thrown out an airlock. It's a pretty short book."

I looked away. "Where are you going with this?"

"May I sit?"

I looked at him incredulously. "By all means. Big box to your right."

He settled himself gracefully on a heavy red crate. "I've always been a believer in second chances. And it'd be a shame to let your skills go to waste."

"Let me stop you right there. I'm not going to steal for you. Not anymore, anyway. Not after last time."

"You just kidnapped a *judge*. When are you gonna quit pretending you're so much better than me?"

"Better than you? Mr. King of the Remnant?"

"I found something I believe in. I'm not going to apologize for that, either. You're just mad 'cause I'm right."

"Oh, you're really onto something there, Ise." I shrugged at him and forced my voice down a notch. I had no idea why I found his words so irritating. "How's this? I believe in not stealing anymore. Especially not for you."

"We were friends for a long time."

"Until we weren't."

"I didn't have to be your enemy, little bird. I—" There was a long pause. "But you don't hear the things I tell you. You think you know better. But this is the end. It's me or the airlock. So maybe you'll listen now.

"I said you have skills. I wasn't talking about stealing. There's more to you than that. You care about your family. I may not understand it, but I've always respected it. You want to belong somewhere. No, don't deny it. You always have. 'S'why you got in with those clowns down below," he said, referring to the group of thieves I'd run with back on Earth. "And you can be very convincing when you want to be. You keep a level head." He looked thoughtful. "I can work with that."

"Work... how? What did you have in mind?"

"My life... your life. I find I believe in more than just the people in the Remnant. I believe in the fact that we're all still here. They did their best to keep us off the Arks, but here we are. We're alive. We're fighting."

He rubbed his hands together, and it occurred to me that he was nervous. He was trying to convince me of something, and he actually cared how this turned out. Regardless of how he was acting.

"And I think that, in spite of everything that's happened, deep down, you do too. You may not see it yet, but on some level, you and I are on the same side. And none of this would matter except for one last thing: we both believe in second chances. A clean slate." He looked up from his hands. "You and me."

I couldn't even imagine what that might look like. He was right the first time: I was trapped. I couldn't exactly waltz back into the Remnant on his arm. I was their enemy. "So, that would mean…"

"I thought about this a lot. It's like, we betrayed each other. I'm not sorry that I used you. I had my reasons, but I could have gone about it differently. No one should have died." He took a breath. "You have to forgive me, Charlotte." He swallowed. "I've forgiven you."

I frowned at him. "For what?"

He took a moment before answering. "For always choosing *everything else* instead of me."

There was a slow silence between us.

My mouth hung open until I spoke, uneasily. "I'll come with you, but I'm not your friend, Isaiah." As much as I had once liked him, six weeks in his prison had given me plenty reasons to remain cautious. I shook my head. "I think you know that." I paused, so that my last words hung in the air like poison. "And I don't forgive you. For anything."

He laughed, and the bin was full of the sound. It wasn't a real laugh, and it didn't sound like Isaiah. It lacked confidence. It was too loud. "So." He clapped once and stood up. "You're in."

"It's like you said, Ise. I don't exactly have a choice."

"Good enough for me. Let's get out of here."

I crossed my arms, still standing. "Where are we going?"

He shook his head. "Still not listening, are you? Don't even pay attention at your own sentencing. The airlock, little bird. The airlock."

Six

He was gone before I stood up, and I was left alone to wonder just what he was up to this time, and why he thought I could help. Possibilities piled themselves around me with no clear answer. Breaking into Central Command, which governed the vast majority of the North American Ark, to steal another program, maybe? Luring Eren back to the Remnant's prison? My certain death in the void of space? He'd mentioned my family, but he was in for a big surprise if he thought I'd ever betray them.

I took a moment to scan the bin for anything I might be able to use. Sure, Isaiah and I were pretending to be friends again, as far as I knew. But I still had plenty of other enemies out there. Best to be prepared.

I already had a gun. Why Isaiah hadn't asked for it was beyond me, but I sure wasn't about to give it up without a fight. I ran a finger back and forth over the tape on a small plastic bin until it warmed slightly, liquidating its bond to the bin, then eased it off and used it to secure the gun to my upper thigh, making sure the safety was engaged. It wouldn't hold for long, especially if I started running, but at least I could get to it easily. I found several crates full of identical rolls of electric wire, complete with wire cutters. I unspooled it greedily and wrapped several feet around my waist, high above the band of my prison pants. I looped one of the smaller wire cutters into the center of my bra and tucked its handle into my wire-belt, then pulled my shirt down over it.

There wasn't much else worth taking. I couldn't tell most software from scrap metal, so I sure as heck couldn't make use of most of what was there, but I did find a few tiny computer chips sharp enough to pass for razors. I grabbed a few of those before leaving. I took one last look around the bin and nodded. I had weapons. Isaiah had been right: I wasn't dead or back in jail. Yet.

Things were looking up.

Isaiah, it turned out, was waiting patiently at the end of a long, double row of Remnant guards.

I had never seen a Remnant guard in livery before, but these were dressed in black, Central Command-issued uniforms. The kind that blocked bullets. I spared a moment of appreciation for Isaiah's people, who had probably gone to some trouble to procure them, while simultaneously suppressing a shudder at the memories the uniforms evoked. The result was something like an ungainly shrug.

If anything, it should have been encouraging. It meant the Remnant had conducted raids on Command supplies. It meant they hadn't given up.

"Nice outfit," I said to the first. She closed the bin door behind me without responding.

"You all right?" Isaiah asked me.

"Yep," I said slowly, eyeing his army of personal guards. "Just fine."

"Get the team out here," he said to the guard nearest him. "Have it locked. Let's go."

The guard behind me took my arm, and I jerked away. "Hands *off*."

She sighed and turned to Isaiah expectantly, giving me a clear view of the shock of bright red hair sticking out from under her cap.

"She'll be fine, Mars."

The guard lifted her hands in resignation. "After you," she said tersely.

"Wait," I said, studying her face. "I remember you." She'd been at Isaiah's side when he came to retrieve me from Central Command during the battle, to beg me to return to the Remnant with him. I hadn't exactly come quietly, so to speak.

She raised an eyebrow. "Congratulations."

Our little tussle had ended with her on the ground, unconscious, thanks in no small part to Isaiah, who'd turned on her at the last minute to keep her from hurting me further. I gave her a fake smile to go with her sarcasm. She did not return it.

As we wove through the bins, the guards flanked Isaiah and spread out ahead of him. They'd clearly had some practice with their formation. I tried to fall in with the ones right behind him, but they kept slowing down at the end of each bin, checking the aisles before allowing Isaiah to proceed through the intersection, so I kept nearly tripping. To make things worse, "Mars" seemed not to want me to walk directly behind Isaiah, so she kept placing a hand on my arm whenever he stopped. I kept right on knocking it away. She'd give a little snort, and we'd start walking again. It was all a little awkward, to be honest.

After about the fourth snort, Isaiah turned around.

"Why don't you walk up here, Charlotte? Give me someone to talk to."

"Sir, I really can't advise—" Mars began.

"It's fine," he said shortly.

She sighed again, and I avoided shooting her a smug look as I sped up to take Isaiah's outstretched arm.

"Hey, you think you've got enough guards?" I asked, not quietly.

Isaiah chuckled. "My jail must not be so bad, since you're still telling jokes. They're doing their job. This area is not under control, at the moment," he said grimly. "Not yet, anyway."

"Don't you have a ceasefire?"

"It's more than just that. There are lockies, some of which are ours, and another group we've tried to monitor," he said.

"What other group?"

"We don't know. Some kind of soldier-types. They come out at night. Probably just part of Central Command, but we can never prove it."

We fell into step, and I remembered the way it felt to hold his hand back on Earth, when everything was dying all around us. I gave his arm a little squeeze, and he leaned in to me and spoke quietly. "You shouldn't give Marcela a hard time."

"I know, I know. She's just doing her job."

"Well," said Isaiah, "Sure. But she's not so bad, if you get to know her."

"Pass."

"All right, then. Don't say I didn't warn you."

I was still trying to figure out exactly what he had warned

me about when we came to the end of the cargo hold. But instead of the dark space that led to the Remnant, we were someplace I'd never been.

The Ark was shaped like a huge, flat wheel, with the cargo stored in the large outer rim. The wheel was divided into sectors, like slices of a pie, and it spun as it traveled through space, which gave the effect of gravity. Unfortunately, the passengers who were farthest out experienced far more gravity than those toward the center of the Ark, the "sweet spot." Every last member of the Remnant was an illegal passenger—a stowaway—and they inhabited the outer rim of Sector Seven. During the battle, Isaiah and Adam had cut the air to the rest of the Ark using a life-support program I'd helped steal: the Noah Board. If they hadn't done that, the Remnant wouldn't have stood a chance against Central Command.

The corridor was well-lit and industrial in nature, save for the patterned weave on the carpet beneath us. We were still on the thick outer rim of the Ark, where Central Command considered the gravity too heavy for living quarters. I guessed it had belonged to them, but like I said, the Remnant had secured it—and their continued existence—during the battle. Two of his guards rushed ahead with key cards, and a series of doors slid apart before us. Isaiah barely broke his stride before reaching the door of his choice.

We entered a small room with a thin metal platform, which Isaiah led me to.

"We're gonna need a better grip," he said, and pulled me toward him. His fingers found the wire around my waist, and he gave me a silent look through his dark glasses.

Four guards joined us on the platform, Marcela among them, and Isaiah reached past her to hold a thick cable at one corner.

"Ready, sir?" called a guard from the doorway.

"Let 'er rip," said Isaiah.

I realized, too late, that we were standing on a sort of elevator, and it shot down into the black shaft beneath us before I was ready. I lost my footing, but Isaiah's arm was solid around me.

I shrugged it off in a sudden surge of inexplicable anger. I hardly needed his help to stand up. When we passed the next floor, there was an instant flash of visibility from the light on its door, and I noticed Marcela's arm hovering around my other side, carefully not touching me. I upgraded my opinion of her by a tenth of a point, then remembered her kick to my arm during our little scuffle several weeks ago and slid it right back down again.

"I really wish I could see the look on your face right now," said Isaiah.

"I've been on an elevator before, you know." I loosened my grip on his arm with considerable effort. "I just didn't realize there was a floor beneath ours."

"Not the elevator," he said as the reason for the extra bracing became apparent. The platform jerked to an unsteady stop just below the bottom floor, throwing my knees forward and my center off-balance. Isaiah's grip solidified around me at the same time, and I didn't fall. "*This.*"

I inhaled involuntarily. We stood at the edge of an enormous room. It was brightly lit, and pale blue, except for a series of shiny white stripes down each wall. The stripes led to heavy black ports, each equipped with a tangle of code-based locks.

The floor was a series of black catwalks suspended over the outer hull of the ship. The main drag branched off at certain intervals, giving access to each port in the room, and of course the entrance. The platform had landed between levels, so that I was nearly at eye level with the floor. I made to climb up onto the walk, but Isaiah placed a warm hand on my shoulder, stopping me.

"Not that we're going in that way," whispered Isaiah. "But I hear it's quite a view."

"Oh no?" I asked.

"The platform stopped halfway for a reason," he answered, pulling me down until we were nearly lying flat. A complicated series of shafts and wires spread before me, in sharp contrast to the bright, open room on the floor above.

They lay against the platform, barely able to squeeze into the space beneath the floor. I followed, my tongue thickening in my mouth, and stumbled again, harder this time.

"Careful," Isaiah warned. "Tons of gravity down here, and we gotta crawl. Try to keep your neck relaxed, or you'll tweak it. We need you in fighting shape."

We went a few steps before I could manage anything resembling a normal crawl. Isaiah continued to talk, leading us toward a particular port on the wall. "Shoulda seen me, my first time down here. It's terrifying."

I had to agree, albeit silently. There was something about the crawl space beneath the floor that was even more off-putting than it should have been.

"Just over here," he called back. "Few more yards. I think you'll appreciate where we're going."

"Is that—" I bit my lip, nearly afraid to ask. "Is that an airlock?"

"Why, yes it is! She can be taught. It's the side of one, anyway. But that's not the important part."

"The airlock isn't important?"

"We're in a hangar, little bird." He slid delicate fingers across the panel before us, then jerked it suddenly. It came off in his hands, and he placed it quietly to the side. It was bigger than me. "Or underneath one, anyway."

I swallowed, with difficulty. "And?"

"And maybe it's time you flew."

Seven

I stared into the space the panel had revealed. It was dark, but I could make out some wires, and beyond that, a control panel of some kind. "You got them to give you an Arkhopper?"

Isaiah gave me a withering glance through the shadows.

I blinked at the airlock, which I figured had to be part of a hatch. "You *stole* one?"

He looked at me patiently. "Not exactly. But you're getting warmer."

"You're about to steal one?"

"Warmer."

I looked from Isaiah to the hatch, avoiding Marcela's openly amused expression. "*I'm* about to steal one."

"Bingo."

I sighed.

He pulled the white panel back into place and settled himself down in the narrow space so that he and Marcela were both facing me, their outstretched legs bordering mine on either side. "It's strange to think about, isn't it? This is the outer rim of the ship. We're right next to space. Makes me feel fragile." He curled his knees into his chest. "And heavy. That's the gravity, though."

I stared at him.

Marcela cleared her throat. "We've intercepted a series of communications between Central Command—the Commander himself, actually—and the Asian Ark. Apparently, he's not so jazzed about continuing our little ceasefire."

"So threaten to cut his air supply or something," I said. "Wasn't that the whole point of stealing the Noah Board?"

Isaiah wiggled his shoulders and settled a little further down, giving his neck more room to straighten out. From where we sat, barely underneath a walkway, we could see into most of the hangar above us. The flooring was only solid on the footpaths, giving the hangar the illusion of being suspended in space. "Yes and no. They update it; Adam rehacks it and overwrites their progress. Rinse and repeat. We can handle it."

"Then why exactly do you need me to hijack an Arkhopper?"

"It turns out we have a weakness."

I raised an eyebrow. "Like other than the fact that they have all the good weapons? And all the supplies? And all the trained soldiers?"

They ignored that. "We—the Remnant—are on the outer rim of the ship and confined to Sector Seven. All our efforts to penetrate the rest of the ship have failed," said Isaiah.

"We don't need to take the rest of the ship," I said. "We just need the rest of the ship to leave us alone."

"Command alone, we could handle," said Marcela. "We have a strong enough grip on their tech that we can probably survive until we get to Eirenea. The problem is that we're right up against the hull of the ship."

I bit my lip, hesitant to be persuaded. Eirenea was the

planet the Arks were trying to reach. The plan was to build some kind of electromagnetic field, then terraform and colonize it. Like a newer, smaller Earth. Even if everything went perfectly, we were still years away from reaching it.

She paused, watching me. "It would appear that the Commander has embarked upon a more... comprehensive strategy for our defeat. Thanks to Adam, we have reason to believe he's going to ally with Asia. Convince them that we need to be wiped out."

I considered that. "You're saying they're going to blow a hole in the ship."

"The engineers took the possibility of projectiles pretty seriously," she said. "There are ways of saving the rest of the ship if the hull is breached. But they didn't take the Remnant into account."

I nodded, understanding. "No one was supposed to live on the outer edge of the Ark."

"We weren't supposed to live at all," she said. "And if they hit us, we won't survive the blast. Especially not if the Commander disables the defense systems first."

"One shot, we're out," said Isaiah.

"They'd never do that," I breathed. "Asia would never intentionally..." I stopped. Fear was a powerful salve for the conscience. If the Commander had convinced Asia that we were some kind of threat to them, I wasn't sure what they'd be capable of. And in my experience, the Commander could be very convincing.

"Oh, now," he said. "Don't look so upset about it. We do have a plan."

"Ah. As long as there's a plan."

"And here he comes now," said Marcela.

I looked around, but apart from the three of us, the crawl space was empty. "He?"

Marcela pointed through the floor above us. I squinted over the walkway and across the length of the hangar. A hooded figure swept into the room, accompanied by a change in the air, perceptible even from as far away as we were. As I watched, the guard on duty rushed toward him, but he held out a hand, and I saw that he was young: his hand was smaller and less muscular than Eren's, or even Isaiah's. The hand touched the guard, and the guard fell to the ground, writhing, and then was still.

The hooded figure barely noticed. He swept toward the panel on the wall, and the door closed. His face was shrouded, but if my creeping suspicion as to his identity was right, that door wouldn't open again, no matter who was on the other side.

He turned toward us, and my guess solidified into ice: Adam.

Adam was a genius, a prodigy. Those were the only words appropriate to describe his fluency with the burgeoning technology of the Ark's various systems, some of which he'd created himself, and nearly all of which he'd modified to suit his own strengths. I didn't know much about his brief life on Earth, but, up here, the only family I'd seen of his was Amiel, his sister.

He worked for Isaiah. We'd done exactly one job together: the Noah Board.

At first, I'd liked him fine, in spite of the fact that he reminded me of myself, minus the tech proficiency. But during the heist, he'd killed without thought, and his methods were ruthless. It made him unpredictable. If you asked me, which apparently no one had, it was dangerous to work with a person like that. And not just to our enemies.

To us. Surely Isaiah could see the need for limitations, for distance, with someone like that.

I shivered, allowing the weight of the ship to pull me down into myself. "Isaiah. No," I whispered. "He can't be controlled."

"I don't need to control him. I just need him to do his job. Sound familiar?"

"Yes, you do," I said.

He approached at a leisurely pace, his hood anchored around his face for the length of the catwalk, and I felt my nerves set themselves on edge as he passed panel after panel on his path through the hangar.

Of course he was coming for us.

When he reached the panel above our hiding spot, he produced a long, thin black rod and swiped it over the controls. They *zwipped* and fizzled before going dark and rebooting. When the subsystem came back online, he pressed a hand against the biometric scanner, and we watched, breathless, as it keyed to his vitals. A moment passed, and the panel was his.

Only then did he turn to us.

He stooped to work an opening in the pipes around the catwalk, then assisted Isaiah through the floor and onto the platform in front of the hatch.

Marcela went next, giving me an appraising look as she accepted Isaiah's outstretched hand. I popped myself up through the hole before anyone could reach for me.

Now that he'd taken control of the security systems in the hangar, Adam let his hood fall back to his shoulders. His face was as young and bright as I remembered. He flicked lightning-quick fingers over the panel, and the hatch popped open.

The airlock was exposed. It lay open at our feet, awaiting us, barely longer or wider than a body. We couldn't access the Arkhopper without it, but the mere thought of crawling into it made my fingers go cold. I decided not to look at it. I couldn't afford to take my attention away from Adam, anyway.

"Hi, Char," he said, his voice softer than I remembered.

I gritted my teeth. What was the play here? "Adam."

He smiled robotically. "Sorry about last time."

Last time, he'd shot me, rather than let the mission fail. His intent to kill had been as plain as the nose on his unlined face.

"So," he continued after my silence, "you and me. Together again." There was an eagerness in his voice that belied his youth, but he showed far more restraint than I'd have otherwise credited him with.

"No." I directed my response at Isaiah. "We're not."

Mars and Adam blinked. Isaiah's face was outwardly passive. I continued. "I don't want anything to do with him. Least of all now that the other Arks are involved."

"Not all of them," said Adam.

Isaiah spoke as though he hadn't heard us. "This is a standard two-seat hopper. It can be piloted remotely, or with the manual controls. Pretty self-explanatory, from what I've heard. I'll be in constant contact while you're in transit."

"Two seats? I'm not going. Not with him."

A brief tension pressed Adam's jaw forward, then he was calm again. Unreadable.

I swallowed. "He's dangerous, Ise."

Isaiah regarded me mildly. "He's learning. And I thought you believed in second chances."

"This is my chance to learn from our mistake: send him away."

"Get in the airlock, little bird."

My lips went numb. "No." My voice was pathetically quiet.

Adam looked from me to Isaiah, eyes wide, but said nothing.

"Don't make me threaten you," said Isaiah. "It's bad for our friendship."

I wet my lips, unsure of myself, of everything. Except this. "Take my hand, Isaiah. I need you to understand me. I'm not doing this mission if Adam's a part of it. And if you know me at all, you know this: *you can't make me.*"

"I'll go," said Marcela.

We looked at her. My hand was still tightly wound around Isaiah's.

She spoke again. "You need two people. I'll do it."

I took a breath and tried to think, but the airlock lay beside me like a grave. If we were trying to stop the Asian Commander, or whoever it was, from blowing a hole in the Remnant, Adam was nothing but a liability. To everyone. Whether or not I was there. I had to stop him from getting on the hopper.

"It should be me," I said softly.

"I agree," said Isaiah.

"Well," said Marcela. "That's settled, then."

"But I... I have demands."

Isaiah raised his eyebrows. "Demands. You. That's cute."

"I mean, yeah. You can't just expect me to—"

"No, no. It's fine." He straightened up and nodded his head, like we were playing some kind of game together. "I'm actually curious about this. Let's hear these demands."

I took a breath. "Okay. All right. First, no Adam."

"Noted."

"And I want citizenship."

"In the Remnant? You got it. Matter of fact, none of this is gonna work out otherwise." He slung an arm over the top of the hatch.

"No. I mean, yes. The Remnant. But for my whole family. Not just me. I know you have my brother."

Isaiah froze, his hand still on the door of the hatch, his chin slightly out.

"West Turner," I said. "I know you know that's my brother, Ise."

He exhaled. "I thought this might come up."

I made my voice firm. "Permanent, irrevocable citizenship for me, my dad, and my brother."

"Actions have consequences." He gave me a frustrated look. "For most people, anyway. I'm trying to build something here."

"And a full pardon for all of us."

"Oh, is that all?"

"No stealing."

He tilted his head to one side. "No stealing unless you agree to it."

I rolled my eyes. "Okay. Good luck with that. Also, no lying to me."

"No deal," he said flatly.

I looked up at him, surprised. "Fine. Then that one goes both ways."

"Whatever you gotta do," he said calmly. "That about cover it?"

I steeled myself. "No Adam. That one's non-negotiable."

He looked at me in stony silence.

"It can't be done without Adam," said Marcela. She sounded like she was suppressing some kind of incredulous laugh.

Let her laugh, I thought. She's not the one I need to convince. I thought of the dead guards from my last mission, but I could no longer find their faces in my memory. All I could see was Adam, and the look in his eyes as he stepped over their bodies.

When I spoke again, there was iron in my voice. "You have to choose, Ise. Him or me."

"You can't do that," said Adam. "I'm a part of this. You can't—"

"You," Isaiah said simply.

They looked at him in shock.

"You're dismissed, Adam," said Isaiah, without turning his head. "Thank you for your service."

There was a tense moment, then a dark look came over Adam's face. But instead of putting up a fight, he turned soundlessly and left the room. We watched him go.

"Okay. I think that's everything."

I made a move toward the hatch, but Isaiah blocked my way.

"Hey now, Charlotte. I have a few demands of my own."

The hairs on my neck stood up slowly. "Like?"

"This mission. You do as I say—*exactly* as I say—we complete the objective, and we get back here in one piece."

"I barely know anything about the mission."

"I'll explain it on the way. Don't give me that look," he said, correctly guessing my expression. "I'm not the one who can't go a day on the outside without committing a felony."

"You still worried about that judge?" I shrugged. "She sentenced me to death. I barely scratched her."

"Uh huh," he said, like he was waiting for me to finish a thought.

I was still for a moment, then narrowed my eyes in

disbelief. "Wait a minute. Did you organize this whole thing on purpose?"

"Let's just say I knew you weren't going down without a fight. There's a reason I chose to hold the trial so close to the dark space, in a room you were familiar with."

I blinked at him. "*You* sentenced me?!"

"No, little bird. That part was real. You got there all on your own. I got you *out*. I had to get you away from the crowd, out of the system, in order to make this work. You were still mad at me. I know you well enough to realize there was only one way to do that."

"Your entire plan hinged on me kidnapping a judge? What the heck kind of a mission is this, anyway?"

"You didn't have to take it that far. Can't say I really saw the whole thing coming." He gave me a serious look, but spoke mildly. "But I figured you could handle yourself. The mission is critical. That's all I'll say for now. You're not the type to be put off by a little danger."

"No, I'm not. But if anything happens to me, if I don't make it back… my family—"

Isaiah frowned. "I'd take care of them, Charlotte. I thought you would know that."

"I'm just… trying to cover my bases."

He shook his head. "They covered now?"

I paused, then gave a single nod.

"So let's go."

He leaned back, still standing in front of the airlock, until I reached out, afraid he was falling. At the last possible second, he bent at the waist and fell backwards through the hatch, leaving me gaping after him.

"Wait, you're going with me? Not… *her*?" I blinked apologetically at Mars, still processing everything.

"You know what they say, Charlotte. You want a job done, you got to—"

"Avoid a land war in Asia," Mars cut in, her voice like acid.

Isaiah chuckled from the darkness. There was ice in my spine.

"Wait! Send the agreement back to the Remnant, in writing." I hesitated. "In case you don't come back, either. All right?"

"Fair enough. Full citizenship for her family, if I don't come back," he said to Marcela. "Think you can handle that?"

They exchanged a look. Both appeared to be suppressing a smile. "I'm on it, King."

"Thank you kindly," he said easily. "Now. Let's shake on it." He lifted his hand up through the open hatch, and I realized I was gripping the edge of the airlock with the strength of four men. I stared at my fingers, willing them to release it, and fumbled for Isaiah's hand.

He adjusted our grip to something like a handshake, and I caught the barest hint of a smile on his upturned face before he pulled me down into the airlock head first.

Eight

I slid into the hatch. He caught me before I hit the seat, and my hand was like a limp rag in his as we completed the handshake inside the Arkhopper. I was in a tiny, round glass cabin with two metal chairs. A complicated series of straps hung from the seats and was mirrored in the webwork around the glass. Marcela leaned in after me to buckle my seatbelts. I pursed my lips and turned away. The process took a long time, then was repeated with Isaiah.

"Thank you, Mars. Now show her the stuff so we can get out of here."

Marcela turned to me and extended a hand toward the dash. "This is your helmet and a skin. You have four hours of oxygen. If they're not sealed together correctly, your blood will boil as soon as the cabin loses pressure. Get yours on before you do his, or you'll both boil. Not that anything's going to happen."

I tried not to let my rising panic show in my voice. From the look on her face, she was definitely enjoying this. "Who's flying this thing?"

Isaiah laughed out loud. "You don't think I can do it? Come on, little bird. Have a little faith."

Marcela smirked. "Okay, time for your heads."

Without further warning, she pressed my forehead back until my head was against the cushion behind it, then pulled the cushions around the side of my head, securing them with a heavy strap. If I was nervous before, now I was approaching outright dread. I couldn't move my head at all. Sounds were muffled by the cushions, and my vision was almost completely obscured, save for a view of the dash in front of me. My breathing came harder, and my fingers curled into fists.

At the last second, Marcela turned back to me. "Try to keep your neck relaxed, if you can." She slapped Isaiah's headstrap into place on the velcroed side of the cushion. "I'll have auxiliary control of the avionics until you get there," she said to him. "Then I'll transfer."

The tightness in my chest pressed up against my throat. "To whom?" I squeaked.

"The Asian Ark," said Isaiah, louder than usual, thanks to all the padding around our heads.

"That's our big plan? We're just going to pop into the Asian Ark and beg them not to blow us up?"

"Unless we lose pressure and boil first. *Zai jian*, Mars. Thanks for that image."

In response, Marcela slammed the hatch shut. She met my eye through the glass for one final instant while securing the latch from the other side. She was still pretending to suppress her amusement when the port closed off completely.

"Hang on tight, all right?" said Isaiah. "You're not going to like this."

"What do you mean?"

"Right now, we're spinning. Whole Ark is. But when I

hit the release, the airlock will open, and we'll be free floating. Takes a minute to engage the thrusters, so we'll still be spinning for a minute. Then there won't be any gravity at all. It takes some getting used to."

Apparently, Isaiah had done this before. Where had he gone that time?

I took a deep breath. "I'm ready."

His long fingers spread out on the dash, delicately brushing the switches and buttons until they found a square yellow knob. "All right. Here we go."

The pressure that had forced its way up to my throat was joined by the new sensation of my neck being pulled down into my stomach from deep inside me. The tension in my innards spread to beneath my belly. I heard myself make a strange, guttural sound, but I didn't start screaming until the pulling and pressing reached its icy hands inside my head.

I was spinning. Heavy arcs of swinging motion overtook me in waves. I screamed louder and louder, until my voice broke. We were completely helpless.

A dull pain bit into my right forearm, and I realized Isaiah was trying to get me to hold his hand.

Then, gravity gave out, and the stars swung slower and slower around the clear pane of the Arkhopper. We went around and around, and the pressure forced its way fully into my skull, blackening my vision. The stars winked away. The dash went dark.

I kept screaming.

I knew I had to stop, but I couldn't. Isaiah's hand was frantic against my arm. *He's afraid for me. He's worried.*

Then, gravity released us completely, relieving me of what wits I still commanded. My body lifted from the seat.

I think I'm dying. I definitely wasn't breathing. The world was red, with streaks of gray. My face felt cold. Everything was so cold, except my hand.

"Charlotte. Char, baby. Come on. You still with me?"

My throat tried to swallow, but failed. "What was that?! What happened?"

"I don't know." Isaiah was calm, except for an errant muscle working its way through his jaw. "I couldn't hear Control."

"No. Right."

"Because of all the screaming."

"Ah." I looked at him, pulled a face. "Sorry."

"Take my hand, Turner."

I spread my fingers, and his fingers slid across my palm. I folded my hand to his. It occurred to me that this was Isaiah's first order. I laughed. What a stupid waste of an order. The streaks of gray in my vision shrank hard, and the red was abruptly angry.

"Marcela. Come in," Isaiah's voice was tense. It made him sound like someone else. "Mars, you there?"

"I'm here, sir. Cabin lost some pressure right out of the airlock. Some kind of defensive mechanism, maybe, or something standard that we just weren't prepared for. I couldn't warn you because of... the noise. Life support is rebooting. You're two minutes out, but there should be enough air to go on if she calms down."

"This isn't her fault, Mars."

"I wasn't—yes, sir."

"Get us back on track right now."

"Yes, sir. Eighty seconds."

"Sign off, too. I don't think she likes your voice."

There was a moment of silence. My stomach seemed to

float in a space all its own, only briefly knocking into my ribs and lungs.

"Char, you have to breathe slower. You gotta calm down." He gave my hand a little squeeze, and I found I could make sense of his words.

I focused on nothing but Isaiah's hand and its warmth against my own. It wasn't the first time his steady grip had taught me how to breathe again. I squeezed him back.

"Hey. There you are." His voice was warm, too. And tangibly relieved.

"Sorry 'bout that. Space is not really my thing."

"You're one stone-cold criminal, Charlotte Turner."

"I'm so dizzy."

"Just concentrate on your heartbeat. Make yourself slow down. And for real, stop screaming. I'm already blind. Don't want to be deaf, too."

"I don't remember it being like that when the OPT docked." I frowned. The truth was that I didn't remember anything from when the Off-Planet Transport docked with the Ark. I'd been drugged, along with all the other passengers. "Was it that bad?"

Isaiah made a small noise. "It was worse. They had to slow the rotation anytime an OPT docked. When you woke up, they were already back in full swing. Planned it that way. Apparently a lot of people got the Lightness."

"Lightness?"

"It's a thing they call it when you don't have gravity."

"Why not just call it 'zero gravity?'"

"No, that's just the fact of it. The Lightness is about whether you can take the fact, or not. Some people plain can't."

* * *

On my second journey through space, I didn't feel like talking anymore than I had on my first. But this time, I sat with Isaiah, not a wing full of strangers. He was a solid mass in the seat next to mine. He was a co-conspirator and a familiar comfort. For the moment, he was both a captor and a friend. It was a strange mix. In his hands, just out of my reach, he held everything I'd wanted since my mother died. I could not leave him, yet I wasn't completely sure I wanted to. The Arkhopper stopped spinning, and the stars ceased flinging themselves around us.

The sky was full of them. I mean, *full*. The more I concentrated on the black spaces between the stars, the more stars I saw. They were everywhere. My spine lifted away from the seat behind me, pressing me softly toward the straps all around me.

I missed my mother. My grief over her death was a constant companion. It swept along the bins of the cargo hold, barely a step ahead of the guards. It roamed the halls of the Remnant, and lately, it had paced the floor of my cell, sometimes weeping at the loss of her, sometimes laughing at her memory. It lay in my bed at night, wrapping its long arms around my ribs, pressing them in and out as I breathed. At times it spoke to me in tenderness, reminding me that she had loved me. Now, it intoned mercilessly that she had died in this blackness, free from gravity forever. Free from light.

She should have seen the sight in front of me: an infinite flood of stars, each more subtle than the last, filling the voids as my sight adjusted to the dark, then blurring out with my tears until I blinked.

She loved the stars.

My grief raged against me only rarely these days, but as

gravity released its grip on my body, it reached long fingers around my throat, threatening to choke me. In a strange way, sitting with Isaiah was like sitting with an older version of myself, a past I had never escaped, and I didn't try to stop the few tears that fell. He'd seen worse from me. His hand tightened over mine, and my grief lessened its noose round my neck.

I did not squeeze him back.

At length, I spoke, but my gaze remained on the stars. "I'm angry, Isaiah. So angry. I don't know why."

He didn't respond, but he didn't take his hand away, either.

When the Asian Ark came into view several hours later, I found that I had slept. I pulled myself together. I had a long way to go that day and not a lot of information to work with.

I had found my father. My mother would be glad of that, glad that we were no longer angry at each other. But I had yet to find my brother, really find him, and I would never stop until I did. And it all started here.

This ship was massive and built like an enormous round cake with layers. Unlike the North American Ark, they'd engineered gravity via an electromagnetic field generated underneath each layer, and cancelled out, inches later, with every ceiling. It had a single discernable decoration: an enormous circular logo on the "roof" the size of several city blocks. As the pull of the oncoming Ark slid me back into my seat, Isaiah cleared his throat.

"So," he said, "Couple of things. First, your new job description. You're the Remnant's ambassador to the Asian Ark, and fully vested with the authority that brings. Which might not be much, depending on how this goes. Second, you work for me. You represent me and everyone I work for. So don't do anything hasty."

"Ise. What on earth—"

"Tshh," he said, shushing me. "The mission."

I gave him a blank stare. "Enlighten me."

"We are here to get official recognition from Asia."

"We—the Remnant?"

I heard his smile, though I couldn't see it. "Yep. See? You're a natural."

"Recognition as what, again?"

"A sovereign nation-state of the North American Ark."

"Isaiah. You can't possibly be serious that I'm the one you want doing this. And are we even supposed to—"

"You rather I picked Adam? He was eager enough. Can't trust him, though. You're the daughter of a senator. You've met foreign leaders before."

"Yeah. When I was, like, eight."

"You know the inner workings of Central Command, and you understand the Remnant: why it exists, how we do things. And you can predict how bad it'll be for all that if the Commander takes us over."

"Okay, but—"

"We don't want to go to war. We just want to be left alone. And we can't do that unless we have independence. And the more support we get from the other Arks, this one especially, the less likely the Commander will be to blow us all up, so to speak."

"Actually, I'm not sure that's a figure of speech," I frowned as he strapped my head back onto the chair. "But why this Ark especially? You heard something?"

"Let's just say I don't trust them, either." He stopped

fiddling with the strap long enough to fix me with his blind gaze. "Keep focused, Char. Thousands of people are depending on us for everything. They need safety. They need justice. And they need to eat. As a separate nation-state, we'll have the authority to fight back whenever those things are taken away from us, and more importantly, we'll be in a better position to form alliances."

"This proves my point, Ise. I can barely remember any Chinese from middle school. They do speak Chinese, right?"

"And Hindi, officially."

"Officially. Right." I shook my head. "That's not much of a plan."

"Adam reached out weeks ago and established a back-channel. There's a big party tonight. The Commander will be there to state his case."

"I take it we're not exactly on the guest list."

There was a pause, and I pictured him tilting his head, as though weighing his answer. "We're not *not* on the guest list. Adam found us a contact: an ambassador's assistant. They're sympathetic."

"As far as we know," I sighed. "I don't like our odds."

"'S not the first Ark we've boarded without an invitation. This time, we won't even have to hide once the party starts. You gotta remember, most people don't want a war."

"I haven't even read the Treaty yet. Everyone keeps referring to the pre-OPT training that I kinda missed, what with being in prison. And, Isaiah, people go to school for *years* to learn how to be ambassadors."

"You think you're the only criminal we got? No one in the Remnant went to pre-OPT training. That was kind of the point, Char. We weren't supposed to survive the meteor. Most of them don't even accept the Treaty as valid, seeing as it planned for them to die. We don't have years. And we don't have a diplomacy program. Yet." He let out a sharp breath. "But I will build this *nation-state* out of what we do have. And right now, that's you."

I sat in silence, focusing for a moment on assisting Isaiah with his own headstrap. "This leader thing looks really good on you. You know that, right?"

"I think a lot of that is going to depend on you, Ambassador."

"I'm not talking about the outcome. I mean they're lucky to have you right now."

He clucked his tongue. "They?"

"We. Maybe." I squinted at him. "Anything you're not telling me this time? Like, I don't know. Something critical that I'm really going to wish I'd known earlier, or something?"

The airlock before us opened, and our little ship found a harbor.

"Oh, there's plenty," said Isaiah. "Now, let's go be diplomats."

Nine

The hatch of the Arkhopper popped open easily, and we were greeted by silence.

The air was cold—too cold—and I suppressed the urge to hang onto Isaiah. As comforting as it would be, it was far better for us both to be ready.

"Should we... I don't know. Just start running? Look for a place to hide?"

"They should be here any minute. We'll stick around."

I shivered. "May I suggest a new plan? Get me away from this airlock before someone flips a switch somewhere and we end up dying in space."

"Tell me what you see. And get me out of this strap; I can't find the buckle-thing."

I fumbled around his wrists and legs, keeping my eyes on the hatch. If we were walking into a trap, I wanted to know as soon as possible. Not that there was anything I could do about it. "Okay, it's dark," I said in a low voice. "But the airlock opened on both ends of the port as soon as we docked, probably automatically. That's the last strap—you're free. There's a little room on the other end. I guess we should get in there before it locks again. What's his name? Your friend, I mean."

"Her name. An. But I never met her. She was more friends with Adam, to be—did you hear that?"

I froze. His hand brushed my arm, beckoning me forward, and we slid through the port and into the little receiving room. We were both pretty good at sneaking anyway, but at that moment, we were like silent snakes. My metric was off, thanks to my stint in the Remnant, but it felt like we were in reduced gravity. Maybe it was lower on purpose, to help other visitors adjust to regular gravity after space.

I was still resisting clinging to him when we straightened out in the dark room and pressed the lock to seal off the Arkhopper.

"All right, your highness," I whispered to Isaiah. "We're here. What now?"

"They monitor everything. They know we're here. Be patient."

"Light?"

"If you must."

I placed a hand over the lightpad soundlessly, then ended up pressing it a little harder than necessary when it didn't respond. Finally, I slapped it in frustration, and the lights clicked on. My jaw dropped, then flapped shut.

We were surrounded.

Four faces popped into view, each staring openly, and I stopped breathing.

I gave in to my lesser judgment and reached for Isaiah, speaking to him in a whisper. "So, we're—"

"Welcome, Mr. Underwood," said the man seated directly before me. A woman stood next to him, and the room was flanked on two sides by uniformed guards. "Adam informed us of your change in plans."

"Shan," Isaiah said pleasantly.

He steadied his arm without forcing me off it, so that my hand was resting in the crook of his elbow. The motion was smooth, as though we'd planned it that way. Like he was escorting me to a waltz or something.

Like I wasn't terrified.

He continued. "May I introduce Charlotte Turner, our newest ambassador. Charlotte, this is Shan Hui, Ambassador to the North American Ark."

I cleared my throat. "Uh, they have guns pointed at us."

Isaiah's jaw tightened. "Ah."

"Yep."

There was an awkward pause while I collected my wits. Well, awkward for me. Everyone else in the room seemed perfectly comfortable, if oddly quiet. The others continued to stare at us, as though taking our measure.

"I must say, I am surprised to welcome you here in person, Mr. Underwood," Shan said at last. "May I introduce An Zhao, my assistant?"

An bowed. "A pleasure."

Perplexed, I imitated the motion, looking back to Isaiah for guidance. He appeared pleasantly relaxed, so no help there. I squared my shoulders and met Shan's eye. After a moment, he stood.

"You have heard about our little reception this evening. I am pleased to inform you that the Imperial has decided that you should be allowed to state your case."

Isaiah nodded. "Good."

"I am afraid that, as you are here without permission, you will be detained until your appearance."

Neither Isaiah nor I were inclined to respond to that, so Shan motioned toward the door. "If you please," he said, and we preceded him into the hallway.

Now, our arms were positioned so that I was leading Isaiah. We couldn't have choreographed it better.

Whatever grace I'd mustered up to that moment didn't last long. As I passed the first guard, he grabbed me by the hips.

So I elbowed him in the chest.

"Hey!" said Isaiah.

"I'm afraid you are under arrest," said Shan. "And while we don't wish to restrain you, Mr. Underwood, we really must insist on searching Miss Turner."

"No need. She has a gun. Probably a knife, too. Char, if you wouldn't mind," said Isaiah.

The men looked at me in silence.

I looked right back at them, but they didn't budge, so I finally sighed and slid the gun out of the nest of wire behind my back and plunked it onto a nearby table. "All right. Fine. Here."

Shan examined it calmly before pressing it into his robe and returning to his patient stance.

"It's not a knife," I said awkwardly, sticking my hand down the front of my shirt and pulling out the wire cutters. "There. Happy?"

"Certainly," said Shan. He nodded at the guard, who produced a shiny set of silver handcuffs.

On hearing their familiar clink, Isaiah frowned.

"No," I said. "No cuffs."

"I really must insist," Shan repeated. "For Miss Turner, pending our dispensation of your organization's legal status."

"She is a diplomat," Isaiah said in a low voice.

"She has no official standing, Mr. Underwood, and neither do you. Furthermore, she just smuggled a gun onto our sovereign territory. Now, I'm willing to forego any reasonable security measures for yourself, but I really must in—"

"No cuffs," I repeated, coating the room in a glare. I laid a hand on Isaiah's arm to remind them of whom I'd showed up with, invited or not.

The two guards waited, expressionless, while the four of us wordlessly assessed the invisible power structure in the room. Shan glanced back at his assistant, whose expression barely shifted from the look of politely detached concern she'd adopted when the first guard assaulted me. Then he locked onto Isaiah, who, to my horror, didn't seem half as outraged as I thought he should be. After all, I realized, he'd gotten what he wanted: a meeting with the Imperial. I kept right on glaring, for all the good it did me.

"Go ahead," said Isaiah finally.

"No!" I shouted, my voice about eight steps higher than I'd intended. "Go to—"

"Remember our conversation, Charlotte?" said Isaiah. His jaw relaxed, but the tension had spread through his usually-smooth forehead.

The balance was weighed, and my vote was as consequential as a sack of feathers. Shan lifted my wrist off Isaiah's arm with surprising gentleness and clasped the cuffs on as though they were a pair of delicate silver bracelets. I revised my glare to a slight frown. It usually hurt enough to leave a mark.

Didn't mean I had to like him.

No one had touched Isaiah yet, which I supposed was a good sign, so I squared my shoulders as I was prodded forward through the door.

I nearly gasped at the sight before me. A bright red carpet led us out of the tiny hangar. I couldn't help but notice the differences between my Ark and this one. In the North American Ark, only the Guardian Level could be described as decorated. Here, on the outermost edge of the Asian Ark, the path was already beautiful.

Shan stopped, expecting Isaiah to walk with him. Isaiah gave a nearly imperceptible twitch of his lower arm, signaling me to release him, and I realized I'd taken his arm yet again. As we walked, An fell into step beside me. For awhile, we walked in silence, watching the men converse, but unable to hear their words.

I began a mental catalog of everything I saw, so that I could repeat it all to Isaiah later, but I was quickly overwhelmed. The biggest immediate difference was the lighting. It was a trick of the eye, of course, but the lights appeared to be completely natural: open flames alternated with elaborately painted lanterns. The ceiling itself seemed to glow. It was white, along with the walls and the floor beneath the carpet.

The next thing I noticed was the calligraphy. On either side of the red carpet, rows of perfectly balanced symbols lined our path.

"Poetry," said An, noticing the direction of my eyes.

"It's beautiful," I said honestly.

"You read Japanese?"

"I—no, not at all. But it's very pretty." I squinted at the symbols. The artist had pressed the brush hard, leaving the edges rough, in spite of the precisely equal weight he or she had given each word. This was a calligrapher who could easily have produced smooth edges, vanishing the mere idea of the instrument's individual bristles, but had chosen otherwise. As I stared, I could almost feel the artist's frustration. "It seems almost... angry."

An rewarded my observation with another sweeping glance, landing this time at my eyes, but she didn't comment on my thoughts directly. "Each culture has contributed literature to this path, which begins on the outer edge of the Ark and spirals continuously to the center. In many places, the inscriptions are still being created. It is the same on every level, but the words are different." She gave me a sharp look. "We believe we have found unity in spite of our differences."

This time, I met her gaze. "I see."

"I am told you speak no Mandarin?" she asked, holding up a hand to stop me. A guard opened a panel in the inner wall, revealing a black stone tunnel lined with torches.

We turned into the tunnel as the conversation continued. It was perfectly straight, so that I could see almost to the center of the ship. "No," I said. "My education was more... erratic. Did you bring much art from your continent?"

An considered that. "The construction of the Ark itself is art. A perfect circle. Each floor has precisely the same gravity as the others. Our homes are each the same, except the Imperial's. He lives in the center of the *guidao*."

"Guidao?"

"The spiraling path that reaches every room on a level. You are on a *lujing*, a path that cuts through the coil and leads to the center. The *lujing* are for official use."

As we walked, we passed directly across the spirals of the *guidao*, its white and red scheme contrasting with the dark stone walls of the *lujing*. "This is beautiful, too." I reached to touch a part of the stone and saw that it was made from actual stone, cut from the depths of the Earth. My handcuffs clinked, and I pulled my sleeves over them, wishing I could make them disappear.

We bustled down the hall, but I couldn't help squinting at the stone. It had an iridescent shimmer, as though it were specifically responding to the light from the torches. On a whim, I reached up and touched an open flame, allowing my sleeves to fall back from my wrists, exposing the cuffs. They caught the light of the fire, which set the silver dancing. The flame was cold.

An spoke again. "The light is art. It comes from within the ceiling. It is not generated from a single point, but radiates through the rooms like a coil. At night, the torches burn brighter, and the ceiling is dimmed. I sometimes walk at night, just to see the flames."

I nodded. "Well, I can see why it's your favorite part. It's very... peaceful."

She smiled. "It is. Although, it's not my favorite part. That is the water."

"Is that in the coils, too?"

"It is beneath us." She paused, considering her words. "Maybe I will show you tomorrow, when you've recovered from the party. It would be a good thing to show the other delegations as well."

"Other delegations?" I asked, at the risk of sounding like a parrot.

"We've sent a signal to the remaining Arks. The others should be here soon. Each has a right to see how your case is stated. If one Ark goes to war, we are all affected."

She had a point, but I couldn't help thinking that the whole reason we were here was to put an end to any secret dealings with the Commander. I was sure the other Arks hadn't been consulted about blowing a hole in a ship, no matter who owned it. I turned back to Isaiah, and he sensed my glare.

"How are you doing back there, Ambassador?" he asked, smiling.

"Oh, just fine. I'm especially jazzed about meeting all the other delegations." *Hopefully not in handcuffs,* I added silently.

Shan gave An a helpless look, but Isaiah seemed not to mind. "Of course," he said easily.

We reached a large wooden door, and I stepped back, expecting it to swing open, but Shan slid a keycard past the pad, and it sucked open, just like back on our Ark, revealing a wide, circular room with red walls and flooring.

"These are your quarters," Shan said. "I regret that you will not be able to... explore during your stay. I am told that your Arkhopper contained cargo. Your things should arrive shortly."

"After you've search it," I said.

He hid his annoyance well, speaking mildly. "We're proud of our way of life here, Ambassador. Every man on this ship knows that it is only by chance that he lives, while his neighbor does not."

I leaned in to Isaiah and spoke in a voice that did not invite the others to join in. "Okay. It's kind of a small, round room with a red carpet, a red couch, and a little glass table," I began. "Everything's red, actually. Walls, ceiling. Different shades, though." I stopped, noticing that Shan and An were listening with great attention. "It kinda works, though," I added, returning their gaze openly. "Definitely doesn't look as bad as it sounds."

There was a soft rap at the door. "Enter," said Shan in a booming voice.

The door sucked open silently, and I continued to narrate for Isaiah. "It's like, eight more guys with four boxes."

"Shall we sit?" said Shan pleasantly, making himself at home in one of a pair of chairs that faced the bright red couch in the center of the room.

I guided Isaiah to the back of the couch, and he slid around it and into the center seat. I joined him, resisting the urge to put my feet up on the low glass table that split the seating area.

"Thank you, Mr. Underwood," said Shan as I settled onto the couch next to Isaiah. "I trust you find your quarters not too uncomfortable?"

He leveled a pleasant look at Shan. "Red's my favorite color."

An raised an eyebrow, then motioned toward the box behind her. "May I?" She gestured at the table. Shan gave a small nod.

"These first two boxes are the cargo from your Arkhopper," said Shan. "I'm having them sent to your respective bedchambers just now."

The men carrying the first two trunks filed back out of the room upon completing their task. The men carrying the two smaller boxes remained in the little round room, backs to the wall, awaiting instructions from the ambassador.

"Thank you," Isaiah said evenly.

"This one is, ah—" the ambassador continued. "Let's set it there," he said to his staff, motioning at the table.

The box sprung open, and I suppressed a gasp. It was full of food: fruits, nuts, little cakes. There were baskets stuffed with potstickers and even a little tea set, which An set up delicately.

"It's food," I whispered. "So much food. And a teapot."

"I gathered," said Isaiah. "Smells just right. Here, Miss Zhao. Allow me."

Isaiah took the piping hot kettle from An and carefully poured the tea into intricately decorated teacups. His long fingers skated quickly across the thin porcelain rims. "How many?"

"Three will do," said An, cutting him off before he could pour a cup for her.

I took the first cup, holding it gingerly by the foot, but waited until she took a sip before tasting it. Something about the way she was acting set me ill at ease, as though she were trying to butter us up before throwing us in a fire.

The tea, on the other hand, was heavenly, like drinking hot flowers with a hint of spice. "Mmm. That's great."

"Yes, thank you, Ambassador. An," said Isaiah, touching his lips to his cup. He fixed An with an open gaze behind his glasses, allowing the momentary silence to ask his next question for him.

The ambassador uncrossed his legs quickly, reminding me of a nervous defendant, and waved at the final box, which was small, square, and black. The men carrying it set it on the glass table next to the food and departed.

An touched an invisible catch, and its lid sprung open. Inside, lying on a bed of black velvet, were two thick, flat gold bands. "So, they're some kind of bracelets?" I said. "And they're really pretty. They have a little jewel on one side. There's also a stick-thingy. Like a screen stem, maybe?"

"Kuang bands," Isaiah said impassively.

There was a visible shift in the posture of the Asian delegation. "We prefer to call them truth bands."

"Let me guess," said Isaiah. "The Imperial will require them at the meeting."

Shan met his blind gaze silently.

"The ambassador is happy to comply," Isaiah said at

last, his voice perfectly even. I looked at him questioningly, but he didn't offer an explanation, so I held my tongue.

An and the ambassador observed my reaction with interest. When Shan stood at last, his entourage moved toward the door. He inclined his head toward Isaiah as he left. "An encouraging development. I leave you to it. I will return at eight to escort you to the party. Do order an hour or two of sleep, should you require it. A pleasure, Madam Ambassador, Your Majesty."

"Thank you, Shan," said Isaiah, as their group departed. "We look forward to the Imperial's gathering with great interest."

Ten

Once we were alone, Isaiah explored our space with careful attention, and I embarked on a serious effort to consume the entire contents of the massive picnic box on the coffee table. Except the olives. Obviously.

"Were you raised in a barn?" he called from across the room. "Seriously, Charlotte. Look into chewing."

I opened wider and added a potsticker. "Depends if the Upper Regional New York State Juvenile Correctional Facility counts as a barn. Although there were plenty of cows."

He snorted and continued to ooke around. I pulled out a basket of hot rice. One prison was much the same as another, if you asked me.

"Okay. Two rooms," said Isaiah, when he returned to the couch.

"Mm," I said through a mouthful of grapes, in spite of our mutual irritation. "They put the trunks in there. You'll never guess the color of the wallpaper. Safe guess the beds are red, too. Here, try one of these." I squished a steaming shu mai precariously between my chopsticks and aimed it at his face. "Hold still. Seriously."

He laid a hand on my forearm, lowering the dumpling toward my plate. "I'm sorry about the hardware," he said abruptly.

The cuffs were tight enough that I couldn't slip out of them, short of breaking my thumbs, but loose enough that they never quite warmed up to my body temperature, so that every time I shifted, they were cold and sharp against the soft part of my wrists—a biting reminder of the life I'd never escape, no matter how far I ran.

So I left his apology unanswered, and it floated untethered through the bright red sitting room.

"Remind me again why I'm here, Ise," I said quietly.

"Relax. It's not like you're giving the main argument, anyway. I'll do that."

"Why am I giving any argument? Why me?"

"Look here, little bird. I have artists. I have teachers. But I don't have anyone I know like I know *you*. We've been through a lot together, Char. I know what kind of person you really are. That's why you're the best I've got. I know that, deep down, you love the Remnant. You understand us. And you're smart. You can talk your way out of almost anything, when you feel like it. So talk."

We sat in silence for a long moment. I wasn't angry, exactly, but I wasn't dumb enough to fully trust him, either. I considered his words. Did I really love the Remnant as much as he seemed to think? I wasn't sure. "Yeah, well, I know you too, Isaiah. You're not telling me everything. You've got something else planned, or I wouldn't be here."

"Show me around the room, Char," he said abruptly.

I sighed. "Not much to show. There are two doors off this one, not counting the one we just came through."

"Show me to a keypad," he said, taking my arm. I released

my chopsticks unwillingly, but stood without protest. As I guided him around the couch, he leaned in close to my ear. "Gotta assume we're bugged."

I gave a terse nod. "There's a keypad in front of you."

A moment's investigation revealed that the keypads to the bedrooms had been deactivated, but the door to the hallway remained locked, in spite of considerable coaxing on our end.

The bedchambers were sumptuous, yet sparse: a soft, flat space for sleeping was set into the floor next to a single hard space for walking. Behind the bed, an oilcloth curtain revealed a spacious bathroom, with fancy lighting, a big tub, and a long mirror. I wandered into the smaller of the two bedrooms and sank down into the bed, which lay even with the floor. I was suddenly very tired.

Isaiah popped back into my little space, and I started describing the room to him out of habit. "So, it's a tiny bed, built right into the ground, and a massive powder room behind that. Also, there's a weird tube thing coming off the wall. It's attached to some kind of keypad."

"Same as mine, then. That's a sleep machine," he said. "You punch in how long you want to sleep, suck on the tube, and you wake up exactly that much time later. I think they go up to eight hours."

"Sounds pretty great. I know a lot of people who would have loved this back home."

"They were around. I've never known a careful man to use one."

"I'd have liked one in lockup," I said, thinking of countless nights I'd spent staring at the bunk above mine. "I guess part of prison is having to lie awake at night thinking about all the things you'd do differently, if you could."

"It's unconstitutional to drug juvies without a psych override," Isaiah said, his face tight. "And they'll have this one monitored. Don't use it."

"Oh, is that an order?" I asked, teasing.

"Yes," he said, simply, and disappeared back to his room.

I awoke to utter comfort and began stripping off my clothes before even leaving the dense pool of silk sheets around me. Halfway through, I realized I was still wearing handcuffs, which made the stripping a little too complicated for my half-awake brain.

I'd barely worked up the wherewithal to stand when the door chimed, interrupting my elaborate plans for the longest, hottest bath since the fall of Rome.

"Charlotte, you decent?" Isaiah's voice perfectly matched the low tones of the chimes.

I rolled my eyes. "Come on in. I hope you packed me something pretty to wear tonight." I held up the cuffs, which now had my shirt wrapped around them. "I'm probably going to have to cut this shirt off."

He stepped into the doorway with the assurance of a tamed tiger. His posture was more like a friend than a king, but with Isaiah, the two could not be separated. "Check your trunk. You should have what you need."

"Is it a robe?" I said sarcastically. "I bet it's a robe." I flitted back toward my room. "People really do love their robes around here."

"You noticed that, did you?"

"I'm a very important diplomat. It's my job to notice these little cultural differences."

Isaiah shook his head. "Give it a look. At least tell me you like the color."

I popped open the trunk and rustled through the packing paper. "My first official mission, and I'll be wearing pajamas. Seriously, though, I can make that work. I'm sure it's fi—" I stopped, seeing the pool of silk before me.

It was a blazing ember, tinged with amber, in a bed of white paper, as solid and bright as the final gasps of flames that had completely claimed the thing they burned. It was the last shade of a fire before everything was charred and black.

The robe was the exact color of the meteor.

I ran a hand over the delicate silk, then looked up with a start. Isaiah was still standing in the doorframe.

"It's beautiful. Really."

He didn't move. "Good. I spent enough time explaining the color I wanted."

"Of the meteor? But how? You were blind by then."

"No, not the meteor," he said, frowning. "Of your eyes."

He still wasn't moving, so I wrestled my shirt back over my shoulders and put a hand out. His tone was like I'd leaned against a fence made out of rubber. You expect it to be hard, but there was softness instead. It was the giving in that put me off-balance. "Hey, what's going on with you? We'll be fine. I can diplomat."

"I know you can."

I stared at him. "At least come in here. Stop standing in the doorway. Seriously, Ise, what is it? I put the cuffs on without protest. No blood was spilt thus far. You're at the top of your game, here."

"It's not the cuffs," he said. "There's something else. I thought I was going to do this differently, but..." His voice thinned out, making him sound like someone else.

"You're scaring me, Ise," I said quietly.

"Yeah. Me too. Listen, Char. I'm having second thoughts about my plan."

"You? Never. I'm sure it's a good plan."

He looked away. "It's a great plan. It's perfect, actually. There's just one problem."

I shifted uncomfortably, pulling my shirt even though he couldn't see me. "Pins and needles, my old friend."

He crossed the space between us to take both my hands, but when he began to speak, he lost his nerve again.

I broke the grip and put a hand on his shoulder. When he raised his head to look at me, I spoke barely above a whisper. "You can do this, whatever it is. I know you can. And listen, I may not be cleared for top secret, defcon-level-one conversations, but you know you can talk to me, right?"

Isaiah shook my hands off his shoulders and visibly gathered his resolve. "I'm just going to ask you one thing. And I'll know if—" he took my hands, "if you're lying, Char. I'm gonna know."

"For Pete's sake, Isaiah. The suspense is killing me."

He swallowed. "That guy, Eren. The Commander's son. We drugged him a little, asked him some questions. He said your name in his sleep. Coulda been a fluke, or something, but then you came back for him."

"That's not much of a question, Isaiah," I said quietly.

"Fine, here goes: him or me?"

I could not feel the softness of my shirt, or the warmth of his hands as they found mine. Only the steel of his blind gaze and the hardness of the floor beneath my feet. "What?"

"Never mind. Bad question; assumes too much. Let's start over: do you love him?"

"Eren?"

"Don't play dumb, Char. There's a lot at stake right now."

"Sure. The fate of nations. Right here in this room."

His jaw tightened. "Do you?"

"This is crazy." I shook my head, then let out a breath. I wasn't even sure what that meant. I'd spent three days with Eren back when I'd first arrived on the Ark. The *closeness* of those days, the feeling that I could reach out and touch him at any moment, was on my mind almost constantly. "I don't know. I guess. Maybe. I'm a little young to worry too much about all of that."

"You and I cannot afford to be young anymore. He's a good guy? He seems good, in spite of his father."

"He is, Ise. It's weird. He really is."

"Has he ever hurt you?"

"What? Look, Isaiah. *No.* But first of all, what's gotten into you? He's fine. You're fine. I'm fine. Everything's fine. I don't see how any of this affects the mission."

"That's what I figured." He squeezed my hands harder, stopping just at the point of pain. I winced, and the pressure was gone.

That was when I saw the kuang band. He held it in one hand and my exposed wrist in the other.

"They can't make me wear one," he said absently, touching the skin around the silver cuff. "Well, he can't, anyway. I outrank him." He said the last part thoughtfully, as though he'd needed to remind himself. "Or I should. Guess it depends on how you see the Remnant."

"Is that supposed to be some kind of explanation?"

He straightened suddenly. "A k-band is a lie detector. It has a sensor that goes under the skin and continually monitors your pulse. As I understand it, when the green gem is lit, it means you're telling the truth. They aren't much use to me," he said. It was the first time I'd heard any hint of bitterness about his blindness.

"And you expect me to wear one?"

"I do. And you will."

I thought about that for a moment. "That's why you haven't told me anything about the mission, isn't it? I can't lie about what I don't know. Smart man."

He smiled at me. "I do what I can."

"Why are you here, Ise? I mean, here in this Ark? Why not just send Mars with me?"

He looked up. If he was surprised at the directness of the question, he didn't let it show. "Put on the band, Charlotte."

It lay over his hand like a spider, thin wires protruding like delicate limbs. The thought of it made me step back involuntarily. "No," I whispered. "Ise, it's scary. You see that, right? I can't let it— I can't put that on."

He didn't say anything, but lifted it gently from its cradle, running a palm under the gossamer metal threads, testing their weightlessness against his skin.

"They'll never let you in if you don't. Do it for the Remnant."

"The Remnant wants me to die in space."

He grimaced. "For me, then."

I'd expected him to remind me of my promise to follow orders. I wasn't prepared for an appeal to our friendship, or whatever this was, but something in the tone of his voice put me even further off-guard, and my hands reached for the compressed metal band.

I didn't look up at him again.

I just clapped it on, fast, before its tentacles crept any

further around my brain. I winced as a wire pressed through the unprotected skin on the underside of my wrist. "For king and country," I muttered, hoping to mask the pain. "Kip used to say that on jobs, right before we'd break in somewhere."

Isaiah spoke even more quietly than I. "Thank you, Charlotte."

I shook my shoulders, trying to rid myself of the sensation that there were actual spiders on my arms and back. "Well, you're welcome," I said. He was standing halfway across the room, but it was suddenly too close. "But don't get too sentimental. I have my reasons, remember?"

A hand across his neck. A smile. "Glory and honor, obviously."

"Uh huh."

He turned to leave. "You're a real patriot. Get dressed. It's about time."

I rattled the chain between my wrists so that he could hear it from the living room. "I'm still cuffed."

"Like that's ever stopped you."

I sat on the edge of the bed and stared down at the smoldering pile of silk he'd left behind. It was a smart move, having us dress as though we belonged at the party. It put the cuffs even more out of place.

I needed to refocus. This party—or whatever it was—was only a few minutes away. As far as I could see, the handcuffs were the most obvious roadblock. They branded me a criminal. No one ever took criminals at their word.

I wound a bit of the copper wire out from around my waist and straightened the end. From there, it took maybe five seconds to pop the lock on both cuffs. I threw the cuffs to the ground in a heap with what was left of my clothes and jumped in the bath for a lightning-fast soak.

The copper wire remained around my waist, and I crushed it into a flat tangle as I padded across the room to examine the contents of the trunk. I wished I had a way of cutting it, but that was a problem that could wait. Better to see to the fate of the Remnant first.

I wasn't free of Isaiah's words, either, but those, too, could be untangled later. The time might one day come when I could tell him everything, from the moment I leaped into Eren's Coast Guard boat in Saint John Harbour, just before the meteor struck, to the days I'd spent hiding from Central Command in his bedroom, all the way through the end of the Battle for Sector Seven, when he'd rescued me from his father, the Commander. It would be good not to keep secrets from my old friend, Isaiah.

I frowned at the empty room. It hurt to think of Eren. And Isaiah wasn't my friend, was he? Not really. Not like Eren had been. And after all, Isaiah had plenty of secrets himself.

As it turned out, the trunk held little more than the robe, which whispered quickly over my shoulders, plus a pouch of makeup. I tied the sash tightly over the wad of copper wire, so that it could remain unnoticed in the event of further frisking, and headed to the mirror, pouch in hand.

The evening would be formal, and I intended to arrive at the party as though I belonged there, so I put the makeup on, starting with the eyeliner. Lots of it. I smudged it deep into my lashes and turned my face from side to side in the mirror. It looked as though the smoke from the embers in the robe had crept up onto my face.

I liked it.

I cleaned up the edges a bit, hoping not to look too wild, and selected a fairly neutral lipstick. After a moment's thought, I replaced the cuffs around my wrists. We were in, but only just, and I didn't want to jeopardize that yet. I threaded the pointed end of the copper wire up over my ribs and out through my sleeve.

And then there was nothing to do but wait.

When I emerged, Isaiah was waiting for me on the couch. He was a different man: much more relaxed, confident even.

And he was determined.

I cleared my throat. "You look nice."

Isaiah stood and spared a moment to show off a bright silk robe of his own. The purple gleamed against his dark skin, and his voice was as soft and deep as ever. "Thank you. You are lovely, as always."

I smiled, let myself breathe a little, and slid onto the chair across from him, avoiding the couch at the very last second. There was something twisted between us. Maybe it had always been there. But we were professionals, and we had a job to do. So I ignored the way he rubbed his hands on his legs, betraying his nerves. I didn't let myself see the tension in his brow.

A chime sounded, ending our brief wait, and Isaiah stood. "So. You ready for this?"

"I guess we'll find out." I nudged his shoulder with mine as the door slid open, revealing Shan, An, and the same two guards from earlier. "Any last words of wisdom?" I muttered. "Advice? Hints about what I'm getting myself into?"

At last, he smiled. "The first dance is mine."

I laughed, more for Shan's benefit than Isaiah's. If they'd

hoped to cow us before we stated our case to the Imperial, they'd have to do better than a measly pair of handcuffs. "Sure thing, Your Eminence."

He offered me his arm, and we swept out of the room together.

Eleven

An's eyes followed me.

No matter where I stood, I could feel her taking in my robe, my face. My hair was loose from its usual binds, but somehow, its unruly texture seemed suited to the fiery robe. I'd cleaned up fine, all things considered.

We followed the curved *guidao*, the path that spiraled toward the center, until we could access the nearest *lujing*, at which point, An finally fell into step beside me. I straightened my back and let my sleeves fall over the cuffs.

We gave each other a brief nod, and she spoke. "Ambassador Turner. What an elegant robe."

"Goes with my band, right?"

"I must apologize on behalf of Ambassador Hui. He is only following orders from the Imperial himself."

I met her eye. Her words sounded genuine, but there was a hardness behind her expression I couldn't account for. "I'm happy to comply."

Her lips curled up a millionth of an inch, as if to make plain her incredulity. "You are gracious to say so," she said lightly.

She struck me as a woman who didn't need a k-band to

spot a false intention, so I decided to try sincerity instead. "He doesn't need to fear us. We are not a threat to your Ark."

"So you say," she said. "But it is not my place to determine."

"Will you remove the cuffs, at least, before we arrive?"

"It is not my place," she repeated simply.

I gave her a hard look of my own and continued down the path in silence.

The hallway was colder and more dimly lit than when we'd arrived that morning. I guessed the Asian Ark had a weather team of its own. Isaiah's words came back to me: the more the environment was like Earth, the less likely people were to go mad at the lightness of space. That probably included changes in temperature.

At last we came to the end of the *lujing*, which met with the end of the *guidao*. An ornate door, carved like a temple pagoda, opened into a huge, round ballroom.

Actually, ballroom may not be the best way to describe it.

The center of the ship was enormous, for one thing. It was open and airy, and set in two tiers. The circular dance floor was surrounded by three staged areas and recessed slightly, so that we were looking down onto it. Two pods swung around overhead on raised tracks built into the space between the tiers. One was empty, and a larger one held a band of musicians. On the dance floor, a troupe of artists performed an elaborate dance. They were outfitted in robes with hundreds of long, carefully crafted streamers, so that when they moved, their limbs blurred through the air.

Above us, just beyond a chandelier hung with every gemstone imaginable, was the night sky, black and deep and spattered with infinite stars, all beyond our reach. I had to wonder how their engineers had created such a vast porthole. I stared at this the longest.

I was yanked from my slack-jawed reverie by the conclusion of the performance. A man and woman, bound together by silk streamers, unfurled themselves from a long silk sheet secured someplace above the chandelier. They began horizontally, holding each other tightly. As they hurtled toward the floor, the sheet unrolled around them, and they flipped around more and more quickly as they fell. We stood below, utter captives to the spectacle. If they hit the ground at that speed, we would stand witness to their certain deaths.

The sheet ran out, but the couple were still spinning around, held in a violent embrace. I saw then that they were not bound except by each other's arms. They were twenty feet from the ground, then two, in the space of half an instant.

At the moment of contact, the gravity generator beneath the floor reversed, and the couple swung out of its reach.

They would live.

We gasped, then burst into desperate applause.

The sound filled the expanse of the ballroom like thunder, but people only clapped harder. I saw more than a few tears among the observers, and I myself struggled to comprehend what had just happened. The dance had been flawlessly executed; the music breathtaking. But the applause was more intense than that: a couple bound themselves together and invited an inevitable death. I understood in pieces, then grasped the whole at last: we applauded their defiance.

But An did not clap. She looked from me to Isaiah and back again, until her delicate features locked onto my wrists.

I'd removed the cuffs when we entered, letting them slip

down the inside of my robe and into an urn near the door. She didn't call the guards. She didn't even appear to disapprove. Instead, she took in the rapt, unguarded expression on my face and my bare wrists with the look of a birdwatcher who finds that the sparrow she tracked is actually a raptor.

"You are perhaps more dangerous than you seem, Charlotte Turner."

But I had found some conclusions of my own. "I think the same could be said of you, An."

The extent of her acknowledgement was the slightest lift of the brow. She disappeared into the crowd without saying goodbye. Shan's eyes followed her and were soon joined by the rest of him. I blinked, somewhat surprised. Even Isaiah was nowhere to be seen. A slow smile caught my lips.

I was free to crash the party alone.

Twelve

I turned my attention to the three scenes surrounding the center floor, starting with a hanging garden generously speckled with red flowers. Not lotus blossoms, but something similar. Lilies, I thought. Dark red lilies. They hung from the ceiling in triplets and wove their way through the lush green trenchers that lined the walls. They were tied to the ropes of a long, willowy swing.

Next around the floor came a rock garden strewn with embroidered cushions, complete with a short, babbling stream, and last was an area set in twilight, draped with sheer red canopies. The overall effect was cohesive: a gorgeous, large-scale scene of silk, marble, and mahogany strung together with varying blood red accents at every stage.

And of course, there was the food.

Long, slender banquet tables ran between each stage of the party, nearly buckling under the weight of their bounty. The table nearest me was a work of art on its own, boasting layers of exotically carved vegetables and a selection of cheeses that would make a Frenchman blush, all draped with figs and honeycombs.

There was a seafood table so big it extended nearly half

the length of the cavernous room, which I prowled with wary interest. Tiny cards marked the name of each dish in Mandarin, Hindi, and finally English: fried rice with black pepper and anemone, tom yam kung, scallops with oranges and watercress, crab laksa, rose wine, shrimp soup, and lobster bao. The stacks of platters were intertwined with rubbery lengths of pickled octopus tentacles that tapered into slender, artfully positioned curls. I thought them best avoided.

I recognized nothing on the most beautiful table of all: the sweets. Glazed buns bursting with what must have been jam overflowed onto a platter of pillowy white pastries, frosted cakes in the shape of tiny dragons, and long brown sticks covered in perfect candy spheres.

My stomach grumbled impetuously.

I made a mental note to hit the cheese table first, followed by two rounds of each dessert table, and planned to round out my meal with enough seafood to populate an aquarium. I hadn't had real seafood in ages. There was none to speak of on board the North American Ark, and in juvy, our options had been limited to microwaved fish sticks harvested weekly from the bowels of the deep freeze.

I'd skip the vegetables for now. They'd take up too much room in my stomach, and we had plenty of those in the Remnant. I pressed my hands together in anticipation. It was a strong plan.

Unfortunately, Isaiah had other concerns in mind. He appeared at my side out of nowhere to crush my dreams of glycemic, near-coma bliss. "Somewhere, the European ambassador is here with his wife," he said, all business. "She started out on the Asian Ark. They've been building bridges here since day one."

"So we have some catching up to do."

"Sure do. But they're not necessarily against us. Haven't made any public statements either way. I reckon they've got their suspicions about the disappearance of Ark Five, but that'll affect the Commander, too," he said, referencing the sudden, unexplained loss of one of the Arks immediately after the meteor struck. "If we can get Europe on our side, their support would go far." He smiled easily, as though we were discussing the music. "I wonder who else is here."

"It's a lot bigger than I expected."

"The party?"

"The Ark."

"You'll do fine. Come on, let's say hi."

Duty called, so I steeled my stomach for the time being and slipped into the mingling throng, still holding Isaiah's arm. He followed lightly, conscious of the slightest pressure from my fingertips, and easily missed running into anyone.

Shan stood at the other end of the dance floor, wearing a golden robe and black pants. An, on the other hand, wore a silver robe and hose combo made of raw silk. It was tailored to her slim build like a second skin, making her look perfectly modern, as though she were attending some upscale holiday party back on Earth. She stood slightly behind Shan, but as we drew nearer, it became apparent that they were involved in a conversation of some kind.

From the size of the forced smile on Shan's face, I'd say it was something important.

I pulled Isaiah to the right, hiding our path among the more innocent partygoers.

"Mr. Underwood," said a strange voice. "Madam Ambassador. Welcome."

I turned to see a pale man, maybe twenty-five years old,

wearing a matte brown robe, make his way through the crowd behind us. "Good evening to you both."

"Hi," I said, extending a hand. His grip was not warm, exactly, but it was not so cold as to bar easy conversation, especially when coupled with the eagerness of his tone.

"How intriguing to meet you in person, Your Highness." His voice was naturally quiet and marked by an unmistakable French accent. I had to wonder whether people kept addressing Isaiah with different titles on purpose in order to slight him, or if they were genuinely confused as to how to refer to his position. I, for example, was solidly in the latter category.

"Just Isaiah will do," said Isaiah. "The king thing came with the election. I'm afraid we weren't thinking how it would look to the rest of the world when we came up with it."

"A man of the people."

Isaiah returned the handshake while appearing not to notice the barest hint of sarcasm in the man's words. To me, he seemed to walk a fine line between good-natured and cautious, like a man who genuinely needed the information he sought, and I was reminded of An's statement that what affects one Ark affects them all.

"I am Charles Eiffel," he continued, as though any pleasantries would be a waste of our time. "Do tell us about this Remnant you've managed to create. Do you consider yourselves a democracy?"

"We are," Isaiah answered. "With respect to our hosts, it was the only way to ensure we were fairly representing everyone, circumstances being what they were."

"I see," he said. "It is curious that your American republic seems to have failed you, then." His tone achieved an impossible blend of kindness and directness. In spite of the sharpness of his words, I found myself liking him.

Isaiah was unaffected either way. "Meaning?"

"Your choice of Commander Everest for the North American Ark. Your government's signature on the Treaty of Phoenix. Any of the things your elections have brought you. The Remnant recognizes none of these."

"None of those things recognize us, either. But we are prepared to support it, given an equal foothold. Was it Sartre who said, 'Freedom is what we do with what has been done to us?' We came close to that on Earth, as did your own continent, toward the end. And now, we must win it back."

"Well," said Eiffel, with considerably more warmth, "freedom will have its champions, *n'est-ce pas*?" He nodded to Isaiah, who slid gracefully back to the crowd, presumably intending for me to continue the conversation without him.

"Hey, Mr. Eiffel," I said, "are you related to the guy who designed the tower?"

"Please, call me Charles. And yes, that was my great-great-great grandfather. I owe him a considerable debt. It is undoubtedly why I was selected as an architect of the European Ark."

"Which part did you work on? Wait, did you design the Biosphere?" The European Biosphere was the greatest wonder of all the Arks. Apparently, it boasted more trees than the Black Forest. In the years after its announcement, West had spoken of little else. When he spoke to me at all.

"That honor went to my colleague, Madam Schiff. I believe she is around here somewhere," he answered brightly, observing my enthusiasm. "I thought I might be asked to work on the Biosphere. I'm an engineer by training, but popular opinion seemed to support my invitation to oversee the Nouveau-Louvre. I've always had an affinity for nature. I must say, I greatly admire Madam Schiff's creation."

"My brother does, too," I said, grinning. "Back on Earth, he had a greenhouse. Biggest tomatoes you ever saw. I think he must have bio-engineered them, somehow."

"Is that so?" Charles said appreciatively. "You and he will have to visit my Ark, one day. I have heard that the new tomato strains will be cause for some celebration." He offered me an elbow, a gesture I'd lately associated with Isaiah. "Now. On to our present business." We took a turn around the dance floor, our voices lowered slightly. "I see you've been placed at a similar disadvantage."

"Oh?"

He placed a hand over my arm, which was carefully draped around his, and pressed my sleeve back several inches. "A kuang band."

"Ah. That."

"Take heart," he said, pulling on his own sleeve to reveal a similar band. "It's not just the upstart republics they've tagged."

I had to smile.

"So we have some things in common," Charles continued in an easygoing manner. "But unlike your Monsieur Underwood, who calls himself a king, the Queen of Europe actually is a monarch."

"Wait, so no Parliament? Or Congress, or whatever?" I asked.

"We have one, certainly, but her decisions are final. Theoretically, in any event. She has yet to contradict their orders. Only the South Americans have attempted a direct democracy in advance of our arrival on Eirenea." He looked at me sideways. "And now you, the Remnant."

"Well, it's working, right? I mean, the South American Ark is at peace," I said. "That proves that success is possible for the Remnant as well, given the chance."

He inclined his head. We wended our way through the thickening crowd, smiling and remarking at the decorations. Every so often, Mr. Eiffel introduced me to someone, and we'd exchange pleasantries. Then after we'd passed on, he would whisper little comments in my ear. "He was lately the Minister of the Global Seed Vault. Delightful man." Or, "Marvelous lady. Discovered the plant genomes that allowed us to engineer the Biosphere. I doubt we'd have survived without her!"

At last, we were seated in the rock garden section of the party, next to the river. I took a careful seat on a wide rock near the water. Eiffel waved at a tray of drinks, which made its way quickly toward our little circle. He lifted a long stem and passed it to me, then took another for himself. "So, Charlotte," he said, giving me an evaluative look. "To what shall we toast?"

I lifted my glass. "To peace. To Eirenea."

"Hear, hear," he said, settling himself on an iron bench opposite me, and we sipped together. The drink was bubbly and sweet, and it appeared to be extracted from some exotic fruit.

Exotic. What did that word even mean anymore? A pine tree was more rare than a ghost orchid up here. I shook my head and took another sip.

"Who has a river in a party, anyway?" I said aloud.

"It sends a message, you know," said Charles. "Loose-running water is quite the feat on a spaceship. A few buckets of this in the right vent, and we'd all be taking a nap together while life support sorted itself."

I considered that. "Almost makes it more like a threat than a treat."

Charles looked me over again, this time with a slightly more appreciative eye. "I do tire of all the secrets," he said.

I lifted my wrist, letting the sleeve fall back. "You're not alone there, apparently. So tell me about the Nouveau-Louvre. That couldn't have been an easy undertaking."

Charles fiddled with the stem of his glass. "It was not. But I think, in the end, we got it perfectly right."

"Was it just the Louvre you got your art from?" I asked.

"Oh, no, my dear. Certainly not. We drew from every collection in Europe, public and private. Applications were coming in every day for ten years, down to the very last week. And how does one even choose? The ancients, the moderns. Statues. Paintings. High concept. The Impressionists. The lot of them, even the artists who'd yet to make a name for themselves. And only us to judge them. An impossible task, to be sure."

"So, how did you choose, in the end?"

Charles leaned close, letting his hand dabble through the water. "There was quite a team we pulled together. Historians, architects. Archeologists, of course, and even some artists. In the end, there were twenty of us. We got to be close, working together all those days. We were so diligent, especially at first."

His tone obscured some deeper emotion, but he didn't seem sad, exactly. More like hesitant, as though he'd decided to tell me something, but wasn't sure what I'd do with it.

"That sounds... well, that's good, right? You had a lot of work to do."

His smile was somewhat distant. "And we were so proud of all our work. We mapped every possible metric for consideration: the popularity of the piece, its influence, the artist's

94

other contributions to the form. And over time, we arrived at a singular conclusion. There could be only one consideration that mattered."

He paused, straightening, and splattered the water from his hand. Then he pulled a crisp cotton handkerchief from his coat and dried himself methodically, pulling the white cloth across every knuckle and between each finger.

I wasn't sure how to proceed. "Just one?"

Charles nodded.

"I can't even imagine. What was your conclusion? I mean, which pieces did you save?"

He met my eye with a perfectly steady gaze, which he seemed determined to hold. "In the end, almost none of them."

Now it was my turn to fiddle with my glass. "None."

He spread his hands in front of his knees. "We had so many resources. So many workers. They'd build anything we wanted. All that bureaucratic nonsense was over with. Whatever we wanted, we snapped our fingers, and it appeared at our door. The machines, the workers, the scientists! Any work of art on the continent. And do you know what we did with it?"

I shook my head. My tongue felt dry, and I took a nervous sip of my drink, but suddenly, its sweetness was cloying. What was he telling me?

He continued, his intensity building. "We built our room on board the Ark. We were given an entire level. Full oxygen, life support, everything."

My breath came harder, and I slid back involuntarily.

"And we brought in incubators. And formula. And the nappies, Charlotte. So many nappies."

"*Nappies*," I gasped. "Do you mean—"

"Diapers, of course. Instead of art, we saved babies. Hundreds and hundreds of babies."

I could not have been more surprised if he'd told me they'd resurrected Picasso and Da Vinci for a tea party with Giotto.

"You see, Ambassador, we twenty thought long and hard about what made a thing worth saving, and we could only ever have arrived at a single answer, working as earnestly as we were: *life*. To create art is an essentially human endeavor. Without life, the greatest masterpieces of history turned to so many splotches on canvas before our eyes. We needn't worry about art at all if there were never to be any more artists. So that is what we did, Ambassador. We saved art itself."

He sat back, nodding to himself, and allowed his words to sink in. I had a sudden flashback to a sketching class I'd wandered into one night in the Remnant. It was taught by a man so old that his hands appeared to be carved from gnarled wood around the stump of his charcoal. He hadn't even been famous back on Earth, but word of his talents had spread, and I'd wanted to see his work for myself. He sketched, and as the night wore on, hands, faces, arms, and whole people blossomed upon his paper. It was the most popular event the Remnant ever organized. By the end of the evening, his hands were beautiful to me.

I thought that I understood Charles Eiffel.

I looked out over the center floor, where the streamer-clad troupe was just finishing its performance. The gravity generator beneath the stage must have been set to reduced power mid-show, because now, the dancers were leaping through the air at impossible heights.

Impossible on Earth, I supposed. Up here, I never knew

what was possible or not, and just like that, another word lost its meaning. If I were only a little different—perhaps if I'd never been to juvy—the thought would have made me want to curl up in bed with the covers over my head.

Instead, I tightened my jaw against the imbalance of reality and forced myself to remember my purpose. He was awfully friendly, and I was pretty sure the information he'd just given me would upset more than a few people. And experience had taught me that nothing was free. Least of all information. "Why are you telling me this?" I asked sharply.

Charles raised his eyebrows in mild surprise. "Ambassador, my Ark has yet to develop an opinion regarding the Remnant's bid for status. We may support you, and we may even be prepared to express that support to the Imperial this very evening."

"And in return?" I asked.

"In return, should the situation in the Nouveau-Louvre ever come to light, we expect to avoid any sanctions from the other Arks. The children are to be counted as citizens, in full recognition of the Treaty of Phoenix, and our share of trade credits will be adjusted accordingly."

"You're worried about being punished for saving babies?"

Charles adjusted his tie. "Not for myself, as such. My concern runs to the children, you see."

"You have my word," I said quickly. "No matter what you do tonight." Of all the impossible things I'd seen or heard since leaving Earth, this was the one that pulled on me the hardest. It was as though I were suddenly, inextricably, bound to the European Ark. I'd once felt the same about the Remnant. I recalled the rushing wonder of my first weeks there and was again hit with the staggering *hopefulness* of a community reckless enough to save as many lives as possible, in spite of the consequences.

He appeared surprised.

"Thank you, Ambassador. I'm sure it won't come to that," he said. "But I am glad to hear it, all the same. And you may as well know, we kept a few of the paintings, in the end."

"Well," I said, breathing normally at last. "Where did you put them?"

"Why, we lined the ceilings, of course!"

"What about the art you didn't take? What did you do with it?"

"Ah, but that is my favorite part!" Charles exclaimed. "In the end, we saved them all!"

"So, you scanned them?"

"Well, we did that as well," said Charles. "Every Ark has a significant amount of storage on the servers of every other Ark, and we used ours to save our books and music, treatises and things of that nature. And of course, copies of the art, right down to their very molecules. But that's still not the best part.

"The originals were also saved! We constructed a cube. It's many stories high, vacuum-sealed, with indestructible walls, and it is packed to the gills with the great works of human history, right down to the last Greek sarcophagus."

I felt my smile stretch to a grin. "You're kidding."

"In fact, there are five such cubes," he said.

"Like the Arks," I said. "So, where are they now?"

"Who knows? We left them on Earth, in the hopes that one day, the archeologists of the future will find them. They each emit a signal, with enough power to last ten thousand years. One way or another, Ambassador, art will survive."

I thought of the pieces of Earth, trapped in eternal orbit around the sun, and for the first time, the tragedy of the image was tinged with an impossible hope. Archeologists. A return to the first home of our species. "That," I said, lifting my glass once again, "is what we should have toasted the first time."

"To art, Ambassador," he said, and touched his glass to mine.

"To art," I agreed. "And nappies."

At last, Isaiah found me. He nodded a greeting to Charles. In the overhead pod, the musicians took up their instruments and began to play. He turned to me and held out a hand, leading me away from my companions, who bid me a warm goodbye. Isaiah's hand was warm, too, and I was full of hope for the future.

We danced.

It was a tango, long and slow, and my robe slid around me like a snake in water as I moved in Isaiah's arms. His grip on my waist was solid through the slippery fabric.

The dance ended before the spell of silence was broken between us, and instead of speaking, Isaiah lowered me into a slow, steady dip. His face leaned in towards mine, and I thought for a moment that he might kiss me.

Instead, I gasped, breaking his grip. "What—"

The blond-haired, blue-eyed figure to our right stepped forward, but his assistance was unnecessary. Against all odds, Isaiah set me back upright without tripping, and gracefully released me from his grip.

Blue eyes. A slightly crooked smile on a perfectly square jaw. A voice downloaded directly from my dreams. "Charlotte. Mr. Underwood," he said, and, taking note of my open mouth, "Well, thank goodness we're all here. I was beginning to worry this would be awkward."

I remained at a total loss for words, but Isaiah was as collected as ever. "Eren Everest," he said calmly. "So good to see you again."

Thirteen

The two men squared up to each other, shades of anger and grim resignation riding the current between them. "I really can't say I share your sentiments," Eren said at last. Then, turning to me, he smiled. This, in combination with the blue-eyes-and-square-chin thing I was already dealing with, effectively stopped me from breathing, let alone speaking.

Again, Isaiah was unfazed. "Thank you for the dance, Ambassador," he said to me. "Good luck this evening. I really should find Shan."

I stared at Isaiah, unable to process that Eren was here, and safe. And *here*. My hand reached out to Eren even as I struggled to respond to Isaiah. "You're leaving me?"

"Why, Miss Turner. Do I detect a hint of jealousy?"

"I—of course not. Actually, I was just—"

"You kids have fun," Isaiah said, and disappeared into the crowd.

Eren and I turned to each other.

"Charlotte," he said simply.

I tried to think of something to say, but the only strategy my brain could offer up was to wrap myself in his arms as soon as possible. Something behind the warmth in his voice made me hesitate.

"How are you?" he said softly, as though the cavernous room held only the two of us. As though we weren't surrounded on every side by dancers, musicians, and dignitaries. "It's been, what, six weeks, and that... *Isaiah* wouldn't tell me any—whoa, hold on there."

Six weeks of separation, and all I could think about was pressing my face into his neck hard enough to feel his pulse in my teeth.

Instead, I found myself unable to get anywhere near his neck, let alone his pulse. His hands were clasped against my upper arms, pinning them to my sides and holding me away from him. "Steady there," he said softly. "We're in the middle of—"

"I do not care," I said, finally finding my voice, "where we are, or what they're all thinking right now. I don't care."

He concealed a smile. "Wouldn't want to cause a scene right in the middle of your first diplomatic mission, would we?"

"Aren't you happy to see me?"

"Trust me," he said seriously. "You don't want to do this here. Not yet."

Something in his tone made me take a step back and relocate my self-control, if only temporarily. "What's that supposed to mean?"

"Nothing. Nothing yet. You hungry?"

"My stomach has digested itself. My ribs are starting to dissolve."

He smiled. "Why am I not surprised? Come on. Let's hit the tables."

"Great. I have a whole plan worked out," I said eagerly.

"Oh?"

"Yeah, we're starting at the cheese and working our way out from there. And then you're going to tell me what's going on and why you're acting like we aren't—"

He gave me a solemn nod. "Cheese, then. I'll help you carry your plates."

"Plates?" I said, noticing the hint of a smile behind his eyes. "No, stop it," I pulled away from the hand he'd placed on my lower back, a feat far more difficult than it sounds. "Are you making fun of me?"

He swept an arm toward the closest cheese tower and held the other hand up to prove he wasn't touching me. "I'm not *not* making fun of you."

I drew myself up to my full height and brushed past him. "I can carry my own cheese plates, thank you."

In the end, I piled a single plate high with as much cheese and dignity as possible, and Eren did the same. We decided to sit in the twilight section of the party, since neither of us had explored it yet. He settled in and watched me eat, an amused expression on his face.

"I didn't peg you for a dancer."

"Cotillion classes," I said, as daintily as possible through a mouth full of honeyed brie. "Raised by a senator, remember? Also, Isaiah and I took a class together once."

"In juvy?"

I frowned. "In the Remnant. They're into all that stuff."

He gave me a questioning look.

"You know. Art, learning. Dance classes every night. You don't have to look like that. It's not so bad."

His amusement faded half a shade. "Agree to disagree."

I changed the subject. "So I was thinking dessert next, and then more cheese. No, wait. Seafood. *Then* cheese."

"Say no more," he said, standing up.

"Don't skimp on the chocolate," I called after him, then added an embarrassed "please" as an afterthought.

He raised a hand to his heart in mock-offense. "I wouldn't dream of it, Ambassador."

I watched him go, then sat for a moment in the near-darkness. There were pinpoints of light directly above my head, and beyond that, the sky outside the porthole made for an impressive ceiling. The musicians swung through the scene, beautiful and unobtrusive, now playing something closer to pop than classical. The floor was full of dancers. It was, undeniably, the coolest place I'd ever been.

I'd been on board this Ark for a few hours, and I was sure I'd found at least one ally. I was out of jail and, most notably, I had not been executed yet. And of course, I was with Eren.

It should have been the best night of my life.

So what was going on with him? Why didn't he want to hold me? Six weeks ago, our feelings for each other had been unambiguous, and after all, I was the one who'd secured his release from the Remnant's prison. Nothing had changed, right?

I wondered exactly what Isaiah had done to him. Surely his feelings toward the Remnant hadn't gotten in the way of his feelings for me, had they? I made up my mind to force the conversation, one way or another. Just as soon as I'd finished eating.

He returned, and again, the sight of him took my breath away.

"So," I began.

"Not yet. Just eat. And why are you so hungry? Are they not taking care of you?"

"Eren, I've been in prison for six weeks. They took care

of me fine, but it's not like you get artisanal cheese towers on lockup. Or literally anywhere else."

"They kept you in jail?!"

I set down a pastry and dusted my fingers in the air, holding my hands away from the robe. "I betrayed them, remember? Noah Board, dead guardians, Command prison. Ring a bell?" I picked up the seafood, but my appetite was significantly lower, whether from the cheese or the conversation, I wasn't sure.

"Did he—did they hurt you?"

"I'm fine, Eren. Really. I'd be even better if you'd tell me why you're acting so weird."

"I'm not acting weird. But I do need to talk to you."

I put my plate down. "You don't say."

"We can't just disappear right away. We need to pick the right moment."

"Why's that?"

"Just trust me. Want to dance?"

"Not really. It's like being on display. It's weird."

"How about right here?" He pulled me up, finally letting my hand rest on the back of his neck, and swayed me around as though we were dancing. But the music was lively, and we were barely moving, and certainly not in rhythm.

That was likely my fault. His hand was around my waist, millimeters from my skin, and warm through the robe. It was hard to focus on anything else.

"Charlotte Turner," he said quietly, as though he still couldn't believe what he saw.

I angled toward him slowly, so that my lips were ten inches from his, then six, and wrapped another arm around his neck. But when I pressed in closer, he stepped back, stopping me again, and glanced around the room.

Flames bit my cheeks, and I pulled my arms away. "What the heck, Eren!"

"Not here, Charlotte. Have a little self-control." His face was inscrutable, except for the barest hint of a smile behind his eyes.

"Are you... *laughing* at me? Wait a minute, are you *enjoying* this?" I whirled around, stalked out of the twilight area, pulse still racing. Maybe Eiffel could introduce me to the inventor of the chocolate fountain, or something.

Eren followed, barely concealing his laughter. "All right, Turner. You win. Let's get out of here. The only thing my father ever taught me about diplomacy is this: the important stuff never happens at the official shindigs."

"Shindigs, huh," I said, my voice a bit sharper than I intended.

"It's a real word," he said.

"I know it's a real word. Just not the one I was expecting."

His face turned serious, and he leaned toward me, still careful not to kiss me. "Come with me to the balcony," he whispered.

I trotted after him, letting my fingers find his, letting him lead me. "Balcony? On a spaceship? That's a little more of an adventure than I'm looking for right now, to be honest."

"Well. Wait till you see it." He pulled me out of the ballroom and through a papery divider. There was a small white staircase built into the outer wall of the ballroom, before the start of the spiral, leading to the ceiling over the dance floor.

I wasn't in the mood to watch people dance, but it looked like a great place to be alone with Eren, so I hopped up after him.

He stopped me when we got to the top. The landing

ended in a large rim that stuck straight up toward a massive overhead porthole. I looked around and saw a series of chairs lining the rim. They lay on their sides, like a hundred bicycle spokes, with their backs toward the stairs we'd just climbed.

"This is kinda trippy, if you haven't done it before," Eren warned.

"Done what? *OH*," I shouted, planting my hands on the floor.

A man was standing on the rim. Not the edge of the rim, the side of it, and he was walking around. A woman in a long blue robe swept toward him, taking his arm.

Sideways.

"The edge of this thing is kind of like a microgenerator for the grav simulator. So they made it into a big round deck and called it a balcony. It's a great place to see the stars, actually. They say the Imperial comes here all the time when he needs to think. Here, take my hands."

I complied, perhaps a little too eagerly. Something in the back of my mind noted that he had a bracelet like mine. That made sense, I thought, before dismissing it. He's one of Central Command's envoys, so he was here as a diplomat, too. Of course the Imperial would require a k-band from the other delegations.

"That's it. Now just *step*. Don't think about it too much. It'll catch you."

He peeled me off the floor and helped me onto the "balcony," which was shaped like the neck of a mason jar, and the entire party was inside it. Eren was right; it was trippy. I'd have lain flat if I thought it wouldn't upset him. The gravity did indeed catch us, and whether I wanted to or not, I was soon sitting sideways, oriented so that the woman in the blue robe could look me in the eye. I remained glued to the floor. I could still feel the faint pull of the gravity in the staircase, too, so I thought maybe I'd just stay put for a good while.

The lady came over to me. "It will pass," she said, with a faint accent.

"Don't be scared." Her escort nodded sympathetically. "If you've never been afflicted with the Lightness by now, it is extremely unlikely at this point."

"The Lightness?" said Eren.

"It's what they call it when you can't stand being in space anymore," I said weakly. "Apparently, it happens on every Ark, but that's what they call it here."

He led me to a chair out of view of the staircase, which, from my current perspective, was now sideways. I closed my eyes and focused on breathing. And him.

After a while, I was well enough to stand, and we took a cautious stroll around the perimeter of the ballroom. There was the wall lined with chairs on one side, the balcony beneath our feet, and on our other side, the stars, safe behind several feet of plexiglass.

So many stars filled the vast blackness of space. I felt cold.

"Was that the Lightness?" I wondered out loud. "Not too bad. I feel fine already."

"Didn't look like it, from what I've heard on our Ark," said Eren. "I don't think we have a name for it, but it gets pretty rough. Maybe you just had a small attack."

I shook my head and leaned closer to Eren. We didn't bother walking any farther around; we just stood. The sky stared back at me, and I couldn't help wondering how many other humans could see the stars at that moment. Almost no one on the North American Ark, of course, with our spinning doughnut shape. And not too many people on this Ark, either, since only the outer spiral could have windows, plus the top and bottom layers. It hit me that space extended out in every direction, with no real up or down at all. I pictured a room on the bottom level, with a window instead of a floor, and felt dizzy. I certainly hoped whoever lived there could handle it better than I was.

"Do you think we're going to make it?" I asked.

Eren knew exactly what I meant. "To Eirenea? Yes, I do."

He was quiet for another moment, then spoke again, as steadily and confidently as he had in my memories. "I believe that peace is not only possible, it's inevitable. My father disagrees, certainly, but I know we're going to make it. Maybe not this year, but eventually. We're going to colonize that planet. The human race will survive."

"You sound so certain."

"I don't have any doubt, Charlotte. I never have."

"I, on the other hand, feel that there is a strong possibility that everything will get blown up in the near future, and that your father will be involved in some way, and furthermore, that that's probably why he has his doubts about peace."

"Second thought: let's not talk about my father tonight."

"Yeah, sorry. Fair enough. I'm sure he's just swell, deep down."

Eren rolled his eyes.

"Like, way, way deep down."

"I get it, Charlotte."

"A million miles down. Past all the ragey, angry stuff."

Eren laughed. "You don't know him like I do."

"Let's just say that goes both ways. Hey, this is a bit off-topic, sorry," I said. "But remember that time he tortured me? Then tried to have me killed?"

The humor drained from his eyes in an instant. He did not answer me, but there was a darkness on his face I hadn't seen before.

"Hey, I'm just kidding around," I said lightly. "I mean, not about your dad. He's actually the worst. But I'm fine now, and look! We're here! Together."

I smiled up at him, hoping to regain something of our usual rapport, but instead of smiling back, he kissed me.

Finally.

I leaned into him, wrapping my arms around his neck, and kissed him back. Slowly, at first, and then more deeply. His hands left mine and wound their way into my hair, causing the ship to vanish around us, along with the stars and the coming war.

I lost myself in his arms. I hoped he would never let go, but at last, he stopped, smiled, and looked straight into my eyes. I felt, in that moment, that he was right about everything. We would find peace. All of us. Eren was with me, and everything was possible.

"Well," I said. "That's one small step for intra-ark relations, anyway. Seriously, though, I am such a good diplomat right now."

"I don't think that's what they meant when they wanted us to—"

"Shh," I said, leaning in for another kiss. But Eren took a step back, still smiling, and I kept right on talking, high from being in his arms after six long weeks of separation. "I mean, at this rate, we'll have them laying down arms by next weeken—Hey, Eren. What are you doing?"

He held me at arm's length, taking both my hands in his and joining them together between us.

"That was the hardest six weeks of my life, being without you. I couldn't think of anything else. I just wondered what was happening to you and if I'd ever see you again. And you're right, you know? We can stop the conflict forever, as long as we're together. With you by my side, I know we will."

"Eren," I began, but quickly lost my voice.

Eren turned around to see what had so surprised me, and squeezed my hands tighter when he locked eyes with his father.

The Commander took a steady step toward us.

I fought the urge to step back, but I could not stop my hands from going limp in Eren's.

I looked from one man to the other, feeling warm and numb at the same time, and felt my head shake in disbelief. The Commander's eyes were every bit as blue as Eren's, but somehow a different color entirely. His gaze turned to me, and we were frozen, the three of us.

"Father," said Eren, choking on the word.

But the Commander ignored him and spoke directly to me. "Ambassador." His voice was like ice and steel, and tempered by years of absolute authority. "The Imperial has arrived. You are expected downstairs."

Fourteen

I hit the stairs with a lot less difficulty than before, probably because the rest of the ship, other than the "balcony," was oriented in the same direction. Eren came flying down after me.

"Charlotte, just a moment," he said. "Let me escort you in."

We entered the ballroom to the obvious notice of nearly everyone there. I squared my shoulders and smiled as calmly as I could.

"I still need to talk to you," he said in a low voice. "It's important."

"Yeah, well," I whispered back. "Right now I have to talk to the Imperial. That's the whole reason I'm here. But Eren, listen. If you're trying to get me to come back to Central Command, that's not gonna happen."

He flashed me a pained look, but adjusted his face to something more pleasant almost immediately.

"I mean, it's just a bad idea," I said hurriedly. "Anyway, your dad will never go for it."

The Imperial's private escort, including An and Shan, were waiting on the far wall of the room, and he led me through the near-silent crowd without much of an expression at all.

"Greetings, Ambassadors," An appeared from her place in the Imperial's escort to take my free arm, and I released Eren. He gave a little nod and left us. An led me through the crowd. "The Remnant's delegation will undertake the first negotiation with the Imperial, followed by a rebuttal from Central Command. Then the pod will open for any other Ark whose delegation would like to speak with the Imperial."

"Thank you, An," I said.

"My pleasure. You are well acquainted with the Commander's son?"

"I—uh, yes. I mean, it's a surprise, seeing him here."

"Not an unpleasant one, I think. You do not smile in this way for many others."

"Am I smiling? I hadn't noticed."

"It must be difficult," she said, staring past the crowd at the Imperial guard. "Knowing that what is desired cannot be obtained." Her gaze caught Shan's attention, and he gave her an oblique nod, to which she did not respond.

I didn't have an answer for that. But then, it didn't sound like much of a question, anyway. In fact, the way she said it, it barely seemed like she was referring to me at all.

She guided me to a circular pod behind the brightly robed escort and lowered her head. The pod reminded me of a giant teacup, especially when the nearest guard opened a door at its handle. Inside sat a small, elderly man. He looked exactly as I expected the Imperial to be: richly dressed, with a long, thin white beard. His delicately lined face was the perfect blend of grandfather and headmaster.

"Your Imperial Highness, may I present Charlotte Turner,

Ambassador from the Remnant of North America. Ambassador, this is the Imperial of the Asian Ark, Sovereign Protector of His People, Defender of the Treaty of Phoenix, and Sentinel of the Peace of this Galaxy."

I bowed, aping An's graceful motion, and tried to get my head around what kind of person needed that many titles. Even the Commander got by with only one, and he had the most inflated ego I'd ever known. Which, to be honest, was saying something.

The Imperial inclined his head a millionth of an inch, and I took an unsteady seat in the pod next to him. The guards shut the door, and I looked up at him expectantly.

"Your Highness, thank you so much for hav—oh, we're moving," I said, and grabbed his arm out of instinct. My seat was lifting toward the glass ceiling. Actually, the entire pod was going up.

His eyes widened, and I released him immediately. "I'm so sorry. That was definitely not on purpose, your, uh, Imperial Highness."

But instead of throwing me out of the pod, he began to laugh. "Ah, Ambassador Turner. I was told that your team did not brief you with any degree of thoroughness. May I assume, my dear, that the Remnant values your honesty as much as I do?"

"I—yes, sir. They do. I mean, we do."

He smiled. "In that case, I choose to view your lack of preparation as a sign of respect, and we may proceed accordingly."

I sensed that things were not off to a great start, but if the Imperial was going to be all calm and smiley about this, then darn it, so was I. "Thank you, sir."

"You are in the Imperial Coach, which is how a foreign

dignitary such as yourself may be granted a personal audience. It will make one complete circle around the ballroom, after which time it will descend, and you may leave. Our present situation serves as a reminder of the awesome responsibility placed on our shoulders by those who crafted the Treaty of Phoenix. Had they not given each Ark power over the others, you might never have sought our approval for the creation of your burgeoning nation. It is a responsibility I undertake with great care, Ambassador. Once I have heard from each of the delegates, I will make my decision."

I nodded. "Sounds good, sir."

"I will remind you of your kuang band," he said, touching my wrist with spindly fingers. "As you may be aware, this band will light green if your words are true and red if they are false. Such a thing has its limitations, of course, as it cannot see beyond your perception, but as a tool for diplomacy, I find it to be of great value."

From this angle, I could see nearly everyone at the party, except for those on the outermost edges. There were those who danced and small groups who remained leashed to the mountains of food. And there were quiet minglers, standing in pairs, their hands in their pockets.

I did not see any k-bands.

The pod swung to the side, and we began our slow circuit around the dance floor, just inside the rim of the balcony. I saw no track that it followed, nor any mechanism by which it remained against the wall. Instead, it simply slid up, as easily as an arm travels through a sleeve. It must have had its own grav pack, or it followed one embedded into the wall. I closed my eyes, thoroughly unsettled, and forced the issue out of my mind.

From where I sat, I saw that Eren was engaged in a fairly

tense conversation with his father, who wore no band. I shook my head and sat up straight. If this was to be my only meeting with the Imperial, I couldn't afford to blow it.

"Ambassador, if you could state for me the premise of your case, please."

"I—we, the Remnant, are here to seek your official recognition of our status as an independent nation-state." I let out a sigh. The gem was green. That much I had worked out ahead of time.

"If you would indulge my curiosity," he said slowly, "I am plagued with questions about the reasoning behind your position. Why do you not instead seek to obtain citizenship for your people under Central Command? Not a single Ark would oppose you, even in spite of your criminal status, given that we have already lost Ark Five."

"Yes, Your Honor," I said. "But we're not like them." My k-band lit up, and I blinked down at my lap. It was bright green again.

The Imperial nodded his approval. "Not like Central Command?"

"What I mean is, we want different things."

"Surely, if you should have some grievance against the Commander's authority, you could take it up with the Tribune?" he said. The Tribune was the highly protected group of thinkers who were charged with upholding the Treaty of Phoenix, and they arguably wielded as much power as any individual Ark's leadership.

"It's more than just citizenship; it's a way of life. They may care about order, but they aren't preserving *justice*."

"The Commander tells me that you lack any semblance of order. How can such a system maintain balance? How can you hope to govern yourselves effectively, if you are made of nothing but criminals?"

"We aren't criminals!" I said abruptly. The band flashed red, but only briefly. Seeing the shock on his face, I lowered my voice and chose my words carefully. "Not most of us, anyway, and not by any standard that matters." I took a moment to match the calmness of his tone. "We're the people who were meant to be left behind. They've always intended us to die. You're older than forty, Your Honor. Surely you can see the value in the people they've discarded. That is what the Remnant does as well."

"I see nothing wrong with saving as many people as we can, but you must see the issue from the point of view of the rest of the world. If we grant you this status, you will find allies. You will build wealth through trading. You will have the authority to create whatever laws you deem necessary. And this is a problem."

I raised my eyebrows. "May I ask... how?" I asked carefully.

"You cannot hope to achieve peace. I have spoken with the Commander. He is a man capable of leading."

"A leader needs checks and balances, Your Honor. Like you were saying. It's a good thing. That's how our entire system is set up—every Ark in space. It's why they gave you power over our food supply. It's why we have the technology you need to maintain weather, and to fight against the Lightness.

"And," I continued, "only half of us on my Ark are North American. I know you care about everyone from your continent, not just those on your Ark. We have plenty."

"The Commander is a forceful man, and these are diffi-cult times. He is perhaps not as fair as you would like, but as you have pointed out, sacrifices must be made to attain that which is worth having: peace. He is precisely the kind of man who can restore order and end this folly."

"Pol Pot was a forceful man," I said, unable to stop myself from interrupting. "Is that the kind of order you want?"

The Imperial flinched slightly, giving the barest hint that he'd even heard me, and continued to marshal his argument. "I am convinced that, without the Commander, you North Americans will never achieve stability. Your system is fallible, and your claims are paradoxical, Ambassador. How can we promote unity by dividing the Ark's leadership in half?"

"Our system within the Ark is no different from the system that binds all the Arks together: it depends upon an even distribution of power, Your Highness. Surely you can see the value in providing some balance against the Commander's reach."

He remained unpersuaded, impassive. "As long as you fight him, your Ark remains a threat to the rest of us. We cannot afford to be drawn into your war. It is better to allow him to annihilate your little faction and rebuild his government unimpeded."

I felt cold, then angry. How could the Imperial be so cruel? And how had the Commander already gotten to him? "But that's exactly why you have to give us our independence!" I said, all thoughts of forced serenity abandoned. "He's a monster, and *you need us*. You need the Remnant to be strong enough to stand up to him. You can't afford to write off my entire Ark. If you want stability, give him something to keep him in check. Legitimize us, so that he won't keep fighting."

He pressed forward, but the tiniest drop of resolve had

drained from his voice, and he spoke as though he was determined to regain it. "You are a warfaring people. Your entire continent runs red with blood. It is in your very nature."

"Show me a continent without blood on its hands, Your Highness, and I'll show you Antarctica."

I'd landed a blow. I knew it. The Imperial gave no outward indication that he'd even heard me, but I sensed a shift in the tone of the conversation. His eyes were less narrow. And even though his back was as straight as ever, his posture was somehow less rigid.

And yet, if he could not see me as anything more than a young convict determined to be a thorn in the side of the established authority, I would fail. And if I failed, we had so much to lose.

What was really at stake here? More than just the Remnant. Of that, I was certain. And that was what I had to make him understand.

"We want to live, Your Highness."

He looked at me.

"This Ark is beautiful because it contains life. Your people are worth protecting because they are alive. My Ark is no different." I lowered my voice. "The Remnant is no different."

At last, he seemed to hear me. "There are rumors of extra survivors on every Ark," he said softly, matching my tone.

"And, with one exception, no one has tried to wipe them out. No one wants them punished. And do you know why that is, Your Highness?"

He looked at me, waiting.

"Compassion. I am making an argument for large-scale compassion. It's the only thing that matters anymore anyway."

The pod lurched downward, and I realized that the circuit was complete. My turn in the Imperial pod was over, and the fragile connection we'd forged was jolted back to reality. His entire demeanor changed before my eyes.

Seconds earlier, I'd been so sure I'd made an impression, but suddenly, the iron returned to his posture. "Even if I wanted to help you, Ambassador, my hands are tied. Your Ark is... *unruly*, and there is only so much I can do from this position."

"I'm only asking that you consider it, Your Highness. Consider whether our lives are worth living. Worth saving."

At last, the rigidity returned to his voice as well. "I have very little faith in your proposal, Ambassador, and if your faction cannot find peace with the Commander, your entire Ark will be destroyed."

Fifteen

I was escorted from the pod without much decorum, and Isaiah was waiting for me when it opened. It was strange: the Imperial genuinely seemed to agree with me. It was as though some unseen force was making him act otherwise. Was he in thrall to the Commander in some way, or was some other intrigue playing out? Or had I misread him entirely? I needed time to think.

I guided Isaiah to a spot near the edge of the ballroom, but close enough to the dance floor that I could see the faces of Eren and the Imperial, who were taking their own flight around the room.

It felt weird to know that, right at that moment, Eren was fighting against me, seeking to destroy the Remnant at his father's bidding. Once, after a long stint in juvy, I'd come home and thrown my arms around my scruffy, yellow dog. It was a rough, impulsive, joyful moment. But she'd grown old since I'd seen her last, and she bit my shoulder, sending me flying backwards in shock. It hadn't hurt, really. It was nothing more than a warning nip, but it made me realize how much I'd clung to the thought of her when I was inside.

It made no sense that she didn't act the way I expected her to. Didn't we love each other at all? I'd cried for hours, until West came home from school.

He doesn't know how bad it would be, I told myself. *He still doesn't realize what his father's capable of.*

"So." Isaiah leaned in close, causing me to stop staring at Eren. "How did it go?"

"Um, not great? He said we should have appealed to the Tribune for citizenship in Central Command, not independence. And he sort of threatened to blow us up if we can't keep the peace."

"I reckon people are still jittery about Five."

"Yeah, fair enough. But we *can't* be under the Commander. He'll never give us a fair shake."

Isaiah grinned. "Careful there, Ambassador. You sound dangerously close to believing in the cause."

"What was the point of letting us in here, anyway?"

"How do you mean?" he asked.

"It's just that he seems to have made up his mind already. And I got the impression there's not much we can do to change it."

Isaiah nodded. "That's not all. There's something else kinda strikes me as funny."

"The k-bands?"

"No, I knew that would happen, eventually. I can't rightly say, just yet, but something's off. Maybe the way they keep hinting that they'll destroy us if we don't play nice."

"Not much of a hint. He about spelled it out for me. Hey, looks like you're up. I'll walk you over."

We crossed the floor just as Eren stepped out of the pod. The Imperial stood, and Isaiah was welcomed into the enclosure with a deep, ceremonial bow.

"Your Highness," said the Imperial, and the pod lifted them up and out of earshot.

I was still staring after it when I felt a tap on my shoulder.

"May I have the next dance, Ambassador?"

Still mesmerized by the flying, floating teacup, I steeled myself with my most diplomatic expression before turning. "Yes, Mister…"

"Commander. Everest. But I think we're a little past introductions at this point, Miss Turner."

Sixteen

"A dance. With you." I could think of a billion things I'd rather do before dancing with Eren's father, the High Commander of the North American Ark, several of which involved a combination of my teeth and a pair of rusty pliers. "Uh, no? Thanks, but no, never. Not ever."

He simply stared, his once-handsome face broken by the stern, ugly line of his mouth. "Don't you want to prove your worth as a diplomat? Might be nice to show the Imperial that we can get along for the space of a waltz."

"See, my main issue here is that I never want to touch you, ever. Also, I make a point of not waltzing with the people who've tried to kill me."

He laughed, as though amused, but the smile didn't reach his eyes, and I took a few steps back, involuntarily. He stepped forward, and I felt my lungs freeze. "Come now, Miss Turner. Surely we can tolerate each other for a few moments."

He was standing too close. I tried to work out the reason why my feet seemed rooted to the ground, but a vision of his sneering face and a crackling stunner made my mind blank out and my mouth pull down into a stupid, helpless frown.

"No. We can't." I tried to sound forceful, but to my horror, my voice came out like a whisper. "And I'm not particularly interested in showing the Imperial you have a soft side."

"Neither am I, in fact, given that I don't." He grabbed me by the waist, in front of every soul in the room, and swept me onto the floor. To my astonishment, not a single person stepped in to pull me away from him. Even my own legs didn't run away. What was wrong with me? The stunner cracked through my mind, and my arms were like a toy, unable to resist him as he arranged them in preparation for the waltz.

In that moment, I would have undergone any amount of pain to stop myself from crying. He was the kind of dangerous that likes to kill the things that show weakness. And right then, I was nothing but weakness.

"You can't kill me on this Ark," I managed at last. "They'll know."

"While I appreciate your advice, Miss Turner, I'd already worked that much out for myself. Steady, there."

I staggered off-balance, but he swept me around as though it was part of the dance, forcing me further into his control.

"Let me go."

He ignored that. "May I offer you a trade?"

"There's nothing you can offer me. Except maybe public acknowledgement of—"

"Yes, yes. The Remnant. Let's spare each other the time, shall we? You are well aware of my disinclination toward any such imprudence. My offer is this: stay away from my son, and I will spare your life."

"That's probably the most predictable, least useful thing you've ever said."

"I'm glad to see you haven't lost your pluck since we last spoke. I imagine you think it's charming." He pulled me in, and my arms found the will to press back, finally, but my position was too far compromised, and he was stronger. I couldn't stop his face from looming towards my ear. "I want you dead, Turner. You are a threat to everything I've tried to accomplish, and I cannot make my son see reason. But you're not like him. You have none of his innocence. I give you my word that, if you release him, I will spare your life, when the time comes."

I battled a considerable urge to spit in his face. People were watching, I reminded myself, and they were probably the kind of people who liked their diplomats to solve problems without phlegm. "Your word is worthless, and my life doesn't need your protection."

"Don't be so naïve, my dear. It hardly suits a girl of your background. The Remnant is outnumbered, outmaneuvered, out-trained, and without access to a meaningful supply line. Sooner or later, and likely sooner, my engineers will outrun the *child* who handles your security, and the Remnant will fall into my hands. I will own you and everyone else in it. Until then, I expect you to fight against me, to seek to prevent this from happening. You will fail. But if you give me this one, tiny thing, when that moment comes, I will not have you executed."

"You know what I think?" I hissed, catching myself before I could stumble again, and stopping him from pulling me further off-balance. "I think you sound scared."

"You should see yourself," he scoffed, finally allowing me to press him away from me. He stepped back gracefully, as though it were part of our little dance. "Chin up, Turner. The Imperial is descending, and, from what I've heard, you have quite a decision ahead."

With that, he released me.

I ran directly to Isaiah. He was still speaking, and the Imperial listened respectfully.

"There are thousands of people in the Remnant, Your Highness," said Isaiah. "By supporting our right to govern ourselves, you prevent rebellion against Central Command. And by recognizing us as independent, you will motivate Central Command to stop trying to bring us to heel. They cannot govern us fairly. A two-state system is the only way to gain stability."

"An interesting proposition. I will consider your proposal with great care, Your Majesty."

"Mr. Underwood," said An. "If you would be so kind as to allow the European delegation to take the pod."

Isaiah stood, giving her an odd look through his dark glasses, but he exited, and I slid between the guards to take his arm and guide him away.

Eren came to stand on my other side, and the three of us stared after the Imperial, who was by then touring the room with another delegate.

"Any luck?" I said to Isaiah.

"Some," he answered. "I gave them my plan."

"You think they'll go for it?"

Isaiah turned to me, but no sign of triumph lit his features, nor did he seem remotely comforted by his belief in his victory. "Yes, I do," he said softly.

I looked back at Eren, who was staring at us both.

"You still haven't told her, have you?" he said to Isaiah.

"I'm a man of my word, Everest."

"Told me what? What's going on?" I said. "Since when do you boys keep secrets together?"

"Isaiah may have found a way to—" said Eren.

"Charlotte," Isaiah said. "You still want to go exploring?"

I looked at him blankly. There was no getting past Isaiah when he stonewalled like this. Staying near him would be the quickest way to figure out what he was up to. In any event, the idea of exploring a new Ark was far too strong a temptation to resist. "Yes, Mr. Underwood," I said slowly. "I believe I do."

Isaiah turned to Eren. "Ambassador Everest. Care to join us?"

"Shouldn't we stay through the end of the party?" said Eren. "I mean, we're the main envoys here. Won't they be expecting us to hang around?"

"We don't have to stay away all night. They're busy with the Europeans right now anyway," I said eagerly. "And besides, An told me the whole Ark is open to the public. It's not even illegal!"

Commander Everest stepped over to our group, forcing a deliberate chill onto the conversation.

"Father," said Eren. "Perhaps you'd like to stick around. Keep an eye on things."

"I would indeed like to keep an eye on things," said the Commander. "Which is why I'll be coming with you."

"We don't need a chaperone," Eren said.

"Private party," I said, threading my fingers through Eren's. "We'll let you know how it goes."

"If you're leaving with my son, I think I'll join you. It is, as you so eloquently stated, not even illegal."

128

"Nothing good can come of this," said Isaiah. "Maybe you should stay here."

We gritted our teeth as the Commander took his place in our circle. The three of us met each other's eyes for a long final moment before he spoke again. "Enjoy your freedom," he said darkly.

We turned to leave, casting intermittent glances behind us. By the third time I looked back, the Commander was gone.

Seventeen

Isaiah seemed to have an idea of where he was going, as was ever the case. I figured he'd gotten an idea of the Ark's layout before we left, possibly from Adam. I stayed near to him, to guide him when necessary, and Eren remained next to me, so close that our arms kept brushing. I gave him a little smirk of pretend-annoyance, and he finally grabbed my hand.

I put the Commander out of mind. I couldn't say I was entirely comfortable being alone with Eren and Isaiah, especially as they barely seemed to tolerate each other, but I trusted them both, and the further I got from the Commander, the brighter the situation became.

Still, we broke into a steady jog by unspoken agreement as soon as the door to the party closed behind us. Before I knew it, we were sprinting down a *lujing* we chose at random, slowing less and less every time it crossed the *guidao*. We found our way to the outer rim of the ship several minutes later, and from there, it was all too easy to locate an elevator.

The elevator was uncomfortably small, probably intended for one-person deliveries, and we huddled together on the enclosed platform. Eren selected the lowest floor, and the grav generator eased us down into the bowels of the ship.

"I can almost smell the water." Isaiah smiled. "I have heard rumors of this place since before we left Earth."

I glanced at Eren, but he only laid a hand on his hip, as though thumbing for his sidearm. Which was, of course, back in Central Command.

The atmosphere changed, one piece at a time, starting, as Isaiah had predicted, with the smell.

In space, nothing has an odor. Each Ark was enormous, and this was the biggest of all. There were so many machines, and so many filters, that smells were the first to go. The air never lingered, and even if it had, the monotony of the oxygen converters had all but robbed us of our ability to smell anything but the ship.

Not so here.

It was a warm smell, and humid, miles from the sterility of space. It was salty and fishy, but there was more to it than just that.

The doors of the platform opened silently, but the wall continued to spread apart long after they'd disappeared, splitting further and further, folding back into itself all around us, until it was gone, and we were left with an unencumbered view of our new surroundings.

We gazed around, nervously at first, then with the kind of open, slack-jawed wonder most of us hadn't used since childhood.

We were on a beach. A real beach, with frothy waves, and a bright, white moon overhead that turned the tips of the tiniest distant waves to silver in the blackness.

"This is... oh," I breathed. "This is amazing."

The steady sound of waves crashing along the shore reached the platform, and I could no longer resist running.

Eren was right behind me, stumbling through—was it possible?—*sand*.

"Take off your shoes!" Eren shouted after me, laughing. "We have to!"

I did so, as did Isaiah, and we left them half-buried in the perfectly sculpted dune, and kept right on running. Sand spilled down around the tall, thin stalks of grass, and I blinked, sliding, when I saw a crab burrow out of our way.

"It's the ocean! It's—but, how is this even possible?!" I said, tripping through cool, broken water of the shore. "Is it safe? Is it okay that I'm about to be *swimming* right now?" I let my feet carry me a bit deeper into the water, so that it was up to my knees. The weight of the waves pressed through my lower legs.

"I'm not even sure I care," said Eren, scanning the tops of the waves. They were perfect and silver in the moonlight. "I can't believe this."

"I saw a crab. A CRAB, you guys." I was giddy. Here, after the end of Earth and all the oceans, we stood on a real, actual beach.

Maybe anything was possible.

"I bet there are fish," Eren said.

"Think how much seafood they must have in there. No wonder no one wants to upset them—Wait!" I shouted. "What about the robes? They'll be ruined!"

"And the kuang bands," said Eren.

"Nothing can ruin a kuang band," Isaiah said quietly.

We chose not to hear him. "I don't care a thing about this stupid band." I pushed my arm into the water, holding the sleeve of my fiery robe barely above the surface, and met his eye. He grinned back and pressed his hand into the water right next to mine.

"Never mind about the robe either, Char," Isaiah said, his voice as low and deep as ever. He dove in, then flipped onto his back and swam away from me. "The *ocean*. The only one in existence. Maybe the last one ever. That's worth more than silk, surely."

Wonder overwhelmed me, and I sank into the cool water, grinning. Eren jumped in, too, and I followed him further in. We spun through the salty crests, which exploded all around us. Eren and I stayed a bit closer to the shore than Isaiah, who stretched his long legs and kicked out past the first silvery peaks.

"I can't believe it," I said again. "I can't believe we're here. You know what the Remnant needs? One of these." I spread my arms wide, feeling the ocean breeze through the thin, wet silk of my robe, and dipped under again.

"Or a lake," said Eren, breaking through the surface. "Even a pond. I'd consider joining if you had a bathtub, honestly."

"You'd make a terrible rebel, Everest," I teased.

The moon lit the water that ran through his hair, down his face, and over his outstretched arm as he studied me. "You think so?" he asked.

"Take it from me. They tend to frown on anything related to the Commander." I looked away from him, and toward Isaiah, almost out of instinct. He was treading through the second set of silver crests. "Isaiah! Not so far!" I shouted. "You're making me nervous."

"Not to worry. I don't plan on drowning tonight." His voice somehow reached us without rising in pitch or volume. It was maddening and comforting at once.

"Well, that's good to hear," Eren said dryly.

"What's a matter, soldier boy?" said Isaiah. "Surely you think we'd all be better off if I died."

"I'm pretty sure no one will be better off if anyone drowns tonight," I cut in nervously. "Inter-ark relations being about as tense as they get right about now."

"Don't worry," said Eren. "It's just a threat. Asia won't really attack us."

"You think not?" Isaiah called, slipping through the water, coming in closer.

"I do, Mr. Underwood. They can't afford to. They need to populate a planet. They need our supplies to survive until that day comes. The system doesn't work without us."

"That wouldn't stop them from bombing our life support and scavenging the remains around our dead bodies," I observed.

"That wouldn't be right," Eren said. "They wouldn't go about it that way."

Isaiah heard him. "You sure about that, Everest?"

Eren lowered his brow. "Believe it or not, there are people who would rather fix what's broken than blow it up and then burn the ashes."

Isaiah pushed further and further away, into the black and silver waves. "Ashes don't burn."

"If we can't find a way to stop the war—permanently— *everything* will burn, Underwood," Eren called after him.

"Oh, come *on*, you two," I said. "Isn't that enough for one night? I think we can safely assume everyone is on the same page as far as not wanting to die in a—AAHH!"

"What?" said Eren. "What is it?"

"Something touched my foot! Isaiah! Get back here!"

"I'm not sure they heard you on the other Arks, Charlotte. Say again?"

"There's something in the water. I can't even see the bottom," I gasped, splashing frantically back to the shore. "What's it doing in there?"

Isaiah's laugh floated across the waves. "Swimming. It's a fish, Charlotte."

"What if it's a shark? We did not think this through." I glared at him from the shore, ignoring his shining smile in the waves, and immediately began to shiver in my silk robe. Wet, it clung to every possible part of me, sapping my warmth with remarkable efficiency.

Eren appeared at my side to rub my arms.

I made a face. "These robes are not as fun when they're wet. Come to think of it, it's a little weird. It's not like they dressed like this in Asia before we left Earth. So at some point, someone decided that now, we're all gonna wear robes. What's that about?"

"I can't complain," said Eren, tightening his sash a bit. "They're pretty comfy. When they're dry, anyway."

Isaiah turned toward me from his place in the water. "It's the same as the uniforms in Central Command. No one wore jumpsuits down below, either."

"I wonder what they wear in Europe," I said.

"Maybe it promotes unity?" said Eren. "You know. Like the way the Arks all have half their population from the rest of the world?"

"Hey, speaking of uniforms," I said softly, laying a hand on Eren's arm. Across the beach, at the peak of the dunes we'd just crossed, three figures advanced toward us.

Eren sucked in a breath. The darkness obscured their

faces, but the figures were unmistakable. "Guess he didn't like being uninvited."

Isaiah rose from the water, but remained at its shore, feet submerged in rolling dregs of foam and water.

"It's An and Shan," I said quietly for Isaiah's benefit. "And the Commander's with them. How did they find us?"

"We weren't exactly subtle, Charlotte," said Eren. "Besides, where else would anyone want to go?"

Isaiah was silent.

When their group reached ours, I regretted our little romp in the water. The Asian delegation looked as fresh as daisies, and the Commander cut his usual authoritative figure. But we were dripping wet, hair ragged, and shivering in the moonlight.

Eren cleared his throat. "Shan. I hope you don't mind our exploring."

"On the contrary," he said. "I'd have been terribly sad if you didn't, seeing as how you are leaving so soon. It's a self-contained ecosystem." He waved an arm around, causing An to release her grip. "Our Ark has artificial gravity generators built into every floor, plus one more up there," he said, pointing up at the moon. "It makes the waves by simulating the pull of the moon back on Earth, but on a graduated scale, since this ship is much smaller than an ocean, of course. The floor and the sand are hydrophobic, so that the water cannot escape. And look!" he said, drawing near and nearly laughing himself, "there are even sandpipers."

I gasped, following the line of his outstretched hand into the sand, and barely caught sight of a fat bunch of white feathers as it disappeared, sleep disturbed, into the night.

"A bird," Isaiah muttered, almost to himself.

"It's beautiful," I said through chattering teeth. "Unbelievable, really."

In response, Shan bowed slightly.

"It's good you are here," said An. "Together. If the other Arks can achieve peace through diversifying the populations, I must believe that it is possible on your North American Ark as well."

The Commander interrupted her with a snort. "Did you really think the reason we split the population of each Ark was to promote unity?"

I stared at him. "I wasn't exactly invited to be on the planning committee, Commander, but I assume that was the idea."

"It's so that no one nation is wiped entirely out of existence. There are Americans on board every ship. Egyptians. Israeli. Russians. And they *will* find each other." I could hardly breathe from shivering, in spite of Eren's chafing, but the Commander's words brought their own special kind of chill. "The only way to promote unity is to increase the strength of the leadership."

The Asians watched our interaction calmly. "Here," said Shan, "we've brought blankets. The night air can be a bit chilly at this hour for those who swim." He distributed a blanket to me and Eren, and we wrapped ourselves together. I twisted around and into him, like we were wrapped in a giant, warm tortilla.

"I never want to leave," I said suddenly. "It is safe, you said? No sharks."

"We have a few moments before we must return you to your shuttles," said Shan. "There are sharks. We've tried to preserve as many species as possible. But they are corralled, at the moment. We've been unable to allow all the fish to swim freely, but they are multiplying, and we should be able to populate a true ocean again, one day."

I continued to gape at the horizon. "Are there starfish? Sea horses? *Holy cow*. Do you have octopuses?" I frowned. "Octopi?"

"Yes to all of the above, and more," said Shan. "Most of the volume is dedicated to the fish we eat, but we tried to save as much as possible."

An did not reply. Instead, she stared at our Char-and-Eren burrito thoughtfully.

Shan stared at An, who had taken a step back and was now perched near the top of the dune.

But Isaiah hadn't moved from his spot near the water. Finally, he joined us, planting his feet in the sand directly in front of An. "So, Madam Imperial," he said casually, "when may we expect your decision?"

Eighteen

"Imperial?" the Commander blustered. "But—"

Shan moved to the side, barely placing himself between us and An. I froze in Eren's arms. Eren looked from Isaiah to An and back again, frowning.

"You are an observant man, Mr. Underwood," An said calmly, looking down on our group. "What gave me away?"

"Oh, there's been plenty," he replied. "Mostly the fact that you downgraded my title even after the 'Imperial' kept calling me a king. There were always rumors on Earth that a secret Imperial was chosen after the meteor was announced. Someone much younger than the last one. So you're the right age. And Shan acts more like a bodyguard than a diplomat, at least around you, Your Highness. You sure don't act like you work for him. And he just said we were leaving. That's news to me. Probably to all of us, except you."

"We have reports from your Ark," said Shan. "The fighting between you has resumed. You will return immediately."

An arranged her robe, allowing the Imperial medallion to hang in front of the belt at her waist. It glinted briefly in the moonlight. "I have one goal." She spoke quietly, as though fully assured that we would strain to hear every word. "Peace. For me, nothing else is possible. But your Ark is not peaceful. I would rather eliminate you completely than risk your attacking another ship."

"But we didn't do that!" I said suddenly. "We are not responsible for whatever happened to Ark Five."

An narrowed her eyes. "I like you, Charlotte, but I warn you not to take me for a fool. Perhaps you are not personally responsible, but your Commander is armed."

"He's not my commander. I answer to Isaiah. And Isaiah wouldn't hurt a fly. That's why you have to help us."

"Even if I grant your innocence in the disappearance of Ark Five, you remain a threat. You are bent on killing each other. Here are my options: One, I could destroy you all. This is risky. It lowers the human population too far." An looked out over the water. "We are one disease away from extinction. One war. One missed step. I prefer not to bring us any closer."

I nodded, letting out a breath. Wrapped against me, Eren did the same.

"Two. I could ignore you—all of you. Refuse to resume trade. You are unstable. The other Arks will follow my lead. You would eventually starve. Again, this is risky. Your people will riot. Your leadership may change, or disappear. Instability would increase, and I am afraid I would still have to destroy you outright."

"Please consider not doing that," I said nervously.

An smiled grimly. "Three. I could lend my full support to the Commander. Together, we would crush the Remnant."

I stopped, took a breath. "An. Ambassador—I mean, Your Imperial Highness, please. Please don't put that man in power."

She gave me a cold look. "I didn't. You did. You North Americans are the ones who voted."

"The Remnant didn't exactly choose him."

Her head tilted a bit. "If you say so. My final option, of course, is to grant your request, in the hope that you are telling the truth. I could help you create this two-government system you seek and expect you to keep each other in check peacefully."

I froze, afraid to speak, in case I ruined the moment.

"But it's very important that you understand me, Ambassador. I have a single objective, and it is this: there must be peace among all remaining Arks. Should I choose to grant your petition, I will reopen trade. Should you form other alliances, I will not interfere. But if you threaten the peace in any way, I will destroy you," she said calmly. "All of you."

Up until then, the others had remained silent, watching our exchange with interest. But now, Isaiah spoke.

"Your Imperial Highness. It seems that your conclusion must be to ratify our petition for independence and resume trade immediately."

An nodded toward Shan, who began to speak. "The Imperial would like to pose a solution for the benefit of all people: Asia will reopen trade with North America for a limited time, on a trial basis. We will keep our fighter ships from your sovereign territory in space. In exchange, the people of the North American Ark will declare an immediate ceasefire among themselves.

"The Imperial has also reached a decision regarding the fate of your nations and your Ark. She finds His Majesty's proposal holds the most promise." An inclined her head gracefully toward Isaiah, who was nodding his approval.

"Central Command will join Asia in agreeing to recognize the Remnant as an independent nation-state," said Shan.

An cleared her throat and took over from there. Her voice was brazen in its youth and its sweetness, daring us to challenge her power. "In exchange for this concession, Asia will further agree to become an ally of Central Command and the Remnant alike. For so long as the cease-fire remains in effect, we will forbear to fire our weapons as well.

"Years may pass before Eirenea is terraformed. We cannot hope to build a new life out of our present situation should this war continue. We cannot afford to lose another Ark, but if another Ark is lost, it will not be the one entrusted to my care.

"I acknowledge the fears of my people and the other Arks. You are not to be trusted blindly. To that end, I place two conditions on my offer, to be met within twenty-four hours. The first: we will continue to monitor blast frequencies on board your ship. We will stop your reign of death from extending any further. You will effect immediate peace among your people. I will not tolerate continued warfare among your Ark."

We straightened. She certainly had our attention.

"And two: in the spirit of cooperation, you will each give a valued member of your delegation to the other." An fixed the Commander with a chilling gaze. "You alone, Commander, have stood in full opposition to the Remnant, in every circumstance. You will give your son in its service, so that I may be assured of your future compliance."

"My son?" The Commander paled. "What do you mean?"

An didn't answer right away. Instead, she studied him. His face was marked with genuine concern, and his voice was higher pitched than usual, as though he'd cast aside an act he'd been playing for years.

"What do you want with my son?" he asked again.

"For myself? Nothing. You will give him to the Remnant, and receive their ambassador in return."

"My son belongs in Central Command, with me. He has a job to do."

"I'm not talking about death, or imprisonment, Commander, or even citizenship. Your son will live with you, along with his wife. This pact will be sealed with more than ink and blood." She gathered the length of her robe in her fist and extended a hand to Shan, who rushed to prepare to escort her off the dune.

Her gaze swept across us all. "Therefore, citizens of the North American Ark, hear this: your treaty will be ratified on the wedding day of Ambassadors Turner and Liaison Everest."

Nineteen

Shan bowed. An nodded again to the group before accepting his outstretched arm, and they headed for the platform.

"Wait!" I said, and began to frantically untwist myself from Eren's blanket. "Your Imperial Highness, please!"

Eren put out a hand to stop me, but I ran past him, shivering, and crossed the dune to walk next to An and Shan.

"Your—did I hear you correctly? You want me to marry Eren?" I studied her face in the moonlight, but she was serene, implacable.

"Ambassador. May I call you Char? I like this name for you. It is as though you have burned brightly."

"Char is—yes, that's my name, Your Imperial..."

"Likewise, you may call me An. There are many forces at work here, Char, and those of us in positions of authority are not generally able to find the happiness we seek for ourselves." She moved closer to Shan, who clearly wanted her to. "But here, we may be able to find a pleasant outcome for everyone. There are others who are not so lucky."

"You mean you and Shan? But you're the Imperial. If you want to marry him, why not just do it?"

144

"It is five o'clock U.T." An's smile dimmed. "My decision is final. Good luck, Char. You have one day."

I waited until the platform walls had closed around the two of them before stomping furiously back to Eren, fists tight. "How could you! How *could* you! I'm not some kind of, of—"

"I don't speak for the Imperial, Charlotte," Eren looked at me. His face was hard, with a trace of pain, like he'd known I would take this badly. "This wasn't even my idea."

"Well, it wasn't hers! She was all set to blow us up this morning. She basically told me that."

"Actually, it was mine," said Isaiah. "Although it's not exactly original. Treaties and informal alliances have always been sealed with marriage. Started back when we were all just tribes. And now, here we are again."

I lowered my voice to a whisper in a futile attempt to keep from sounding shrill. "I mean, I don't exactly trust your father not to kill me in my sleep, so where would we even live? Are you just going to join the Remnant? Has it occurred to you that we are too young to be making life commitments here? Oh," I said, as my whisper became a hiss, "and I am *not* having a baby, whether or not they start giving out bonuses."

The three men stared at me, each momentarily at a loss for words.

"So this was your big plan all along?" I said. "This is why all the secrecy? I hope you two are happy."

"Actually, I am," said Eren. "Word of an alliance will reach the Ark before we've even landed. Because of us, people will have hope again. It'll be all over the news on every ship. They'll sleep safe in their beds tonight because of us."

I glared at him, refusing to grant him any points, no matter how much sense he made. How dare they leave me out of this? I thought of my father reading the news of my marriage before I could reach him. Before I had returned his son to him. Had I failed him again so easily?

I shook my head. This wasn't over yet.

"That was the mission," said Isaiah. "Recognition from Asia. As goes Asia, so will Europe and South America. It's going to be a lot harder to crush the Remnant when we have equal standing to any of them." I opened my mouth to scream, but Isaiah crooked his elbow at me and spoke softly. "Take my arm, Charlotte Turner. Let's take a stroll by the sea. You and me."

I turned back to Eren one last time, but words failed me. He'd clearly planned this out with Isaiah from the beginning. Maybe even since he'd been their prisoner.

He looked pained. "This way, I can protect you. The Remnant will be safe. It's a good plan, Charlotte."

"You have to be kidding me."

He gave me a hard look. "I thought we could fix everything, if we could be together. I thought you felt the same way."

"And now?" I said, letting my anger show in my voice.

"And now... it's still worth it, for peace. But maybe you're right. Maybe everything is different."

"Yeah," I said, marching down the beach to where Isaiah still stood, arm out, waiting. "It is."

The waves crashed in carefully metered moments, and for a long time, I walked in silence on Isaiah's arm. It was an easy pace, enough to put some space between us and the rest of the group without wearing me out after my six weeks in an eight by ten.

Nevertheless, my breath ran short. "Isaiah, please. If I marry him, the Commander will kill me. You know he will."

"You can handle yourself. And Eren won't let that happen. He loves you. But you know that already." He ran a hand over his head, as though thinking, but his face was an unreadable mask.

"You once told me that you loved me. You were manipulating me, even then. Do you even remember the day we decided to live? The day we started running? Was everything a lie between us?"

"You were always running. Always trying to get somewhere. But not me. Not that day. I was done. My journey was over. I really believed that."

"Why are you telling me this?"

He stopped walking. "I just needed you to know that there was a time when you were the only thing I had."

I shook my head at him. The familiar heat of my anger crept up through my chest, burning my face, and I gritted my teeth. "So why are you giving me up?"

"I could still be your friend, Charlotte, if you'll have me. But you know where my priorities are. Where they have to be. There's nothing more to say."

"Oh no? How about this: you can't make me marry him."

"You forget that I have what you want." Isaiah's voice was low and deep.

I considered that. "You're not threatening West, are you?"

"He's a good kid. Nothing like us. No, I'm threatening *you*."

He faced the water, as though watching the waves fall against his feet.

"Ise, this isn't like you." My throat was tight. I tried to

147

take his hand. His arm was like stone. "Don't send me back there. Please."

But my friend was long gone, and only a king remained. He stood suddenly, like a cat, and turned to leave. "Marry him, Char. That's an order."

Twenty

I was a wooden puppet, guided by unseen forces, on the trip home. I did not speak to Isaiah. What would be the point? We understood each other.

I let myself be strapped into the Arkhopper without a word. When Shan bent to secure my forehead, I caught a view of the rest of the tiny receiving room off the Asian hangar. Eren and his father were being prepared for their flight back, too.

Eren met my eye for a single moment. It wasn't a pleading look. His eyes did not ask me for anything. He wasn't angry, either. He was merely searching. Trying to guess what I felt.

I looked away.

The hatch was sealed; the coordinates set.

We were released into the weightlessness of the endless sky.

The docking at return was as bad as advertised. We aimed for the center of the wheel, and the thrusters engaged, causing us to spin. I reminded myself that that was good, that we needed to spin before we docked, and the thought was comforting. When we were fully attached to the North

American Ark, the hopper slid out to the edge, and gravity claimed us more and more heavily until at last the hopper selected the proper hangar.

The stars spun hard around my head, but I didn't scream. I had bigger things on my mind.

When the hopper unlatched, I dutifully assisted Isaiah with his straps. I had the feeling he accepted my help out of kindness rather than necessity.

"Where is everyone?" I asked, gasping more than I'd expected to. "Marcela should be here at least, right?"

Isaiah shook his head. "She'll be here. She's never let me down."

I suppressed an angry look. Good for her, then. I still wasn't sure I'd marry Eren. I'd always hated being forced into things. Pretty dresses for my parents' parties, for example, were grating enough. Let alone a life partner I'd had no say in choosing.

Near us, the Commander was stalking through the hangar, flanked by an official I wasn't sure I recognized.

"Jorin should be here, too," I half-muttered.

"Who?" said Isaiah.

"Lieutenant Malkin, the Commander's second in command. As I understand it, his job is to make sure the stunners are charged. Real nice guy; you'd like him."

Isaiah smirked, but it was cut short. The platform had barely dropped into place when a low, unearthly rumble shook the floor, and I redoubled my grip on his arm.

"Easy, there, little bird. I'm not made of steel."

I made an admirable attempt at unlatching from him before settling on what I hoped was a light, casual death-grip on his lower arm. "Honestly, and I am still kinda recovering here, but did this room just move?"

150

"I'm sure it's nothing to worry about, yet," he said in a low tone.

"That's the thing about a spaceship, Ise. When one thing rumbles, that means *everything is rumbling.*"

"I will agree it's not ideal."

"Well. So long as I'm not crazy. Hey, there she is!"

Marcela and her flame-red hair came sprinting toward us across the long white hangar. "King! They've breached the cargo hold."

"That is the point of a demilitarized zone, isn't it? No one's guarding it?" I asked.

"Oh, we guard it," said Isaiah. "We just don't interfere in it. Mostly." He turned to Marcela. "What's going on? Tell me everything."

"A report came in about an hour ago that you had struck a deal with the Commander, details to follow, and that the treaty was backed by Asian nukes."

She paused pointedly, as though waiting for Isaiah to confirm. Instead, he frowned. "And?"

"We had your orders. No fighting. But they started it. Fired on everyone in the cargo hold. Lockies, our guys, everyone. And somehow, we're locked out of HQ."

"Wait," I said, "You're locked out of headquarters? In the Remnant?"

"We'll figure it out," said Isaiah. "Probably just a glitch. I'll get Adam on it."

I looked out over the blue and white of the hangar just as the Commander reached the door to Central Command. "HEY," I shouted after them. "Hey, Commander!" He turned back, and I continued to run toward him. "You're firing on the DMZ? What does that even get you? More bins?"

He paused, waiting for his aide to open the door, and gave me a tired look. "My son tells me you play chess. He was keen to list it among your attributes."

"I've played before."

The Commander nodded. "Well, I play a little chess myself. Fascinating game. Do you know the secret of winning?"

"You'll have to enlighten me."

"You attack the king, and you keep attacking. None of the other pieces matter. They're nothing but tools—they're weapons, in fact. You attack the king, over and over, until he cannot escape you."

"What a nuanced analysis. You should teach classes."

"I do have a point, Miss Turner, if you would be so kind. You exploit your opponent's every weakness until his defenses are dismantled, and the king is exposed."

I felt my face begin to heat up. "I'm learning so much right now."

"You would be surprised, Miss Turner. Lesser players will cling to the other pieces, even to the neglect of their king. Easiest way to defeat them. They will insist on saving their favorites, their bishops and their knights. They assign them values quite apart from their usefulness as tools. Especially the queen. She has her advantages, but she is only a weapon."

"I wouldn't be so sure of myself, if I were you, Commander. I've played a lot of chess with Isaiah."

"Oh?"

"When we were kids, he used to sneak me into his cell. Had a chessboard in his room. The one condition of getting me out of my cell was that I had to play." I met the Commander's eye. "He needed someone to practice with."

"I'm sure that's usually the way of it, when a young convict entertains a female prisoner in his quarters."

"You're charming. You know that?" I cleared my throat. "Anyway. Isaiah is scary good at chess. When he gets checkmate—and he always does—I never see it coming, with one exception."

"Do enlighten me."

"When he sacrifices the queen, you've already lost. You just don't know it yet."

There was a short moment of silence between us, and the door sucked open. The aide stepped aside. To my surprise, the Commander laughed: a short, humorless staccato. "Those aren't my weapons, Miss Turner. Same as with Ark Five. Now, if you'll excuse me, I have a battle to prepare for."

I took my time in returning to Isaiah and Marcela, walking deliberately, using every step to think. By the time I reached them, I'd made up my mind. If they were going to use me as a game piece, so be it. But I was going to play, too.

They waited for me at the exit, still discussing the situation. There was a clear look of annoyance on Mars's face.

"Take me to West," I said firmly.

They stopped talking long enough to stare at me. Isaiah shook his head in disbelief.

"Char, there's a war on."

"I do not care about the war. I want my brother. I will marry Eren and ratify your stupid treaty, although I highly doubt it's going to solve all our problems. But only if you take me to West. Now. And give me back my gun."

"We can't," said Mars. "He's gone out to get the lockies."

"Then take me to the lockies."

"You can wait for him at headquarters. I don't have time for this," said Isaiah. Marcela gave me a strange look, as though I were something she recognized, but couldn't quite believe she was seeing. A zebra, for example.

I returned her stare with one of iron. "One way or the other, the Remnant is about to fall. We won't win against Central Command in an all-out battle once they outrun Adam's tech. They have ten times the people and the weapons. But even if we did, we cannot survive a direct attack from the Asian Ark." I held out my arm to him. The gem on the k-band glowed bright green against the pale underside of my wrist. "Take me to West, *right now*, or I will never marry Eren for as long as I live. Look at this. Tell him, Marcela. Tell him the light is green, because I'm telling the truth."

"Like I need a light to tell me that." Isaiah's frown deepened, but Marcela put a hand on his arm. He inclined his head to her, maybe for an instant, then took a deep breath. "Take her, Mars, and report back to headquarters. I'll be in the control room with Adam. Maybe he can help us make sense of all this." Isaiah pulled my gun from his bag and placed it in my waiting hand in a single, deft motion.

He disappeared into the darkness as Marcela and I exchanged a final look. At length, she spoke. "This way."

Twenty-One

The battleground wasn't anything like I'd pictured. When we stepped into the cargo hold, Mars held up a hand, stopping me. I hadn't heard an explosion for awhile, but the evidence was everywhere. The air in the hold was smoky and electric. The light was diffused, making it darker than usual, and creepiest of all, it appeared to be deserted.

Going by the look on her face, it wasn't what Mars had pictured, either. "The lockies are that way," she said. "It wasn't this bad half an hour ago. There must be some soldiers, too, but we haven't located any. Everyone's hiding. So keep an eye out."

Hiding from what, I wondered. But I nodded and crept along as fast as I could, letting her lead me through the rows at her chosen path and pace.

Our route was straightforward, and we passed only Remnant locks on the bins. The air had a smell, too: like rain and melted plastic. Seconds later, I found out why.

A long yellow bin lay marred and partially open. Its bright color was muted to a charred black at one end, and the roof was, for lack of a better word, *melted* down over the opening. "Is this what the bombs are for? They're trying to open bins? Is this a fight among the lockies?"

"No. I don't know. I don't think so. For one thing, lockies work for their governments. They won't fight without orders. They're barely armed. For another, look. No one's been here. Nothing's been taken. You'd have to lever off what's left of the roof first. No one can fit in there. It's gotta be something else."

For an instant, I watched her mouth move, and the sound was progressively muted. Even the noises around us, the sounds of our feet, for example, stopped making noise. And there was pressure in my ears, just for a second, until they popped.

Then everything returned to normal.

I looked around nervously, trying to see in all directions at once, but when I glanced at the ceiling, I grabbed Mars's arm. "Look up. What *is* that?"

The cloud above us was slowly swirling into a defined circle. My brain was engaging in a similar endeavor—mixing around and around, searching for the answer that was right in front of me.

Or rather, right *above* me. I was so close. What was I missing?

Think, Char. Think.

"Hey, Mars," I hissed again. "Is it just me, or is it, like, crazy cold in here? I can see my breath in the air."

"Shh," she said. "That's just the smoke from the bombs."

I nodded. "That's kinda what I figured, except for one thing. Have you actually seen a bomb go off?"

"What? What are you talking about? Didn't you see the bin?"

"I did, and it made me think. I can't say I've ever seen a bomb before. Have you?"

Marcela shrugged and kept moving. "Yeah. Combat training."

"But not in space."

She stopped hustling through the bins long enough to give me a truly withering glance. "No. That wasn't really in the budget."

"Mars. Listen to me. My uncle had a tractor shed. It was probably made of the same kinda stuff as these cargo bins. He lived upstate. Lots of open land during the winter. No trees. Just a metal shed in the middle of a field. Plastic walls. We visited once during a thunderstorm. A real bad one."

Mars shook her head, ignoring me. "This is where they should be. He must have moved fast. They're probably back at the Remnant by now. Keep moving."

"Look at that. The clouds are swirling in an *actual circle*. They're getting thicker."

"Probably due to the air differential. You're the one who thinks it's so cold."

We reached the far wall, the one that bordered the Rift, and Mars began feeling around with her fingertips for the invisible door. I tilted my head, watching her. Air differential. She was smart. I'd give her that.

"Yeah. I get that," I said. "But what if we're thinking about this all wrong? How can you have a battle with *no soldiers*?"

She found the spot, knelt down, and began swiping her wrist around in a square. "I'm taking you to West. Then you're on your own. I have to get back to headquarters before the bombing starts again."

My skin went cold. "But you said headquarters was

157

locked. What are you doing? Is this door wired to a sensor?"

"Yeah." She bit her lip, concentrating, and kept right on swiping her wrist at the wall. "Gotta be a glitch."

"It's not a glitch, Mars," I said slowly. "That door isn't going to open. And neither is headquarters. Not for you, or anyone else."

She stopped, breathed out, and finally looked at me. "And why is that?"

"Because the attack didn't come from Command. It's coming from inside the Remnant."

"Char. What are you *talking* about?"

My irritation with her dismissive tone was matched only by my growing trepidation. "Look around. We're surrounded by *clouds*. That shouldn't even be possible. That bin wasn't bombed. This is a spaceship. You can't drop a bomb on the bottom floor of a spaceship. It'd breach the hull. We'd all be sucked out. And so, so dead. They're not bombs."

"Whatever you want to call them, we're trapped. If we can't figure this out, we'll probably get to see one up close. Then we can talk all about it."

"*They're not bombs*, Mars. You'd need something that kills without penetrating, like the bullets. Look around you. Look *up*. That bin was struck by lightning. It's a thunderstorm. And there's only *one person* who could have caused it."

Her annoyance dissipated into understanding and then fear, and her strong, slender arm froze in mid-swipe. "We're under attack from Adam," she said finally. "This is a coup."

Twenty-Two

"We have to get out of here. We're sitting ducks." She stood, instantly calm, pressing me against a bin, and scanned the area. "We gotta figure out his plan."

I looked at her. "Okay, how's this? Step one: build the best weapons *ever*. Like, I dunno, a killer lightning cloud. Step two: take control of all the entrances and exits. Step three: kill everyone who tries to stop you. I'm pretty sure he's on step three right now."

Marcela let her wrist fall back to her side. "Then we'll just have to stop him."

"See, I don't think you were paying attention during step three," I said, but she wasn't listening.

She pulled a comm device from her uniform and held it to her ear. "King, it's Mars. Come in, King. Repeat, Come in."

"MARS!" Isaiah's voice came in. "Don't come back in here! It's—" Static hit the line, buzzing out the sound of his voice. A cold knot worked its way into my stomach. Isaiah never shouted.

"King? Ise, you there? Isaiah!" Mars shouted. The static remained until the transmission was terminated with a short, soft beep. Mars and I exchanged a wide-eyed glance. Then she angled her shoulder at me, hiding her own face, and frantically pressed the buttons on the comm. "West. It's me. You there?" Her voice lowered several decibels, and my expression deepened into a frown.

When no one answered, she looked back at me. "We have to find another way into the Remnant. We have to stop Adam."

For a fleeting second, I wondered how long it would take me to round up West, Eren, and my father, and get them all on an Arkhopper before anyone else realized what was happening. Before the Asian nukes arrived.

Another part of me spared a moment of appreciation for An. She might have been onto something. Adam was dangerous, and he was a citizen of the Remnant. She was right to fear it. I couldn't imagine what damage he'd do if his coup succeeded.

And then I felt sick.

There were a hundred thousand people on this ship at least. Men, women, and children. Families. And loners, too, like Amiel, who were barely clinging to this life, held together by nothing but the hope of a new one.

Marcela was right. We had to stop him.

I had to try, anyway. I didn't know what my life was worth, but surely it was that much.

We took off running. "Do you know of any other way out of here?" I asked. Mars looked back at me expectantly. Oh, sure. *Now* I had her attention. I held up three fingers. "The Remnant. Command. The hangar. Are there any other doors?"

"He's probably blocked them all by now. The hangar is likely our best—*CHAR!*"

A smear of red hair split my vision, and I reached for Marcela. She was barely too far, but if the world were ending here, I supposed it didn't matter. I breathed burning plastic, and my face hit the plyocrete as the universe exploded into light.

I couldn't see. There was only whiteness everywhere.

I could breathe, though, for the moment, so I focused on that for the space of four heartbeats.

Everything hurt, starting with my teeth. Except I was also kinda numb, too. But the numbness was fading, and the pain was about to win.

"Char. Get up. You have to—" Marcela's voice floated across an ocean of agony. "Char, please, you have to get up. It's coming back."

"It?" I shuffled my hands under my chest and pressed the floor down, but it didn't do much good. I couldn't stand up if my life depended on it. Which it probably did.

"*Uunffh.*" Marcela's voice was near my ear, across the cargo hold, and all the way inside my head, entirely at once. Her arms were under mine, and we were standing, holding each other.

Something was burning, and I had a hard time remembering where I was and what I was doing. "I want West," I said, too loudly. My voice sounded less clear in my ears than it did in my head. When my eyes were open, everything was too sharp. When they were closed, everything was fuzzy.

Oh, and it hurt to talk. A lot.

"Charlotte Turner. I will take you to West if it's the last thing I do," she hissed. "But you are heavy. So if you don't listen to me, *right now*, we won't make it. That cloud is coming back."

"Cloud."

"Yes. Cloud. You just got struck by lightning. Now *run*."

I must have tried to run, but it didn't last long. The next thing I knew, we were slumped against a bin a few feet away. Well, I was slumped. Marcela was kneeling next to me, and yanking something out of a hip-pack. It was a needle, an ugly, sharp one, and she stabbed me with it.

That absolute *cow*.

"West," I mumbled, and she gave me a look that told me it wasn't my first time to say it. The pain of the shot blossomed through my thigh, and a brush of bright red hair swished against my face. Marcela pressed her head to my chest, then placed a finger under my chin while staring into space, jaw tight.

Wait. I knew that look.

"You're a doctor," I tried to say, but it came out, "Wwwweeeest." The pain in my leg—and all the rest of my body—evaporated. The room wobbled. Not shook. *Wobbled*. Like the lines of the walls were made of gelatin.

I hated gelatin. Reminded me of prison Christmas.

The bin was waving, too. I squinted, and Marcela's hair waved back.

"West."

"For the love of tiny gophers," Marcela said through clenched teeth, "could you *please* stop saying West."

"I could not," I slurred stubbornly. "You don't understand. He's my brother, and I love him, and you're just a giant red paintbrush."

She directed an exasperated look at the ceiling.

I stuck my lip out. "A giant *angry* red paintbrush, and you stung me."

"It's psychaline. Enough to restart you. It's disorienting,

162

a bit like alcohol. You'll feel dizzy, and slightly anxious, until the first phase wears off. You might hallucinate. Then you'll be in pain again. We have to be gone by then. I don't think the cloud can see us, but—this is strange, but I think it's targeting you."

"My foot. I can't."

She directed an angry look at my ankle, then knelt in surprise.

"Yeah, it's sprained. Okay. Okay." She reached back into her bag, frantically searching for something. "The psychaline will make the swelling go down. Brace it like this," she said, ripping off my shoe and pressing my joint into place. "And don't move. Now shut up while I do a field wrap."

"Ooh, look who's had combat training."

"I'm a doctor, Char. This will work."

I made a grand gesture toward her face. "And medical school!"

She looked supremely annoyed, but finished wrapping up my ankle with quick, sure moves.

I bit my lip. "Hey, not bad. Thank you."

"You're welcome," she said icily.

I looked deep into her eyes, since she was about an inch from my nose, and I didn't have much of a choice. To my utter shock, I didn't see the one thing I expected.

"You don't hate me!" I said, trying a little too hard not to slur. A hint of a smile stole across my face. "You really, really don't."

She looked at me like someone who came home from a long day at work and discovered that her dog had made a mess all over the couch. "I wouldn't go that far."

"We should talk about this! We're making a connection here."

She placed her hands on my shoulders and opened her eyes wide. "Big gun BANG." She waved her hands around her ears for a moment, then mimicked a wild "Aahh!" beneath her voice. Her gun hit her hip, and she finished off the performance by miming sprinting away in slow motion. "We run now," she said, in a drawn-out accent.

I watched her leave. "Yeah. Good talk."

We ran, and my feet wobbled into the floor, one after the other, until we'd put some distance between us and the cloud. Marcela was right; it was definitely following us. For whatever reason—probably the drug—I found that my thoughts were isolated behind some kind of steel wall that separated them from my emotions. I knew I should be afraid, or even angry, but instead, I felt my mind ticking away.

"Adam either locked Isaiah up, or he killed him. Otherwise, this wouldn't still be happening." I tried to picture Isaiah in another cell. The image made my chest feel tight, like I was caught in a vice.

"Char. So help me. You need to keep running. I can't leave you, and I can't carry you, and West will never forgive me if—"

"Your monkey brain is panicking. You have to calm down to engage your higher thinking."

She grabbed my collar, and her angry red hair zoomed toward my face. "You. Will. Keep. Running."

"No, I didn't mean *you're* a monkey," I gave a little laugh. She was actually kinda scary up close like that. Not that I could really feel fear at the moment. "I mean, it's just instinct to freak out, but that's a good way to lose the ga—"

"You run, or I don't take you to West."

"I really thought you hated me. Hey, I'm wearing a copper wire."

"What?"

"Copper wire. Around my waist. That's why the cloud is following us. Lightning needs a conduc—a conducive—"

"A conductor."

"That's the one. A conductor. All aboard."

She stopped trying to run for about one full hair-wobble. "Of all the absolute—*a copper wire?* In a thunderstorm. Of course you are. Get it off. Keep running."

I unspooled myself as we ran past the final few rows of bins and came back to the door to the hangar. The last several loops of wire were tangled, and I had to stop. Marcela swiped her hand around the door.

"Wait, what is that? What are you doing? Is there some kind of invisible keypad here too?" I asked.

"Yeah. Adam installed it. Links to a chip implant in my wrist."

I stared at her. "You let him. Put a *chip*. Under your—"

"It was all very futury, sciency—you know what? It made sense at the time."

I thought about that. "Yeah, yeah." I gave her an understanding nod. "I get it. I mean, we *are* on a spaceship."

"Right?"

"Still creepy though."

She gave a sigh that could have been a laugh and turned back. I scanned the area, especially the ceiling. Tiny gray puffs of clouds swept around above us. They didn't drift, like real clouds. They flew, like hawks.

"He's almost certainly deactivated it, but I can't think of anything else to try," she said. "Do you hear screaming?"

165

I cocked my head. "Lockies, maybe? They're stuck out here, too."

An explosion rocked the cargo hold—no, the entire ship, I reminded myself—and I fell into the wall. It didn't stop Marcela from continuing to try to open the door, and I admired her ability to stay cool in a panic. It was probably something she'd learned as a doctor. Or maybe combat training.

I, on the other hand, had to will my hands not to shake. Stupid psychaline. This was why I didn't do drugs: the thought of losing control of my body, even for a second, was terrifying. A slow tingle built its way up my back, like someone was walking their fingers up my spine.

I just needed some space from the noise in my brain. I needed to think. "Isaiah's not out here. We'd have seen him," I said quietly.

"That's—we can't be sure about that," she said, aiming her sidearm at the wall.

"The bullets won't penetrate the ship, Mars. Just skin, remember?"

"What?" Marcela stopped swiping long enough to study me.

"He would have thought of that. Adam built it. Adam blocked you out. Adam has Isaiah. It's all over."

"Calm down. That's the adrenaline in the psychaline. It makes you panic, once it kicks in, which helps block the pain."

"I'm not panicking. I mean, I am, but that's just because I'm right."

The comm crackled, and some of the tension drained from her shoulders. "West? Thank goodness. West? I didn't hear that."

"It's not West," said a young voice. "It's Amiel. He's here. He's sick."

Amiel, Adam's younger sister? What was she doing in the cargo hold? I yanked the comm from Marcela. "Amiel? You're with West? *Why*? Where are you?"

Marcela leaned over the comm. "Are you in the Remnant?"

"No. We're in the hold. West came for us when Adam moved on the cargo hold, before he sealed the door to the Rift. He got out, but he says he was one of the last. Adam was going to seal the doors. Lots of people stayed in on purpose, to fight." She paused, her voice small. "For both sides."

"West came for you?" I asked, confused.

Marcela took her finger off the comm, muting us. "He takes care of the lockies. Brings them food and stuff. Makes sense he'd go looking for them when this all went down. You know the Remnant. Everybody's gotta work." She said the last part in a disgusted tone, and I understood why. Amiel was young. Way too young to have a job this dangerous.

Marcela pulled at the comm again. "Can you confirm that Isaiah was captured?" she said. "Amiel, where are you?"

"He's not moving. Maybe twenty bins out from the door, and ten to the left. There are clouds. The Nowhere Men haven't found us yet. No one has."

"Hold tight," said Marcela. "We're coming."

Twenty-Three

The drive is long, even for me, an impatient teenager, but anything beats juvy. It's Thursday, early morning, and West is probably still asleep.

Not for long.

I've been away for four months this time. I've missed Christmas, West's birthday. There's a lot to catch up on. I measure the trip in monotonous clusters of trees and forced sighs.

I fiddle with the gift in my hands. My mother picked it out, bought it, wrapped it. West loves presents.

I'm up the stairs before my mom even reaches the front door. "West! West, I'm back!"

No response.

Undeterred, I slam open his door and leap the entire space between it and the bed in a single bound. "Uuuuup! C'mon. You didn't forget about today, did you?"

I stop, breathless. West isn't sleeping. As far as I can tell, West isn't even in the house. I look around, suddenly confused.

"Charlotte." My father is standing at the door. He hasn't changed, of course, but he doesn't seem as angry as usual. Even his tone is lighter, somehow.

But I can only frown. "Hey, Dad. Where's West?"

"School," he says.

I brush past him and into the hallway. Only my father could sound smug in one syllable. It's not like I was expecting some kind of welcome home party, but he doesn't have to be so condescending all the time.

I'm not allowed back at school. Not that it matters. Everything will be blown to bits in four more years.

My father clears his throat. "What are you doing? You are not to leave this house."

"Heeey," I say. "Good to see you too, Dad. Yes, of course I missed you."

"Charlotte, honey—" my mother begins, but cuts herself off with a helpless look at my father.

He physically blocks the top of the staircase.

I snort. "You have to be kidding."

"Go to your room. We're not going to start this nonsense again. Not when your mother's been up half the night driving."

"Get some rest, Charlotte," my mother says. "I'll call you down for lunch, okay?"

I look at her. She really is tired. My father, too. I close the door to my room without slamming it.

"I am glad you're here, Charlotte," my father calls out from the hallway.

I do not respond. Instead, I look down at the gift in my hands. It was a stupid idea, anyway. I wish she'd never thought of it.

When I finally do see West, he is bright and full of chatter. And although his words sound the same, there's something missing behind them. I chew my dinner slowly.

No, nothing is missing. He really is happy to see me. But there's something else, too.

I know he will sneak into my room tonight, so I don't let it bother me.

And so hours later, when my door creaks open, I'm up. I'm waiting.

"Shh. Not so much noise."

"I don't think they care, Tarry." West is the only one who calls me that, and only rarely in the years since he learned to pronounce Charlotte. It rhymes with starry. It is a happy sound, a safe, closed-up place in my heart. "They know we're going to talk."

"What do you mean?"

"Just that they probably assume."

We sit there for the space of five slow breaths. It is a comfortable silence, but neither of us expects it to last. There are things to be said.

"How was school?" I say.

"No recess this year, but we have an actual lab in science class, so that's good."

School is no longer mandatory, but if you want to apply for the lottery, you can't stop going. From what I heard, it's a lot harder than it used to be. But West is smart. Way smarter than me. I bet he loves it. "Dad's going to get me back in."

"That's good," he says. He chews his cheek. "That's good, Tar."

"I know," I say, taken aback by the serious tone. "Hey, I got you something. Mom said you're into this game now."

He opens the gift more slowly than I expect. He really is older. I smile in anticipation.

"*The expansion pack. Yeah, this is great. Thanks,*" *he says. He's not smiling.*

"*West. I'm sorry I missed your birthday.*"

He does not respond. And it's either my imagination, or he's inching toward the door. "*I'm sorry I wasn't here this morning.*"

"*I'm not going to miss them anymore. I'm not—*"

"*Just stop. Stop it, okay? You said that last time.*"

I freeze, unable to breathe. West has never been so tall, so distant.

"*All I've wanted is to see you again,*" *I say. My voice has a pleading tone I haven't planned on.*

But West is leaving, and I understand—really understand—that he hadn't wanted to see me that morning. And I think that maybe he had wanted to hurt me. That I had hurt him. His dark eyes flash. He puts a hand on the door, high above the knob, and stops. "*You can't... Look. This is it. You can't do it anymore.*"

"*I'm out. Seriously, West. I know about the age cut-off.*" *If you commit a felony after you turn fourteen, you're no longer eligible for the lottery to get on an Ark. That's when it hits me that West probably hated missing my birthday, too.*

To my horror, he does not respond. And another thought hits me, heavy: my brother is crying.

"*West,*" *I say.* "*Hey.*"

"*You have to stop. You really—you can't. Please,*" *he stutters, sniffing.*

"*I'm stopped.*"

West looks at me, face red. "*I can't go up there without you. I can't leave you here when the meteor comes. So you have to promise me. You'll never go back in there. Promise me, Tarry.*"

171

I open my eyes wide. I've never meant anything so honestly in my life. But neither has he. My heart pounds nearly out of my chest. "I promise, West."

He stares at me, and I do not look away. He is satisfied.

"Hey," he says at last, and tosses me the game pack. "Turn the board on. You gotta see this game."

I take a breath. "Sure hope you've been practicing. You needed it, if I'm remembering right."

"Hey, don't worry. I'll take it easy on you. Since you're a girl."

I laugh, relieved. My brother is back. He locates the handhelds, and we play side by side, throwing insults and talking about the stupidest things that pop into our minds, and as the hours wear on, the grayest knots around my heart begin to untangle.

We're still sitting like that when the sun invades the bedroom, and when my mother ascends the stairs to wake West for school, she passes his room without a pause and comes straight into mine.

West. After that day, we'd been best friends right up until my final stint in juvy, when everything had changed. West was here, somewhere in the cargo hold, same as me. I'd explained to him a thousand times that I hadn't broken my promise, that I hadn't set a finger out of line, but nothing was ever the same after that. In the days leading up to my ill-fated trial, he'd barely looked me in the eyes. I did not know whether I was forgiven.

The bins blurred past.

My heart pressed into my chest and throat, threatening to spill out from my eyes. The psychaline fueled me onward, and my lungs felt like they were in competition with my legs to use the most resources.

I was about to see my brother.

I felt cold all over.

Surely, I was dreaming. But the ground was hard beneath my feet.

West was here.

The bins burned past.

My lungs were tight.

I felt no pain, only burning.

West.

"West!" I screamed, over and over. "West! Amiel!"

"Shh!" Marcela hissed. "Left here. Stop screaming. They'll find us."

I didn't think the cloud could hear us, but it occurred to me that we couldn't be sure of that, so I stayed quiet.

We turned a corner as if in a dream, and there, lying on the ground, curled into a ball, was my brother, West.

"West." I dropped to the ground, placed a hand on his head. He did not respond. I found I could not speak above a whisper. "West. Wake up."

He shifted, but his eyes were closed. I looked at Amiel, my eyes wide. "What is it? What's wrong with him?"

"It's the Lightness," said Marcela. She placed a hand on my shoulder, but I flinched without meaning to, and she pulled it back quickly.

I looked up at her, then back to West. "Can you fix it?"

She pulled in a breath and gave me an odd look. "It's a form of psychosis. It causes paralysis, shortness of breath. Like a panic attack, but with worse potential complications. It didn't exist on Earth. We haven't had time to study it yet."

"You can't fix it? Give him a shot of psychaline or something?"

She crouched down next to me. "That would make it worse. Psychaline increases the body's production of norepinephrine, the fight or flight hormone. He's already dealing with too much of it."

I felt a surge of irrational anger toward Marcela, not for the first time. "So you're saying you can't do *anything*? What kind of doctor are you?"

"The student kind. The Academy didn't award degrees. We were too young, and there was too much other stuff to cover."

I gaped at her. The Academy was a government-run program for extremely gifted children. It trained them in highly technical fields, the idea being that they would have the equivalent of ten extra years of experience and education when the meteor struck.

It also made no sense. If Marcela had been drafted into the Academy, then she hadn't exactly had time to join the military, too.

I narrowed my eyes. "So, if you went to the Academy, how come you're not in Central Command right now?"

Marcela bit her lip, then jerked her head to the side. "Move over," she said. I complied, and she knelt down next to West, replacing my hands on his head and shoulder with hers. Then she leaned into his ear and spoke softly. I could barely make out the words. "West. Can you hear us?"

She rubbed his shoulder slowly, up and down. "West," she whispered, even more softly. "West, it's me." Then, she leaned down and whispered something I couldn't hear.

Wide brown eyes opened, and my heart was so full I nearly started sobbing. Marcela planted an elbow in my chest, pressing me back, and I suppressed a sudden urge to punch her.

"He's getting up!" said Amiel.

My brother pulled himself into a sitting position, and pressed both hands into his scalp.

"Give him lots of room," said Marcela. "And for heaven's sake, get the rest of the *copper wire* off your body." She breathed in, then kept right on cooing at West. "You're okay, West. You can do this."

I gave her a strange look, but whatever she'd said was working, so I took a deep breath and tried whispering at him, too.

"Hey there, stranger. Remember me?"

My brother looked up at me and smiled. Elated, I reached out to hug him.

Then he wrapped both arms around Marcela.

And then he kissed her.

Twenty-Four

"What just happened?" I looked from West to Marcela, and back again. "Am I hallucinating, or did that lightning strike me harder than I realized?" Obviously my baby brother did not just kiss Marcela. *Marcela.*

"Tarry!" said West. His grin was lopsided, just like always, and I melted. He pulled me into his hug with Marcela, then released her. "That's my Tar. I knew you would make it." He placed his hands on both my shoulders and looked me squarely in the eyes. "I always knew we would find each other again. I never doubted it."

"Me either, West. Never once." I swallowed the lie, trying not to grin like a complete idiot. It was surprisingly hard, given our circumstances. "I found Dad," I added. And then, because I felt stupid, I added, "He misses you."

West frowned. "It's complicated right now."

"He's not as angry with me as he was." I looked away, unable to maintain eye contact. "About Mom."

West didn't answer right away. "Maybe we should be angry with him, for once."

"For once? You just described my entire childhood." I suppressed a shudder at the ice in his voice. It was so foreign, coming from him. "I can't be angry like that anymore. Not at him, anyway."

"How many lockies are out here?" said Marcela.

A steady light flicked on, somewhere in the distance, and Amiel's little head twisted around, trying to locate its source. It was nearly impossible in the haze. Overhead, the clouds grew sharper. "Uh, you guys. That is not our biggest concern at the moment," I said. "Let's get going."

Marcela scanned the ceiling, then grabbed my arm and pulled me away from West. When she had me standing, she reached down again and made an admirable, if unsuccessful, go at pulling West to his feet. "The clouds are back, and two of us are incapacitated," she said in her military voice. "We need to move. Now."

"Clouds, plural?" West curled up a little tighter. He must have seen them in action.

"Yep. Sorry." She tried again, looping an arm around his waist, and yanked him fully to his feet. "Are there more lockies out here? Anyone from the Remnant?" she asked Amiel.

"Also not our biggest problem," I said. My head began to swim again. We started running, a task I found quite suited to my rising panic.

"She's had psychaline," Marcela said. "We are all aware of the killer clouds, Char. That's why we're running away."

"It's a heck of a drug. My brain still won't unfuzz."

Amiel lowered her voice and paused at the end of the second row. "Maxx is out there. He went to find the others. We couldn't move West."

"Others who? Like more lockies? Or the—" Marcela stopped. The sound of hushed, deep voices filled the corridor, accompanied by heavy boots. "Wait. Does that sound like soldiers to you?"

"Ding, ding," I whispered. "And *that* is our biggest concern. I think they're coming from Command."

"Could be the Nowhere Men," Amiel said. "Command never sends soldiers in here. Only lockies."

"It's a special occasion," I said. "And who are these Nowhere Men?"

"We don't know. We thought they were a rumor until we realized the lockies were joining them, or being taken by them, little by little. They're definitely not from the Remnant. Doesn't make any difference now. There's nowhere to go," said Marcela. "No exits. None of the bins are safe from the lightning, either."

My brain, my brain. So much fuzz. What would the old Char do? "I mean, it makes a little difference where the soldiers came from," I said. "Officially, Command is supposed to be an ally now."

Marcela looked at me, deadpan. "Yeah. We should really have them over for tea."

"Point taken. But hey. At least we're armed."

"It's going to be, like, fifty to one if we engage them, judging by the bootsteps," she said, her voice rising.

"Well, sure, if you want to be all pessimistic about it," I muttered.

The door the soldiers had come through closed, darkening the hold, and highlighting the lightning as it flashed in the distance. The psychaline sent wobbles through the area, and as we ran, my lungs began to burn again. West groaned, leaned against a bin, and slid down into a stoop, like he was about to go fetal again.

"Oh, no you don't," said Marcela. "You get up right now. We can't carry you and fight the Command soldiers *and* look for shelter from the killer clouds, all at once."

178

"It's dark," he said.

"The better to hide us with, my dear," said Marcela. "Since that's our only real option at the moment." She pulled him up, gently and firmly, and I pretended not to notice how his hands lingered on her waist.

An instant later, he straightened. "Wait. Did someone say copper wire?"

Twenty-Five

I pulled my shirt up, showing them the nest of copper around me. "It's… kind of knotted up right now."

"You haven't lost that yet?" said Mars.

"It's not like I enjoy being chased by lightning. I can't get it off."

"Thanks to you, we are *all* being chased by—"

West held up a hand. "Everyone just stop." We looked at him expectantly. "What if we could set a wire up on a bin and have it sticking out in different places? Like a lightning rod."

"We'd be safe from the clouds," Amiel said.

"And the soldiers, as long as we could guard the door." I smiled. "That's not half bad."

"Okay, so we need to find a bin," Marcela said firmly. "Somewhere in the middle, something the lockies haven't gotten to yet." She pulled a sidearm out of nowhere and shot the shiny new keypad on the closest bin.

"Hey, I've done that before," I told her, still struggling not to slur my words. The psychaline was slowing down, and the pain was steadily building back. I welcomed it. "It's not as effective as you'd think. The bullets don't go through—"

"Plastic. Yeah, yeah." She scratched her head, sending a few final waves of crimson through the air. I watched, mesmerized, until a bolt of lightning struck a bin an aisle over, and sending us flying out of our skins.

We were running again.

This was accomplishing nothing. At this rate, it would be better just to surrender to the Commander's squadron and call it a day. But West was here, and so was Amiel, and I strongly doubted that the Commander would be inclined to take any prisoners today.

"Can't you break one?" said Amiel.

"What?"

"The locks." Her eyes were huge in her head, and they focused on me intently. "You can break into anything. That's what Adam said."

I stared at her. She was eerily calm, easily the most level-headed among us, as though she had experience dealing with near-death situations. She'd left her brother's side, an act that made perfect sense to me now, for a life—no, an existence—scavenging among the bins, dodging the guards and the Nowhere Men. She had no parents, and something about the set of her chin told me she hadn't known any on Earth, either. Was there no one left to worry about her? My chest tightened against my lungs, making everything heavy.

"I don't know, Amiel," I said. "Maybe I could have a long time ago. If I had my sack. And if these locks weren't brand new."

But she shook her head. "He said you disarmed the lasers in the control center without even touching a computer."

I had done that. One of the worst mistakes of my life, as it turned out.

"She can. I know she can," my brother said.

"West. Not helping." All I needed was my brother's misplaced faith in my criminal abilities. The boots thudded closer. They'd be armed, and except for Marcela, we weren't wearing uniforms. The bullets would cut right through our clothes.

They had a point, though. I was good at breaking into things.

I shook my head, begging it to sharpen up, willing the last of the psychaline to burn off into space.

And to my surprise, it did.

"Okay," I said slowly. "I have an idea."

"Just anytime you're ready," said Marcela, wincing at a crash of lightning.

"It's... kind of iffy. But if we can expose a wire in a keypad, we could use the copper to short the—"

"Lock mechanism!" West whisper-shouted. "Brilliant."

"Um. Thank you. But we need wire cutters."

"Or anything harder than copper," said West.

"We could shoot the wire with the gun!" Amiel ducked at the edge of a bin, and looked back at us enthusiastically.

"Won't work. They only penetrate skin," I said.

"Or we could just use a utility knife," said Marcela. We looked at her. "Like, say, an M9 bayonet. Oh, and hey, look at that. I have one right here."

She drew a scabbard from her hip and pulled out a black blade about seven inches long. At that moment, it was the most beautiful thing I'd ever seen.

West thought so, too, apparently. He was staring at Marcela with a look I'd never seen on his face before: something like a cross between a craving and a grin. I sincerely hoped I never saw it again.

I cleared my throat. "Maybe try loosening the plate, and I'll—"

"Yep. I'm on it." Marcela went to work on the keypad, jimmying it gently apart with the blade, and West went right on staring at her.

"It's a cool knife," he said finally.

"Why, thank you, West," she said, returning his expression before flipping the knife back to the scabbard. "Now. You. Hold still."

I held up my shirt, and Marcela used the scabbard and its blade to sever the knot of wire around me, as though she'd been doing it all her life. "Combat training," I said appreciatively.

"Combat training," she agreed, straightening the wire into a point and handing it over.

I wrapped the end of my shirt around my fingers, in case the circuit board carried a defensive charge, and worked the wire deep into the cable harness, making sure it bypassed the transorb and hooked directly to the negative terminal, so that the surge would have nowhere to go. "I can't find a grounding wire," I said at last. "I'm pretty sure they didn't plan for lightning up here."

Marcela was staring at the circuits, a bemused look on her face. "I'm pretty sure they didn't plan for you, either."

I smiled a little at that. "We're almost set. I just need to make sure the fail-safe won't activate when the controls are shorted. Shouldn't take long."

West was scanning the ceiling with growing apprehension. "I hate to rush you," he said. "But could you possibly move any slower?"

"Rome wasn't built in a day, buddy."

"Rome wasn't dodging killer lightning clouds," he said,

scanning the ceiling. "Which, I should point out, have congregated anew, just for us. Char, they're doing the swirly thing. They're gonna strike any second."

"I'm counting on it," I said grimly. "Marcela, cut here, if you please."

She complied, black blade twinkling in the gathering fog, and I pointed the end of the wire straight up, doubling it back to brace it against itself. Not half bad, all things considered. "Nothing to do now but wait for a bolt of lightning."

"Hang on," said Mars. "Where's Amiel?" She trotted to the end of the aisle, all thoughts of hiding abandoned. "Amiel! Get back here!"

I looked around. The air became electric, signaling the oncoming attack, and the hairs on my arm stood up in response to the sudden cold. Or fear.

"Oh, no. No, no, no," I half-whispered.

The clouds swirled faster, forming a defined circle, sucking the sounds away. At that moment, Amiel came sprinting around the corner.

"You scared me to death!" I said. "Get down. Everyone get lower than the antennae!"

"I went to find Maxx," Amiel shouted. "He's out here somewhere."

I threw myself on top of her. "We got incoming!"

Amiel's mouth moved.

"What?" I shouted back.

"I said, *boots or bolts?*"

"Yes!" screamed Marcela, and the world exploded into light once again.

But this time, I was ready.

* * *

When the smoke cleared, a few things were obvious. Thing one: my plan had worked. The lock took the hit, dying in a blaze of sparks. It wouldn't do for a paperweight now.

The door to the bin hung open impotently, and Amiel didn't need an invitation. She leapt in immediately. Marcela was crouched on the ground nearby, drawing my attention to thing number two, which was curled into a ball half-in and half-out of the bin: West.

"Is he hurt?" I shouted. My hearing had yet to return. Marcela said something that looked like "Lightness," and I bit my lip. That was bad timing, made worse by the arrival of thing three. Which was, of course, the soldiers.

They must have found us before the bolt landed, and they must have decided to take us by surprise from both ends of the aisle, because we were already surrounded, and the gap was closing fast.

Masked operatives crouch-ran toward our position as fast as cats in a rainstorm. Even working together, we'd never move him in time.

I planted my back on the ground near my brother and positioned my feet on his ribs and shoulders, then jammed my legs straight, shoving him over the doorway. Marcela leapt in after him and grabbed the edge of the door, slamming it shut as I rolled in after West.

Almost shut.

The black barrel of an assault rifle blocked the door panel from sealing just as I landed. It entered our space, our almost-haven, directly above my head.

I'd seen a weapon like this before, but it was somehow smaller around than I realized, and sharper. It jerked to one side as its owner attempted to pry the panel, then shifted while he sought better leverage. My breath caught. We were fish in a barrel. The rifle twitched again, this time, accompanied by a grunt.

Amazingly, the door did not budge.

Marcela was *strong*.

She lay into the panel, forcing it to stay where it was.

I pulled my gun off my back and aimed it at the crack in the door. "When I say go, let the door open another couple inches. But no more, if you can do that."

She took in the gun and quickly focused back on the door. "Yeah, hang on." She shifted her weight to her back leg and placed the toe of her forward boot precisely two inches to the left, then nodded at me.

"Go," I said, and the panel cracked open. The man in the mask saw the gun, and I aimed it at the only exposed skin I could find: his eye.

I hesitated, adjusting for the kick, and felt my soul slip down into the darkness below the ship.

I squeezed the trigger.

The hesitation was all he'd needed. But instead of firing into the bin like you'd expect, the soldier fell back, out of the path of the bullet, taking the rifle with him. Marcela slid the door in until it clicked, a soft echo of the unbearably loud shot I'd fired.

"Okay," I said, my voice shaking. "They're definitely Command. Not that we had any question. And I don't think they were ready for the lightning anymore than the rest of us. Is he okay?"

Marcela gave me a long, appraising gaze before replying. "He will be. Are you?"

"Can you wake him up?"

She kept right on looking at me. "You know that feeling

you get? In the back of you mind, when you're walking down the hall, and you realize there's just a few feet of metal separating you from space, and then it hits you that you'll never jog down a street again, or see a tree, or drive a car?"

I nodded, my mouth dry.

"And then you think, none of those things even exist anymore, and they never will again?"

I stared back at her.

"Well, the Lightness is nothing like that. It's a *million* times worse. It's a dissociative disorder that simulates a heart attack, over and over again, and all you can think of is how Earth is dead and we can never go back. And I'm afraid that one of these days, it's going to kill him."

I looked around the bin. My brother was catatonic, brought down by the trauma and madness of space, and we were surrounded.

Marcela seemed to be following the same train of thought. Her brow furrowed, and she placed a hand on West's chest.

I shook my head. "If those soldiers want us dead, all they have to do is take the wire off the keypad and wait for lightning to strike the bin."

"Let's not worry about that right now."

"Sure. What's the point? There's no way we're getting out of here alive, anyway."

"We could surrender," said Mars.

"Yeah, no. I'll take the lightning." It was suddenly all too much. I started laughing. "Isaiah once told me that everyone dies alone. But he was wrong. We're gonna die together. Right here in this bin."

"You Turner kids. You have the emotional fortitude of kittens. Buck up! We're all he's got right now."

I looked at West, *my West,* lying there, and frowned. I'd finally found my family, what was left of it, and against all odds, they didn't hate me anymore. It was a massive step in the right direction, but it still wasn't enough, as long as West and my father hated each other. There had to be something more that I could do, preferably before the Asian Ark blew us all up and called it good. I frowned. I was definitely missing something.

I looked from Mars, to West, and back again. "Actually, no. We're not."

Twenty-Six

I had an idea, or the beginning of one, but what we needed was a plan. "First things first," I said. "That's a full tactical unit. They'll breach the door any minute now. We need to figure a few things out before then. For example, why didn't that guy shoot me?"

"I don't know. You didn't return the favor, though, so I'm guessing he will next time." Marcela leaned over West, rubbing his shoulder and arm in a slow, steady motion.

"I'm guessing he won't. He seemed like he'd had training. It felt deliberate."

"Why not? What's stopping him?"

"Did the reports mention any of the details of the proposed treaty with Command?"

Marcela shook her head and went right on kneading West's arm.

"It's like this: the Remnant will be recognized as an independent nation-state so long as two conditions are met: we stop the fighting on board the Ark within twenty-four hours, and, uh, I have to marry the Commander's son."

"Wait—*what*? You were serious about that?" Her hand paused on West's arm, if only for an instant.

189

"He's not so bad, actually." I felt myself working up to a blush and pressed on hurriedly. "It could be worse. But you were right; it's backed by Asian nukes. Meaning, if the treaty isn't ratified within a day, they're going to destroy us all."

"But, that's—Char, that's insane."

"Not really. They think we have nuclear capabilities, too. They think we blew up Five."

"Did we? Didn't the Commander, I mean? Why not just kill him?"

"Something about blaming all of us for electing him, and something else about how we're really into warfare. I don't know. I don't think it was Plan A. Doesn't matter. Right now, we need to ratify the treaty, and that means taking down Adam."

"Char, we'd need an army for that. He's not alone in there."

I raised my eyebrows. "I know."

"Hold on a minute. Let me stop you right there. There is *no way* we're going to use the Commander's forces against Adam. That's the opposite of stopping a war."

I took a deep breath and hoped I didn't sound crazy. Hoped I *wasn't* crazy. "No, not the Commander. We need to wake West up. We need to ask him about the Nowhere Men."

"The guys who snatch lockies? They'd never help us."

"You might be surprised," I said slowly. "I think they helped me once. Well, tried to."

Amiel shifted next to me. "They come out at night. They never raid the bins."

We looked at her. "Then how do they eat?" said Marcela.

Amiel shrugged.

"They're grown men?" I asked. Amiel nodded. "Armed? Dressed in black? Kinda move together, keep to the shadows?"

She nodded again.

"Do they have a leader?"

"I don't know. Maxx thinks so. He has a friend who was taken. Maxx swears he saw him again, but he didn't want to leave."

"Must not be so bad, then," I said.

"Or they're so bad, he's afraid to try to escape," Marcela intoned. "Let's not go believing in fairy tales, here."

"I think I know who they are. One of them, anyway. I've... run into them myself. And I think they'll help us. Can you get us there?"

Marcela interrupted. "Doesn't matter, does it? If we leave the bin, we'll be shot."

"But just say we were out there, no soldiers, Ames. Do you know where the Nowhere Men go? Could you get us there?"

Amiel nodded.

"Then I think we have a plan."

West rolled from his back onto his front, holding his head in both hands. Marcela touched the back of his neck distractedly.

"Is that it, then?" she said. "Stop the Commander, depose Adam, find Maxx, join the Nowhere Men, and get you married off to the enemy?"

"Maybe rescue Isaiah, if we're making a list." I gave a little shrug. "That about covers it."

"We better get started."

"That's the spirit," I said dryly. "Now. About those soldiers. Anyone got any bright ideas?"

Marcela helped West to a sitting position, but he didn't release his grip on his own head, or give any indication that he knew what was going on. "We could try shooting our way out," she said.

I shook my head. "There's too many of them. We'd never make it. Is he—is he going to stay like that for awhile?"

"Hard to say. It kinda varies. That was a pretty loud bolt, and it's exactly the kinda thing that sets him off."

I glanced back at the panel next to the door, trying to figure out how many guards were still out there. "Can we weaponize the copper with the lightning?"

"Too unpredictable. Plus, we'd be just as likely to get hit as they would," said Mars, sounding irritated.

"I guess none of it matters anyway, as long as West can't move," I said. My brother was still curled up on the floor at our feet.

"Leave West to me," she said. "I can get him to walk, when the time comes. Maybe we should just take a hostage. Worked for you, right?"

I thought for a moment. "Actually, that's not a bad idea."

"It was a joke, Char. They've had training. It'd be impossible to catch one without getting shot." I tilted my head at her, and she laughed. "Are you suggesting I hop out there and kidnap someone?"

"No, not at all," I replied. "That would be crazy. I'm suggesting you already have."

Twenty seconds later, I emerged from the bin, my hands held high. I made my eyes wide and let myself stumble when Marcela shoved me forward into the aisle, maintaining a rough grip around my throat with her forearm. I had to hand it to Marcela. She was really committed to her role.

She pressed into the back of my neck, and I tripped, gasping, toward the nearest raised gun.

It occurred to me that neither of us was doing much acting.

"You shoot, she dies," Mars called out into the space between the bins.

The guard nearest me narrowed her eyes, but her gun, steady in two hands, lowered to point at the floor. "The Commander only wants her, for now. We have orders to take her in alive."

"You can have orders to bite me," I said.

The guard ignored me. "Let her go, and you can still walk away from this. No one has to die."

"You tell the Commander she'll be in touch, if he means it. Charlotte Turner is still a prisoner of the Remnant. In the meantime, we better be all the way outta here before anyone moves," Mars told her.

West followed directly behind her, one arm around Amiel, who held my gun level. When we'd put two bins between us and the guards, Marcela relaxed her grip, and we started running again.

But this time, we knew where we were going.

"Just take us straight there," I shouted to Amiel, letting her take the lead. We didn't need to evade; we needed to arrive in enough time to avoid a shoot-out.

"It's around here," she said, stopping sooner than I'd expected. The guards were still several bins away, but that wouldn't last long, at the rate we were moving. "Right here!" she said. "This is where they go!"

"So how do we get it open?" I shouted.

"I don't know! Knock, I guess!"

We pounded on the door, all at once, until Mars pulled

us away. "Okay, I think we can assume they heard that. Any more, and they'll think they're under attack."

"That's all we need," I muttered.

The door slid open a crack, and I stepped back, showing my open palms to whoever was behind it. "We come in peace, but we're being pursued." Was it wise to tell the guard why I was here? I decided that it probably couldn't hurt, at this point, and it might actually help, so I hastily added, "I'm Charlotte Turner, and I'm looking for my father. So, uh, take me to your leader, please."

Twenty-Seven

The door opened the rest of the way, and I led our little group over the threshold. Two of us—Mars and I—looked around with curiosity. We were in a small, wooden-paneled receiving room lined with Nowhere Men. They returned our gaze with open expressions of their own. The door locked behind us, but I couldn't relax just yet. They weren't planning to shoot us, but we weren't necessarily wanted here, either.

"Hi," I began, "I'm not totally sure who you guys are. I don't know anything about you, actually, but I'm Char—Charlotte—and this is West, my brother, and we were hoping that you could help us find our—"

"Charlotte." My father stepped into the hall and crossed the space between us in a single pace. "You're here." There was a half-breath of uncertainty before he pulled me into a slight embrace. Another breath, and I was fully enveloped in my father's arms.

I laughed into his shoulder, momentarily at a loss for words, and he hugged me tighter.

In spite of everything—the madness of space and the endless prospect of war, the haunting tyranny of my mother's death—my family was together again. I pulled back for as long as it took to memorize the sight of my father's face before mine, then pressed back into his embrace.

I was happy.

It was a strange version of happiness, constrained by the uncertainty of the chaos around us. But for the first time, the heaviness of the years that lay between us failed to mitigate *this moment*. My eyes shut tightly against the once-familiar, starched white cotton of his upper sleeve. *I had won*. Never mind what happened next. We were together, and we were ready.

My father was the first to let go.

"West," he said. It was the same tone he usually used with me. "Welcome."

West nodded wordlessly. His face betrayed no sign of hostility.

"This is Amiel," I said. "And Mar—"

"Marcela Ramirez," Mars cut in, extending a hand. They shook, and she took a step back toward West, suddenly shy.

"They're from the Remnant," I added.

"You are welcome," my father said, looking at them both in turn.

West took a step closer to Mars.

My father cleared his throat and waved us into the next room. "We're a small operation, but we've had remarkable success in gaining traction within the sectors controlled by Central Command. This is the main area here," he waved around a room full of makeshift tables and chairs made from what appeared to be the sides, roof, and contents of a storage bin. The room was short and resembled a wide tunnel, giving it a temporary feeling. This was a place you passed through along your way, rather than a destination in its own right. "There are also sleeping quarters at each of these doors, all full for now. Most of us have an official, legitimate residence somewhere on board the Ark. And that's about it. Welcome to Nowhere."

There was something vaguely off-balance about his tone. It crowded out the meaning of his words until I pinpointed it: He was addressing us like adults. He cared how things worked out, and unusually, he wasn't sure what that would be. As impossible as it seemed, my father was nervous.

Life was strange.

"Is anyone from the Remnant? What do you do? How many of you are there?" I had a million questions, but Amiel was more insistent.

She grabbed my father's arm, forcing his attention to herself.

"Is Maxx here? He's a lockie, like me. Have you seen him?"

Dad was taken aback, but he gave her a friendly look. "The lockies don't come this way unless they're joining us, and there's no one here who goes by that name. Maybe look around."

Amiel's little mouth tightened, and she flitted from room to room off the main hall. Each door she slammed shut was louder than the one before, mirroring the growing panic on her face.

"He's not here," she announced at last. "Maxx isn't here."

Dad gave her a sympathetic look. "We can send out a search party when it's safer. We're missing a few other people. We'll add Maxx to the list."

"No," she said. "That'll be too late. We have to go now."

"Out of the question. It's too dangerous. There's a fight going on. One we're not prepared for, Miss..." He waited while she ignored the request for her name. "Well. We all need to eat. Let's talk about it after."

"But that's exactly why we have to find him! *Because* it's dangerous."

I put a hand on her shoulder. She was all bones beneath her shirt. I wondered whether that was normal for a girl her age, or if her life was as hard as it seemed. Then I shook my head. Of course she was hungry. Of course she was.

I remember the look on Meghan's face when she found me stealing her food after weeks of slowly starving in prison. Meghan had protected me. She'd given her life just to give me a shot at survival. Looking at Amiel, I felt like I could almost understand that.

"Ames," I said, using her brother's name for her. "I get it, I really do. Isaiah's missing, too. Those guards will kill us, even me, if we go out there again. Let's eat. Just a little. Then maybe we'll be able to set foot outside again."

Her worried eyes turned back to the entrance, then up to me.

"Trust me," I said, the words heavy on my tongue. "I'll help you find him myself." I met Marcela's eye over Amiel's head, and she gave me a quick nod.

"Here. Sit with me," said Mars. "We're gonna figure this out, I promise."

She agreed, silently, and my dad motioned us toward a table. He fiddled with a fork as we sat, and several other members filed into the main room. Either it was meal time, or they'd been startled by Amiel's frantic search of their rooms and were coming out to assess the situation in the mess hall. Before long, the short tables were full. Tin plates like something from an army kit lined the long makeshift tables. Dad had been paying more than a little attention to

West since we walked in, but I sensed that West wasn't ready to talk yet, so I took the lead on the conversation, hoping to avert any potential fireworks. Like I said, we were together at last, the three of us, so there was no end to my optimism.

"So, Dad. You have a lair."

He half-attempted to cover his amusement. "Don't be dramatic, Charlotte."

"Hey, I'm not the one with a lair *and a secret army*."

"It's not an army. More like a strike team."

"Doesn't answer the question, though, does it?" said West.

"What question, son?" said Dad.

He spread his arms out, drawing a little attention from the surrounding tables. "The question is why. Why do you have an *army*, Dad?"

"We have our reasons," he said.

At this, West scoffed and shoved away from the table, which had been crafted quickly, cobbled together with a view toward transience. His plate clattered around, inviting instant silence from those around us until it fell back into place, by which time he was nearly out of the room. We watched him go.

"Let him leave," said Dad. "He'll talk when he's ready."

I looked after my brother until the door closed behind him. "He knows his way around."

Dad gave a vague nod, still staring. "He's never come in through the front entrance before."

"There's a back way?"

"Connects to Central Command. Well, to the stairwell." Dad didn't lower his voice, so it must have been common knowledge. I'd thought the Rift was the only unplanned space on the outer hull of the ship, but there must have been a similar area in more than one sector.

Uniformed guardians placed trough-like vessels onto the center of the tables, and I took the opportunity to look around the room. Several people wore black uniforms. Why did my father have so many of the Commander's forces in his little compendium? Not that this was a huge group, but even one Command soldier would have been surprising.

Come to think of it, nothing indicated that all the members were present. There was no telling how big a force it was.

"This is quite an operation, Dad. How long have you been here?" I asked, digging in to the food. It was a stew of some kind—lovely and brown—and it had a slight crunch. It was savory, but without the chunks of meat I expected. Beside us, Amiel ate like a bear in a campsite. She was intense and silent, but I had been right about her. She was *hungry*.

He hadn't answered, so I tried again. "What's in this?" I asked between mouthfuls. "It's good."

He watched me eat with mild interest. "You really want to know? Took me months to try it again, once I found out. Great protein, highly sustainable source. I'll just say that we'll probably be eating a lot of it once we arrive on Eirenea and leave it at that."

I was suddenly pretty sure I had seen a set of tiny legs in the bowl before me. Like, a set of six tiny legs. Dad observed my reaction with amusement while continuing to eat, using the same high manners he'd insisted on every day of my childhood. I gave the stew one last glance before putting as much distance between it and me as I could manage politely, then pushed it a few more inches away for good measure.

"You know, you're quite a maverick," I said. "I have to wonder what you're really up to in here."

"It's hardly nefarious, Charlotte. And I'm not the only one who broke a few rules. Did you know that there's an entire sector of the European Ark that's just full of incubators?"

"Like, for babies? Yeah, I heard something about that."

Marcela piped up again. "I heard a rumor there's a whole floor of the Asian Ark with a bunch of the survivors' grandparents."

"Someone should send them to the incubators with rocking chairs," I said. "Sounds like they need each other."

My father looked at me. "That's a very good idea, Charlotte."

"Who takes care of them? The babies," said Marcela.

"There's a videoscreen," I said. "They picked a woman to be the 'face' of their mother, and she's up on the screen all day, singing nursery rhymes. The Queen spared all the workers she could, when she found out. And the Biosphere makes extra oxygen, so they really can afford to keep them. For now, anyway."

"What a strange family they've all been forced into," Dad said, to no one in particular. "It should be sad, shouldn't it. But instead, it's a good thing, because they survived."

"I thought the European Ark was required to contribute its extra oxygen to the other Arks? As part of the Treaty?" said Mars.

"I don't know," I said.

She gave me an annoyed look. "You haven't read the Treaty yet? I thought they put a copy in your cell."

I gave a noncommittal shrug.

Dad had a hard look. "Every Ark has its secrets. It's just that ours are a bit more... *pressing* at the moment."

The table fell to contemplative silence. At length, my father finished eating and leaned back in his chair, crossing his arms. It was a familiar pose—one he adopted after nearly every family meal we'd shared. "Nice bracelet," he said. "Do you know what it is?"

I glanced at my wrist. "K-band. Lie detector, basically. The Imperial insisted."

"I'll bet he did. It's more than that, Charlotte."

"What do you mean?"

"It's a transmitter as well. Probably does some other stuff, depending on the model."

"A *transmitter*?" I looked down in horror. "Like, with a microphone? We have to get it off." I held my wrist out to him.

Dad hopped up from the table and made his way to the lockers on the far wall. "Can't do that," he said over his shoulder. "Not without causing some serious damage. It's in your skin. We'd need their cooperation. Didn't they tell you about it when you put it on?"

Marcela leaned in with a sardonic expression. "You let them put it *in your skin*, Char? Did I hear that right?"

"Seemed like a good idea at the time," I muttered.

"What was that? I didn't quite catch—"

Dad returned to the table with a roll of aluminum foil and slid into West's seat. "All is not lost," he said in a goofy voice, an obvious attempt to put me at ease. He patted the table in front of me, indicating that I should set my arm on it.

"How do you know so much about them?" I asked. The aluminum extended in a shiny arc, and Dad began wrapping it around my band in noisy sheets. "Senate hearings, or something?"

"No, they never made it that far in North America. Not that we didn't use them. We just never had to explain it."

I set my water down and looked him square in the eye. "Who's we? What's going on with all this?"

"I'll tell you when it's time, Charlotte. We're not there yet. Suffice to say, there are a lot of people who don't find the balance of power among the Arks quite to their liking, and there has to be someone who makes sure those people stay quiet until we get to Eirenea."

"Well. You're doing a fantastic job so far."

"We didn't count on the Remnant. There. That should block the signal."

I studied the flattened mass of metal on my lower arm. "Thanks, Dad."

He gave me a serious look. "All things considered, it could be a lot worse." His eye fell to the silver blob. "The war, not the band. The band looks ridiculous. I'm afraid it can't be helped."

"Nah. Reminds me of that time I was Wonder Woman for Halloween, and Mom made my costume out of tinfoil, a tablecloth, and a swimsuit."

"A classic look for any discerning young hero," said Dad.

I laughed, but when I met my father's eye, the pain of the grief we shared cut the sound short. I continued to stare, studying his face, desperate to know him again, but in many ways, we were like strangers now. The things that once bound us together had, in the end, driven us apart.

But he was still my father. My mother's ghost was bright, and unsatisfied, and visible only to us.

"Dad," I said, leaning in. "Asia's going to fire on us if we can't get the fighting to stop. They're monitoring the blast energy, or something. We have until morning."

"I have some contacts on that Ark. They ran me through the details of the proposed treaty."

"Contacts?" said Mars. "How do you communicate with them?"

My father looked at her. "I have my ways."

"Your ways," I repeated flatly, but Mars looked thoughtful.

"Yes, I—" Dad began.

"The Tribune," said Mars.

Dad weighed her up for a long moment, his face tight. Mars, on the other hand, was as calm as ever, and she returned his gaze frankly. "No one else has the infrastructure to pull this off. You needed blueprints, some pretty advanced comm technology," she said. "Just for starters. And if the Commander knew you existed, he'd spare no effort to destroy you. Unless you were part of the plan all along."

"I thought the Tribune were just supposed to decide Treaty disputes," I said.

"I heard they started that way," said Mars.

I stared at my father. "What does she mean?"

"There had to be a single, unifying power. We couldn't afford to lose a single Ark, let alone fall into warfare. This was the only way," said Dad. "We organized. Gathered the leadership. And this is what we came up with. But not everyone wanted to go along."

"So you're... what, exactly? A Tribune member?"

"It's more complicated than that. We're not as centralized as we'd like to be, but our goal hasn't changed. We just want everyone to survive. We want to reach Eirenea intact. It's trickier than it sounds."

"If you didn't want fighting, why do you have an army?"

"I don't. It's more like a network than anything else. We survive by keeping in contact with each other. We trade in information. We started out trying to resolve disputes, but we had access to every inner circle, and we kept hearing things that conflicted. And then Five went dark, and we realized we'd failed to see what mattered." There was something so strange about his voice, like he was dead set on making our relationship work, no matter what the cost to himself. He handed his plate to a man over his shoulder and spoke again in the same tone of forced politeness. "So we changed our strategy," he finished.

"You're spies," said Mars.

"Something like that."

They locked eyes and, after a long moment, Mars nodded.

My father turned back to me. "So," he said awkwardly, "you're getting married."

I took a deep breath. "It'll have to happen soon. There's a guy in the Remnant. Adam. He took over headquarters, and I don't know what happened to Isaiah after that. He's the one who made the killer—"

"Lightning clouds, yeah. We've had our eye on him."

"Don't blink now." I shivered, thinking of the dead-eyed bodies of the guards Adam killed. "He's dangerous, Dad. More than you know."

Dad nodded, thinking, and I savored the brand-new feeling of being taken seriously by him. The rest of our troubles were at the front of my mind, but it still felt like a solid victory, life-wise. If my biggest goal was reuniting my family, I was so close I could taste it.

And then it hit me: that was my moment. Right then. I'd never have another like it. So I jumped.

"Dad, I gotta know. What happened with you and West?"

Twenty-Eight

"It's weird, Charlotte. Life, I mean." He drummed his fingers on the tinny table, then stopped drumming, then looked back, forward, at the door, and at the ceiling.

At everything but me.

"Weird, how?"

"It's just—it's not what I expected. Not because of the meteor. Here's the thing: there's nothing I can point at and say I'm truly proud of it, with two exceptions. You and West. I did okay by you both, in spite of myself, but I can't seem to keep either one of you. Maybe I should be grateful things are working out the way they are. But I can't help but wonder."

He hazarded a tiny glance at me, looking away before our eyes met, and I frowned. "Wonder what?"

All around us, the conversations were varied. People were serious, or quiet, or debating. Some tables were even laughing. The effect was a cacophony of shared survivorship, and any other time, I might have relished it.

He didn't answer me, but stood expectantly. "Let's find your brother."

I glanced back at Marcela, but she waved me on with an

understanding expression. "You go. I'll stay here with Amiel. We might even get seconds."

"You're welcome to mine," I said and followed my father out of the room. When I looked back, I realized that Marcela had given Amiel her jacket at some point during the meal.

And West was in love with her, and Isaiah trusted her with his life. I had to smile.

I really was a terrible judge of character.

My father's room was painted yellow. *Yellow*. It seemed so unlike him, until I remembered that it was mom's favorite color.

It had two narrow beds made from shipping pallets covered in the same standard-issue foam mattresses found all over the Ark. One bed had been hastily made, and my brother was slouched on the other.

I spared a moment of appreciation for West. He'd always been more mature than I, even though he was years younger. If I'd been the one acting out, they'd never have found me.

He rubbed his face and looked up at us. Then he spoke aloud the words that pounded through the room, making us safe, reverberating through all our minds at once:

"Here we are. Together."

The three of us shared the following thought as well, but its presence took up so much of the space between us that no one thought to lend it breath:

I miss her.

Dad cleared his throat. "For years, I've dreamed of saying this, and when I finally had a chance, I blew it. But we've spoken our mind about the past already, and I can finally say it now: Welcome home, Charlotte."

I laughed. "Thanks, Dad."

"You too, son."

West looked up, then shook his head, a dark expression on his face. "This isn't home."

I plopped down, cross-legged, in the middle of Dad's bed, effectively barring him from sitting there, hoping that he'd sit next to West. But West stretched his legs out, blocking the rest of his bed. Dad paced the room once before leaning against a wall, arms folded.

"You guys," I said. "*What* is going on between you? I know it's none of my business, but come on. It's like you said. Here we are. Together. Can we please make up and be a family now?" They shifted around, and I rolled my eyes. "Whatever it is, I've done worse. I mean, unless someone's committed several felonies since I saw you last."

No response. My face felt warm, and I told myself that getting upset wasn't going to help anything. I rarely made good decisions while crying.

"Ha, ha," I said, forcing brightness into my tone. "But, seriously, you forgave me!"

Another moment passed, and my throat grew tight. Its pressure burned up into the skin on my face. A hot tear splashed onto my hands, and I froze completely, unwilling to expose myself any further to the two people I loved most in the world.

"West," I said, my voice wooden. "This isn't what she'd want."

At that, my dad uncrossed his arms. "I made a mistake."

I frowned. That was definitely not what I'd expected to hear.

"What happened?" I asked.

Dad took a breath. "In the early days, starting right after the launch, West was sick all the time. He'd ball up, not speak to anyone for hours. We didn't know what to think about it."

"The Lightness," I guessed.

Dad nodded. "At the time, we didn't know much. I thought it might be a heart condition, something that would eventually disqualify him from work, marriage." He scratched his head angrily. "If he lived that long. What kind of life would that be? But then we got it looked at, and it turns out it was all in his head. Debilitating, yes. And terrifying. For both of us. But not that uncommon. Reports were coming in from all over. It was happening on every single Ark. Europe was working on this treatment; Asia had another. Not a lot of progress on this Ark. We didn't even have a name for it."

West gave Dad a dark look, but remained silent.

"And it happened almost every night. And your mother was gone, and you were..." Dad looked at the wall.

"Yeah, I was gone, too," I said.

He shook his head. "I'm just telling you what was going on. He was all I had left, and he just... *refused*..." He broke off again. "He took one round of pills. Went a whole week without an attack. We were hopeful. Then he never touched them again. Wouldn't see a doctor. The attacks came back, worse than ever. I'd wake up at night, wondering if his heart had stopped beating. If this was the night I'd lose my son, too."

I looked at West. His face was red, and his cheeks were wet. He was as still as a statue.

"I stopped sleeping. I couldn't..." Dad broke off. He didn't look sad so much as genuinely baffled. "It's an illness of the mind, Charlotte. He didn't know what he was doing. And I'm his father. I had to help him."

West put his face down, resting his forehead against his arms. I couldn't believe how broad his shoulders had become.

"I got several more rounds, enough for an entire year, and started grinding them into his food a little at a time. We spent so much time together, those days. He never suspected it. I was going to tell him; I just wanted him *well* first, so that I could talk to him about it. I wanted my son back."

"Did it work?" I asked.

Dad was staring at the wall. "Yes. It worked."

We both looked at West, but he hadn't moved. His head was still down, his breathing slow and even, if a little forced. Not labored enough to indicate an attack. Just crying, then. Or avoiding crying.

"And the day I told him, he left. I looked everywhere. Found out he'd joined the Remnant, of all things. I couldn't get to him, but he sent a message out. He wasn't coming back; he'd never forgive me as long as he lived. It's funny." He paused, looking at me. "Couple years ago, it could have been written by you."

I shook my head, thinking. "That seems... I mean, no one wants to be drugged, but I can see where—"

"No." West's head jerked up. "You can't. You can't understand *at all*."

"Tell me," I said.

He put his head back down. "It's... you wouldn't understand, Char."

"I'm here, and I'm listening. We used to tell each other everything. You two are all the family I have left."

"What if I leave the room?" Dad said suddenly.

"What?" I said.

He opened the door and stood with his hand on the keypad, looking at us, his children. "Talk to your sister, West. Even if you can't forgive me, she's right. You can't just give us both up. But for what it's worth, son, I believe in the Lightness. I never thought you were crazy, if that's what this is about. The idea that our bodies were meant to live on a planet with changing temperatures and varying light and all that—it's real. Just because it's in your head doesn't mean it wasn't killing you. And me, too.

"But it's also true what they say, that we are a race of explorers. That we were built to survive." He leaned in closer. "And we will, West. You and me and Charlotte. Our family. The Remnant. The other Arks. The kids in the incubators. Everyone. *We are going to survive.* But I'm not going to do it without you. I'm not going to sit by while you waste away." He waited, but West offered no absolution. "Well. I can't apologize for trying to save you, son."

West started talking, his face was full of emotion, but he looked only at the bedspread. Navy blue, same as Eren's. Probably exactly the same, now that I thought about it.

"When I first heard about the Arks, I knew I was going to get on one. I did. I just knew it. We were all going to make it. Mom, Dad. Even you, Char. I knew you'd be here." He choked a little, took a slow breath. We waited for him to continue. "But life is strange. And the things I took for granted don't exist anymore.

"Gravity, Charlotte. They took away *gravity*. And it doesn't even matter, because nothing is what I expected it to be. We were separated, and I tried to hang on. I wanted to be brave." He was crying now, but he didn't seem to notice. "But she never came. And neither did you."

He looked at me, and I felt as though my soul had slipped away from the room to wander across the shards of Earth, haunting the home that had failed us all.

But my brother went right on talking.

"And that's when I finally understood: nothing was okay. Nothing would ever be okay again."

He sucked in a breath, making a little gasp, and I stood as quietly as possible to sit on the bed next to West, who was nearly grown, and pull him into an embrace. West tolerated the hug for a moment before pulling away.

"And here's another thing I never saw coming: grief. That's the name for it, but it's nothing like I thought it would be. I feel like it should be called something else." He broke off again, suppressing another sob in spite of the tears on his face.

"It followed you around," I whispered.

He nodded. "I got used to it."

"It kept you company, because it reminded you of her," I said. "It made you think of her, even when you didn't want to."

"Even when I didn't expect to," said West.

"Especially then," Dad said.

We looked at him. It was almost as though we'd forgotten he was there.

"It's weird. It becomes comforting, after a while," Dad continued, "when you realize she's not coming back, that that feeling is all you have."

"That's what you took away from me," said West. "That's what I lost when I took the pills. *I lost her.*" He looked at Dad, a mix of anger and confusion on his face. "I didn't feel sad anymore, or scared, or anything. I couldn't feel anything but panic, and even then, it wasn't real; it was like someone was playing a joke on me.

"But the joke never ended. I never got better, and everything wasn't real, but I didn't care. I just stopped being able to care."

Dad was staring at him. "I didn't know."

"You didn't even ask! You just sneaked around, and you—"

West cut himself off, making a sound like he'd forced himself to stop breathing, and stood. His anger made him tall. The flimsy bedframe gave a rude creak when relieved of his weight, punctuating the silence as he left the room.

Twenty-Nine

Dad watched him go with a face like a much older man. The only indication that he'd even understood the conversation was the slightest change in his voice, like its strength had dropped a tenth of a power. "Hand me the toolkit, Charlotte. I have something to show you."

I knew where it was without him telling me. There was only one place Dad had ever kept a toolkit: under his bed. I slid it over to him wordlessly, and he selected a screwdriver, which he applied to the vent filter on the wall near the door panel.

"That's a terrible hiding place," I said.

"It's nothing anyone'll come looking for," said Dad, extracting a black box from the ventilation shaft.

I recognized it as a standard-issue personal box. Everyone who boarded the Ark through the legal channels had received one. You were expected to put your worldly possessions in it, and it'd be waiting for you when you got to your assigned quarters. I hadn't had one, for obvious reasons, but it reminded me of the little shoebox I'd kept in prison, which had been stolen from me the day the meteor struck: here, fit your life into a confined rectangle.

This one must have been my mother's. My grief leaned in close, whispering that she had given her life for my place on this ship. As if I ever thought about anything else.

"I think she knew," said Dad. "She knew it'd be hard for us to stay together, when she was gone. She put her wedding ring in here. Part of me wishes she'd kept it, to comfort herself, in the end." He looked up, suddenly, as though he regretted speaking so openly about her. "But she wanted us to have it."

"It's weird to think that she knew," I said.

I took the box from my father's outstretched hands and lifted the lid again. My mother's last will and testament was not a document, but a metal box. My inheritance was our shared memories of her, and the box was full of them.

Photographs. A cheap necklace, which I recognized as one my father had given her for their first Valentine's Day together, when they were both in high school, was now tangled in her wedding garter. A silky, silver-plated baby hairbrush, which had lain on the dresser in my nursery. Handmade Mother's Day cards. West's footprints, smudged onto a certificate she'd received from the hospital on the occasion of his birth. A "book" I'd written when I was six, about Robin Hood getting in a fight with a wolf, who turned out to be Maid Marian in disguise.

I hadn't known she'd kept that.

I sat, frozen, fighting the urge to paw madly through the entire box like a starving man at a banquet table, and my father took it from my limp hands. My throat grew tight when he pulled out a big, familiar square of foam. I'd have recognized it anywhere, even though it was wrapped in plastic. Here was something she'd intended only for herself.

"Mom's pillow," I said softly.

Part of her must have hoped she wouldn't have to die. The thought made me ill. *Of course she hadn't wanted to die*. The reality of it snaked through my limbs, binding me to the coldness of space. Just because she was resigned—*just because she loved us*—didn't mean she wasn't afraid to die. It was too horrible to think of. There was no escape for anyone, was there?

"You know how she was about her pillow," said Dad.

"Believe me, I know. She wouldn't sleep with anything else," I answered, a near-hint of crazed laughter in my voice. "That thing must be twenty years old. Why is there plastic on it?"

"No reason. Just how I keep it," said Dad. He looked down at the pillow again. "Oh, Charlotte. That's not true. I keep the plastic on because when we first got here, it still smelled like her. And I thought if I could make it stay, the scent of her, I would still be able to—" he broke off to stare at the wall. A flash of frustration, or anger, lit his features briefly, then he looked at me. "But it doesn't anymore. We're in space. The air is recycled a thousand times a day. And it doesn't smell like *anything*, least of all your mother."

I watched in absolute shock as the plastic floated to the floor. It was the first wasteful thing I'd seen my father do in my life. He pressed his face into the pillow.

I was unable to guess what was happening until a great, silent sob wracked his body.

My father was crying.

"Dad."

His own words were cracked and muffled by the foam. I leaned closer, unable to understand anything after that, until a single word became clear: "Cecilia."

I threw my arms around him. He held onto the pillow, but his other arm found me. The embrace shook the coldness from the room, from the ship.

Thirty

"Hey, Turners! Mr. Turner!" A loud knock made us jump, and the bed let out another screech as we stood.

"That'll be Mars," I said. "Hang on."

Dad got to the door first, and Mars came running in, her red hair lighting up the yellow room, West trailing closely behind. "It's Amiel," she said, breathless. "She's gone. I went to the bathroom, and when I came back—"

"She'll never make it out there," said Dad. "I'll get the infrared."

"She must have gone to find Maxx," said Mars.

"Who's Maxx?" Dad frowned.

"I have to find her," I said suddenly, surprising even myself.

"Charlotte, that's—"

"Dangerous. Yes." I pushed into the hall. "That's exactly why she needs me."

"Us," West called after me. "She needs us."

"Now hang on just a minute," said Dad. His voice was suddenly so strong, so full of authority, that we stopped and looked at him expectantly. "Who has a gun?" he said.

"Me," I said at the same time Mars said, "I do."

"Mars, just think about this," said West, holding out a protective arm toward her. "You should stay here. I'm sure we'll be back in no time."

"Like heck I will," she spat, her anger flaring. "I will not sit around *hiding* while there's a fight going on. That little girl needs us."

I slid my opinion of Marcela Ramirez up another notch. "Might be good to have a doctor."

Dad looked from one of us to the other, then spoke to West. "Son, go get a gun from the room. You should be armed."

We spared a few tense minutes in the mess room to gather our wits about us, cobbling together makeshift lightning rods with ripped bedsheets, spare wire, and canteen knives.

"So, the plan," I prompted. "We need one."

"Uh, we have a plan," said Mars. "You're getting married. I'm rescuing Amiel." She nodded toward West and my dad. "And they're coming with me."

"Yeah. Me too."

"No, no, no," she said, exasperated. "Surely you can see how bad an idea that is. Point one, you've been struck by lightning. And drugged."

I shrugged. "I'm fine."

"Point two, and I cannot overstate this, you are vital to the survival of the entire human race, so stop being so selfish. At least until your wedding. Then you're welcome to go—"

"This is absurd!" I appealed to my family. "Obviously I'm not just going to sit—"

"She does have a point," West said.

"Three points actually; I'm not done yet," said Mars. "Someone needs to hang back here. Guard the door for reentry. Keep the path clear. That's you."

"She's right, Charlotte," said my dad. "We can't risk it. You'll stay here."

I scowled at Mars, beaten.

She smiled back at me. "There are no small jobs, Charlotte. Only small—"

"Shut up."

"Right, then. See you soon," said Dad. His voice held a touch of concern, which was mirrored in the face of my brother.

I looked at them both, suddenly worried. "Be careful."

"We will," he said. "We'll be right back."

And then they were gone.

I paced the room, then sat. Then I stood, opened the door and closed it again before finally yielding to the slowness of time. It did me no good to try to keep calm, so I gave myself permission to fret as usefully as possible. I took my role as door-guard in earnest, allowing myself to check the passageway as often as I liked. When I noticed a storm cloud gathering, I set up an auxiliary lightning rod nearby before ducking back into Nowhere. Time slipped past in spurts, but only when I was occupied, and none too fast even then.

I thought myself prepared until I heard the lightning crash several aisles away, too far to chase. I ran into the cargo hold, gun drawn, and stuck near the relative umbrella of my lightning rod. Someone was screaming. Amiel, judging by the pitch. My hands curled into fists so tight my wrist began to ache.

I stopped breathing and started running. I saw Mars first, her bright hair a beacon. A lifeless figure was draped across her arms.

"Move! Go!" she shouted.

Behind her was West, moving slowly, gripping hands with Amiel. I couldn't tell which of them was assisting the other.

My father flanked West, matching his pace with an intensity I'd rarely ever seen from him. It was as though he could not stand to be more than a foot from his son.

Time extended into the pathway, giving the impression that they were running through glue.

Mars made it past me and through the door. I did not recognize the unconscious child in her arms. It had to be Maxx.

"Oh, no. Oh, no," I muttered, taking in his small face, but my voice was drowned in a sudden silence. The air became electric, and I tasted poison.

I felt myself begin to scream.

The door to Nowhere yawned open before us.

My father stood in the aisle, waving us in, refusing to enter before us, and my lungs filled with kerosene. The cloud over his head formed into two perfect circles, and despair took root in my heart. Two. Two clouds. One lightning rod.

Not Dad. Not Dad.

I shoved Amiel ahead, practically throwing her toward the doorway, and she dashed forward like a terrified gazelle, still tethered to West. They were in.

My father reached for me, wrapped his arms around me, and threw himself in, taking me with him. I tripped forward, landing painfully on my knees. We were in.

I looked at my hands, senselessly taking note of the tiniest lines of blood that crossed my palms. We made it.

Amiel released West and reached back to close the door.

She was barely inside the frame when a nauseating crack split the air.

Lightning stretched out its long, lethal fingers and wrapped itself around her little chest.

"Marcela! We need a doctor!" my dad was shouting. His voice cracked. It sounded like someone else. "Marcela!"

I traced the line of metal all the way down the grounding wire of my single stupid lightning rod, and looked back at Amiel, who'd fallen barely an inch past the door. She lay face down, with one skinny arm twisted underneath her stomach and the other stretched overhead.

A surge of anger lit up in my chest. She had made it through the door. I'd pushed her through myself. I slammed the door shut in her stead, unsteady on my feet.

I shook my head. We had this wrong. Why were her shoulders contorted? Only a little, not enough to be uncomfortable, but enough that you could see individual sinews across her back. She really was too skinny.

"Amiel," I said. "Get Mars. Get the psychaline."

But Mars was already here, looking at us, an expression of horror on her face, a syringe in her hand.

"Give it to her!" I screamed. "Give it to her!"

"I can't," she whispered. "I gave it to Maxx."

Now Amiel was lying on her back, and my father was attempting chest compressions. Mars threw the syringe aside and knelt at Amiel's head. Maxx lay just behind her on the floor.

West spoke. "Dad, where's your medikit?"

"Doesn't matter. There's no more psychaline. I only had two," Mars said weakly, moving her fingers from Amiel's neck. "Maxx's in bad shape anyway. But Amiel..."

I looked down at her again, as if in a dream. Mars touched my father's shoulder, and he stopped pressing on Amiel's chest. He slumped down.

"Amiel," I said, dumbstruck. "Hey. Amiel."

West put his arms around me, pulling me toward him tightly, but I reached for Amiel, so that I could hold her hand. I realized in pieces that her hand did not hold mine in return.

I stayed that way for a long time, until my muddled mind crystallized into one thought: *This was Adam's work.*

A hot iron burned through my neck and chest, burnishing the steel of my ribs.

I stood up, releasing Amiel. West reached for Mars, whose hand was resting on Maxx's upper arm.

"Dad, we have to stop Adam." I thought of Isaiah and suppressed a chill. Surely we weren't too late. "Gather everyone who will fight. I'll come back as soon as I can, but march on the Remnant without me, if I'm not here in an hour."

"Char. Charlotte. Don't leave. Don't marry the Commander's son."

"What?"

"I'm serious. I have connections on the other Arks. I can get us to an Arkhopper. I've already evacuated half my people. We belong together, as a family."

"Dad, what are you talking about?"

"You. Me. West and Marcela. Even Maxx. We can make it out of here. You know it's not like this on the other Arks. They may have their problems, but they're not all trying to kill each other. We can start over, have a new life."

West and Mars just stared at us, as though we were behind a wall of glass. "I can't do that," I said.

"This isn't your fight, Char."

I made my neck like stone so that I could not look down at Amiel again. But it didn't matter. I couldn't see anything else.

"It is, Dad. It really is."

I jerked away from his outstretched fingers and forced a path through the mess hall and toward Nowhere's stairwell to the rest of the sector, leaving a trail of shredded aluminum foil in my wake. Let the k-band light up. Let it signal every Ark in the sky. I had no secrets left to keep.

I had to get to Central Command. I had to get to Eren. One way or another, this war would end at dawn.

I checked the clock on my way out. 23:00 Universal Time. Six hours to go.

Thirty-One

I hit the stairwell and began to climb. Gravity lessened with every step I took, but I remained barely short of breath.

It didn't stop me from screeching frantically into the k-band. If it really was a transmitter, it was my best shot at locating Eren without being killed or captured by his father. "Is this thing on? An, can you hear me? Please, if you can hear me, patch me through to Central Command."

There was a pause, and I kept going. The stairs pulled forward under my feet, rubbery in the lessening gravity. "Shan? Anyone?"

Finally, I could no longer breathe, and I had to stop climbing. "An," I gasped. "Please."

A soft voice answered. "Welcome back, Ambassador Turner. I have Eren Everest on the line. You may proceed."

"Eren? You there? It's me." There was no response, so I kept talking. "There's a fight going on in the cargo hold, and we're being attacked by lightning. People are dying," my voice broke off, failing me. "I think Isaiah's been captured, and I'm really scared. I need you, Eren. I'm pretty sure I can't fix any of this without you. Maybe I thought I could, but I was wrong." I sniffed. "Marry me, Eren. An's about to kill us all, anyway."

There was silence on the other end for a long time. Too long. I felt myself begin to cry, but silently, like it was my first night in juvy, and I just realized that no one was coming to get me. No one would bring me home.

But the band crackled to life.

"Meet me in the commissary, fast as you can."

"Eren? You'll marry me?"

He laughed, but the sound was distorted by the connection. Surely it would have been a warm, comforting sound, had he been standing in front of me. "I'll marry you, Charlotte Turner, for whatever good it will do us. Of course I will."

I pressed up, toward the big door to the Guardian Level, and ducked into the first room in the hallway, maybe ten feet from the door to the stairwell. It was the commissary, where a young girl had rung the alarm half my lifetime ago. It was also where I'd brought Adam during our raid on Central Command.

Eren was waiting for me.

I rushed toward him, and he grabbed both my hands in his. His grip was light, but there was no softness in his eyes.

Good. I didn't need this to be any more confusing than it already was.

"Here," he said, "take this." He fished around in his pocket for a moment before pulling out a small metal thing.

It was pressed between his fingers, and my mind understood it in pieces: a row of three tiny blue stones. A silver band.

It was a ring.

"Eren," I started.

He met my eyes. "This has to be believable, Charlotte."

The ring slid across my finger without difficulty, as though it were meant for me. I found myself staring at it, a perfect, lovely, delicate thing, barely as thick as the head of a pin.

Eren's eyes followed the ring. I held out my hand, showing him, and his face was masked in an emotion I couldn't place immediately. Not sorrow, or happiness, but something that combined the two, like he was thinking of something he had loved that was gone forever.

"It's not that I didn't want to marry you, Eren. I did. It's just—we're so young, and there are too many things you don't know about me. I thought you deserved..." I looked at him, frowning, unable or unwilling to explain myself. "It's beautiful."

There was a long pause—too long—before he spoke. "My mother's."

"Eren!" I held the k-band away from my mouth, wishing desperately we could be rid of An, and spoke in a near-whisper. "I can't take this. Come on. You know I don't—"

He lay a hand on each of my shoulders, then slid them down until he was cradling my elbows, barely grazing my waist. My skin lit up beneath my sleeves. "Please, Charlotte. For me. It's the last thing I'll ask of you. Just wear it. And let's be done with this."

"Yeah," I swallowed. "Okay."

His gaze shifted from the ring to my eyes. "Thank you."

"So, where should we do this?" I asked, still catching my breath.

"InterArk Comm Con. Let's go."

I nodded, hiding my surprise at his bluntness. "Lead the way."

Thirty-Two

I was escorted to my wedding by enemy guards.

In a way, it was fitting. I had a lifelong habit of attracting police escorts to legal proceedings. Didn't mean I had to like it, though.

Eren turned the corners sharply. He probably no longer noticed the lavish wallpaper on this hallway, or the endless rows of crystal chandeliers. He'd gotten used to it a long time ago. He didn't hold my hand along the way.

I guessed that was fitting, too.

So neither of us wanted to be here, then. There was a subtle change in his demeanor when we reached the door to Comm Con. He didn't touch me, exactly, but he angled his body between me and the door and bent his arm around my elbow. He let a guard punch us into the room.

It was a protective gesture, which made me nervous.

I had no idea why he was acting so distant. It was unlike the forced distance he'd placed between us at the party on Ark Three, easily cast aside the moment we were alone.

The reason for his protectiveness hit me like a volt from a stunner as soon as the door opened. Under a halo of tiny

228

lights, right in the middle of the sunken amphitheater of the communications room, stood the Commander.

He looked about as ecstatic as his son.

I took a moment to collect my wits. This might have been the only move I had, but that didn't mean I had to go in blind.

I scanned the room. The main desk displayed its default screensaver: a flat smattering of pin-like stars. Under the fluorescent circle of ceiling lights, an oversized hologram matched the display on the main desk. Dots of light rotated slowly through the room, with tiny pinpricks darting among the larger dots. They were meant to look like stars, but I had my suspicions about that. Ever since my first visit to this room, I'd thought the large ones looked more like Arks, and the smaller ones had to represent communications flying among them.

This was where he'd first kissed me. Everything felt familiar, but the room was so different in the light.

Or maybe we were different. I couldn't tell.

"Eren, I—"

"Yes?"

He looked at me, an open expression on his face, but I choked on my words. Again, I wasn't going in blind. Marrying Eren was the smart move. The Remnant would be legitimized. The treaty would go into effect. A burst of pressure welled up in my throat, and I pressed it right back down again. Instead of reaching for Eren, I wiped my palms against my hips. I had to get a grip on myself.

This "wedding" would save a hundred thousand lives. Nothing else mattered. Not Eren, not me. Not the strange bubble of hope that enveloped my chest whenever I stood next to him. Not An and not the Commander, who were both planning to kill me, with varying degrees of fervor. Eren stood so straight beside me, making me feel stronger than I was. That didn't matter, either.

This isn't real.

None of it means anything.

We descended into the center of the amphitheater, where a skeleton crew of cameras aimed a few shiny lenses in our direction.

Eren took one look at the cameras and turned to his father. "Should she wear anything else? A dress?"

"Unnecessary." The Commander stood, black robe replaced by his black uniform. The brass medals reflected the lights of the holo. He was impressive.

Eren turned to face me in front of his father. The sight of him threatened my very last molecule of strength. I couldn't think about the cut of his uniform, the blue of his eyes.

So instead, I thought about An, and the ice in her gaze as she announced her decision. She had meant every word.

"Where is Isaiah?" Eren half-whispered, out of hearing of the cameras.

"I have no idea," I lied, holding my k-band against my back. "Does he have to be here?"

"The point is to promote unity, Miss Turner," said the Commander. "Even I am surprised he couldn't see that."

The Commander raised his voice, and it echoed through the room. In response, the cameras activated, transmitting their view to every Ark. Above us, a single point of light sent stars darting to every other point, large and small, creating a luminous spider-web of dewy light.

"We are gathered here so that the citizens of every Ark may stand witness to this, the declaration of ceasefire among the people of the North American Ark. The ceremony of commitment on which we are about to embark shall stand as a testament to the commitment of all our people to peace and cooperation."

At his signal, the lights were lowered, and I stood facing Eren underneath the twinkling canopy.

He took my hands, and my nerves returned in full force. I swallowed. He squeezed, and I saw a flash of concern cross his eyes. He'd only ever tried to protect me, from the moment we met, when I'd believed I would drown in an icy harbor, and he'd guided me past the throng of the walking dead to the safety of the OPT.

But I'd learned a long time ago that safety was a lie that made people soft. That was a lie I could not afford, least of all now, as I prepared to pledge myself to my enemy's son.

I felt sorry for Eren. After everything we'd been through, he still couldn't imagine how broken I was. How broken everything around us had become.

This isn't real.

His hands went limp, having received no encouragement from mine, and he glanced at his father, signaling our readiness.

The Commander wasn't much given to sentimentality, especially in this case, so he cut right to the chase.

"Do you, Eren Everest, take this woman to be your lawfully wedded wife? Do you promise to love her and to keep her, forsaking all others, as long as you both shall live?"

Eren spoke without pause. His voice was firm, and the words came easily. His eyes never left mine. "I do," he said simply.

His father continued without inflection. "And do you, Charlotte Turner, take this man to be your husband? Do you promise to love—" he cut himself off, and looked at his son.

Eren returned the look. There was steel in his eyes.

A deep red flush splashed across the Commander's face, and he locked his gaze on me. My feet burned, and my knees felt weak. My hands squeezed Eren's as though my life depended on it, and the ring twisted in our grip.

The ring. The Commander had seen the ring.

I knew then that I had never truly understood him. But in this gaze, he opened his soul to me, daring me to look, to grasp his true self. In that moment, it held one thing, and one thing only: pure hate.

And then, the moment was over. It passed so completely that I had to wonder if I'd imagined it. But I felt the cold chill of sweat between my shoulder blades, and I knew that the Commander's message was as real as the ring on my finger.

"Ahem," he said, pretending to suppress a cough, "Do you promise to love and keep him, forsaking all others, as long as you both shall live?"

My throat closed up. I felt my eyes widen under Eren's steady gaze. All those people were watching me. Every Ark. I bet my dad was watching, too. Was Isaiah? I had to speak, or all was lost, but I simply couldn't.

Eren's grip on my hands grew tight, and an instant passed before I realized that I was clutching him, fingers aching, betraying my nerves. I didn't know how long I'd been doing that, but his grip held me steady.

I took a deep breath, breaking eye contact at the last second. "I do."

"Then by the power vested in me as High Commander of the North American Ark, I pronounce you man and wife."

Did I have to kiss Eren, in front of the cameras and the Commander? I steeled myself for the possibility, not wanting to screw everything up at the last second, but it wasn't an issue.

The Commander looked to one of the guardians. "Does the Imperial of the Asian Ark recognize the parties as lawfully married?" he asked. The guardian touched a device secured around his ear, then gave a firm nod to the Commander.

The lights flicked on, and the Commander strode immediately out of the room, followed by half a dozen aides and as many guards. I held my breath as I watched him leave.

Was—was that it?

Eren and I were left standing in a near-empty room, still surrounded by the unflinching gaze of the cameras.

"Kiss me, Charlotte."

I leaned in robotically, and his lips met mine for an instant. They were warm and dry and purposeful. I found myself breathing again.

Eren was as eager to leave as his father. "Let's go."

We reached his room in minutes, before I'd fully processed where he was leading me, and he released me from his grip the instant we were through the door.

We stared at each other for half a second, then we both spoke at once.

"Are you okay?" he said.

At the same time, I blurted out, "I have to leave."

He rubbed his face. "Listen, Charlotte. There are things we haven't said."

"It's not the time, Eren. And isn't this room bugged?"

"No," he said, a little too strongly. "I took care of that as soon as I got back. I give you my word that we're completely alone."

I should have been able to relax, if only for a moment, but there was too much between us. I was completely unnerved by the Commander and seconds away from literally shaking.

"I don't expect anything, of course, but we have to be able to pass as married. You have to stay here a little while," he said. The lights flickered, barely enough to be noticed.

"I can't. The—the Remnant is under attack. I need to go."

"Hey, it's okay." He gave me a strange look, his mind far away. I couldn't fathom what was going on in his head. "I'm not going to make you stay. But at least—we should talk."

I nodded mutely.

He crossed the room to the little linoleum kitchen. "Would you like some water?"

I shook my head. "Don't. It's not safe."

"You really think my father would try to drug the water?" When I didn't answer, he gave a defeated sigh and took a seat on the bed. "Fine."

"What did you want to talk about?"

"You. Me. I feel like I owe you an explanation for what happened at the party."

"It's—it's not a big deal, Eren. You wanted to save the Ark, and this was the best way to do it. I understand."

"No, you don't," he said angrily.

His tone was disconcerting, and I felt my own anger rising up. It was familiar, comforting even. "Why are you so upset

234

right now? It's not like I had a choice about any of this!"

"You think you're the only one who doesn't have a say here?"

"You set this whole thing up with Isaiah. You—*of course* you had a say!" I picked up a little gray pillow from the couch and sat down, hard, crushing it onto my lap.

He shifted on the bed. "I did want this, Charlotte. I wanted it so much. I thought we could fix everything, if we could be together. I tried to ask you. On the balcony. I was going to propose, before my father showed up."

We would never be free of him.

The lights flickered again. Eren continued. "I thought if you said yes, then I could tell you the plan for the agreement. And then, no matter what happened, we'd have always had that. A real engagement. Everything else would have worked out."

I crossed my arms and glared at him. His sincerity was infuriating. "And now?"

"And now... I don't know. You're right. It's not the same."

I raised an eyebrow. "No kidding."

"This isn't how I wanted it to go."

"Everything is going to be messed up now. We'll never have a choice."

He lowered his voice. "Not that it matters at this point, Charlotte, but I made my choice a long time ago."

I pressed my lips together, forcing a mountain of silence into the room. It made no sense for us to be tangled up like this. Better to use our heads. People were depending on it.

I had to find my own strength, or I'd never survive this.

When I did speak, several minutes had passed. I was calm. I had thought about what needed to be said and what it would do to Eren. I regretted that, because I understood by then that it would hurt him in some way, but again, I didn't have a choice.

Neither did he. It was a momentary illusion, exactly like the one he'd tried to create when he'd proposed to me. As though we'd ever had a choice about any of this. "Eren. This isn't real."

He didn't respond.

"None of it is real. We were forced to do this, and now it's done. And there are other things we have to deal with *right now*. It's just that the timing's all wrong. Of course I care about you. I care so much that I have to—I have to—" the lights flickered, stronger this time, and I stopped talking.

He waved a hand. "Look, Charlotte. I actually do understand. I think you know that I love you. And I know what I saw. I know what's happened between us in the past. But you're right. We can't deal with this right now."

"The lights, Eren. They mean something. That's what—"

"Yes!" He jumped up from the bed. His feet shuffled back, and he sat down again. I frowned as he continued. "I knew it! I knew you'd seen them." He gave me a crooked grin, and I felt myself slipping a little further down the rabbit hole. *Focus, Char.*

At that moment, the room went dark.

The lights sputtered, then popped on again.

I stared at Eren, but he didn't seem to have noticed.

"Green. Bright green," he said. His words lost their crispness, and his grin became sloppy. "Like yours, Charlotte. Just like—"

"Hang on! Did you see that?"

"See what?" He leaned back against a pillow, eyes unfocused.

"The lights just went out. Where's your gun? I didn't bring one. Wasn't sure if they'd search me." I threw open his wardrobe and tossed a giant pile of rumpled uniforms out onto the bed, then bent to open the wooden drawer at the foot. His pistol wasn't there.

The lights went out again.

Thirty-Three

By the time the lights were back on an instant later, I'd gone through half the drawers in the kitchen. I still couldn't find a knife. Eren was still sitting on the bed like a frog in a pot about to boil. Happy. Peaceful. What was wrong with him?

No knives. No gun. I needed something else.

The door opened, and a hooded figure swept in. My lungs squeezed *in*, and I ducked behind the wardrobe, forcibly suppressing a scream.

"Char, you in here? Don't shoot," said the figure, pulling back his hood.

"Isaiah! What on *earth* are you doing here?" I fought back a deep desire to throw something at him. A fork, maybe, since I was pretty sure at this point that there were no knives in the kitchen.

"I'm here to rescue you."

"*Rescue* me? Ise, I don't need rescuing."

At that moment, Eren slumped from the bed to the ground, unconscious, hitting the floor with all the finesse of a sack of apples. I rushed to his side and cradled his head in my lap.

I looked up at Isaiah, wide-eyed. "Okay. Maybe a little rescuing."

Isaiah nodded and reached behind himself to lock the door. "Is he okay?"

The weight of Eren's head pressed into my lap. It was heavier than I expected, and I felt the overwhelming urge to shield him with my body. Instead, I touched his cheeks with both hands. I had to make him safe. I had to wake him up.

I had to tell him a thousand things.

"This is all wrong," I said to Isaiah. "I keep doing everything backwards."

"Char. Check for a heartbeat, then we need to get out of here. There's only one reason they'd want him knocked out. They're coming for you."

I blinked. "Yeah." He was right. I wrapped my arms around Eren's body, pulling his chest up as much as I could. What green lights was he talking about? I'd thought I was close to figuring something out, but that didn't fit in anywhere. "I mean, he's alive. Breathing. The lights went off a few times."

"That was probably me. I had to disable the surveillance system. May have gotten a few wires crossed. My usual tech guy is trying to kill me. You understand."

"I do, actually. Speaking of which, *how are you here?*"

"Funny story. I was sitting in a Remnant prison, thinking of interesting ways to kill Adam, when your dad showed up with his own little personal army."

"They're more like a strike team."

"Either way, it's on. Everyone's getting ready to fight."

"Nothing good will come of that," I muttered, and froze.

Behind him, the door began to open again. Whoever was on the other side must not have expected the lock, because it stuck for a moment while the keypad reset. Then the lock flicked off.

Someone was using an administrative badge, then.

Weapons, weapons. Someone had swept the room for weapons. I glanced around, frantic. Surely I could find something sharp and pointy.

"Speaking of fighting," Isaiah whispered. "Nothing good can come of this, either."

"Please tell me you brought a gun," I said, ducking behind Eren's desk, which lined the back of his couch.

"I'm really no good with guns, little bird," said Isaiah.

I grabbed a screen stem from the desk and gritted my teeth. As weapons went, I'd done better. "Fair enough. This is the worst honeymoon ever."

"But I brought a stunner."

I rifled through the desk drawer, still in a crouch. "For me? You shouldn't have."

The door swished open, and even though I couldn't see him, I recognized the intruder from the way his bulk blocked out the light from the hall.

Jorin Malkin had entered the room.

Thirty-Four

His mask was off, and his stunner was out. I didn't see a gun, but that didn't mean he wasn't packing.

This was it. I'd married the Commander's son, so he'd sent Jorin to kill me. There would be nothing stopping him now. Our sick cycle would end, and soon.

Around and around and around we go. Where it stops, nobody knows.

At least the Commander and I were done making idle threats at each other. There was something to be said for that.

Isaiah had disappeared behind the bed. I stood up from behind the desk, hunched my shoulders, and held my hands in front of me. "Please, don't hurt me." I raised the pitch of my voice and let it shake.

The stunner cracked to life in response, but I'd expected that. Jorin would almost certainly try to kill me slowly, instead of with a bullet. By the time his face had taken on that stupid, evil grin of anticipation, I was halfway through the distance between us. The lit end of the stunner caught me in the mouth, but not before I'd shoved Eren's screen stem into his side, just above the black strap of his belt.

The room pitched, but the stun was shorter than usual, and I was used to the feeling. Well, to the extent that you can ever get used to the feeling that your body is pulling apart from your soul. When the whiteness in my vision yielded to sight an instant later, I was lying halfway on top of the bed, blinking into the lights.

Jorin hadn't screamed. That was a problem. First of all, it forced me to question whether I'd landed my attack, even though I had definitely felt the pen enter his flesh. Secondly, I had no idea where he was. And third, it was just plain creepy. A reminder that he was a thousand times stronger than I was, and that he'd trained to fight. To kill. I looked around frantically.

My eyes seemed to move a half-second slower than my head, and I blinked. This wasn't the effect of the stunner. I tasted sugar.

I wanted to sleep.

Wait, no. I couldn't sleep. Jorin was trying to kill me.

The bed. Of course. *Of course* the Commander had poisoned the bed.

A dark figure moved near my legs, and I kicked out as hard as I could. The blow caught him in the sternum, but he didn't even slow down. He was like a train, and I was like, well, me. A small-ish teenager with zero combat training who'd been sedated by a mattress.

My other leg swung out instinctively, and I saw the stunner fly out of his hand and onto the carpet. Apparently, even my legs were afraid of dealing with that again.

His hands reached for my neck, and I suppressed the urge to block them, since it wouldn't do any good. Instead, I pressed a fingernail into his eye as hard as I could. He backed up momentarily, and I leaned forward to claw at

242

the spot where I'd stabbed him. The stem was no longer there, so I grated my fingers across the open wound.

That earned me a grunt and a two-second break. I shimmied off the bed onto the floor, then threw myself in the direction of the stunner. I got maybe six inches before his vice-like hands closed around my thigh and yanked me backward. It was enough slack to grab the stunner, though, and I gripped it furiously in two fists before swinging it across Jorin's head like a baseball bat.

His hand went to his head, blocking me easily. I swung again, even harder, but he caught the end of the stunner. I engaged the trigger, and Jorin jumped back at the resulting crack, instantly releasing his grip.

Interesting. He's as afraid of that thing as I am. More, even.

He backed away, and I cracked the stunner again. His eyes widened almost imperceptibly.

"Beetch."

"Just stand right there. Don't move." I pointed the stunner at his face.

Jorin raised his hands, a mockery of surrender, as though to say, *You can't control me*, and began to circle.

I stepped away from him, keeping the stunner raised, then realized he'd blocked the door. I had nowhere to go. I was blocked on two sides by the wall, and the bed was right behind me. Eren slept peacefully at my feet. Isaiah was somewhere behind me, but I didn't want to give him away just yet. Just in case he had a plan of some kind.

Which left... talking.

"So. You drugged the bed."

"A wedding present for the happy couple from the father of the groom."

"It's a shame he couldn't deliver it himself."

I'd have better odds being locked in a cage with a tiger. I needed to get his back to Isaiah, and signal Isaiah to attack. I swayed back and forth, letting the stunner crack a few times. Jorin took a step closer, menacing me. If I stunned him first, I had a shot at surviving. But if he reached me before the stunner connected, it would all be over. I wouldn't get a second shot.

He sashayed to the other side, his sickening smile widening by the moment. I mirrored him, cracking the stunner a few more times for good measure. I didn't know how long we could keep this up. *Stalemate*, as Isaiah would say.

Jorin seemed to have the same thought. He was a calculating man, but impatient to get back to hurting me. He made the first real move: sliding to the side, giving me a clear path to the door.

I knew I'd never make it that far.

I angled my back to the door, and Jorin took the bait, advancing toward me, a teasing expression on his face.

"Now!" I shouted.

Isaiah came flying over the bed and brought his stunner down on Jorin's head with a thick *crack*. He pressed the stunner into the softest part of Jorin's neck, and I cringed as the smack of electricity filled the room.

"Shoot him, Char," said Isaiah. "The world isn't safe while he's in it."

Moving mechanically, I unlatched Jorin's gun from its holster, flicked off the safety, and cocked it, all in one motion.

But something kept me from pulling the trigger. "I—"

The hesitation was all Jorin needed. He lunged at me again, before he'd even stood up completely.

Isaiah stunned him from behind, and the jolt went through

Jorin's body and into mine. I pulled the trigger, over and over, but the gun didn't fire. I blinked. It must have been disabled by the electricity. I never thought I'd miss Earth guns. Reliable, mechanical. Able to shoot through glass and skin alike.

I felt like my teeth were splitting in half and could not stop the desperate cry that escaped my lips. I landed clumsily on my back, my fall partially broken by the edge of the bed. When my head hit the carpet, the blood-covered screen stem bounced into my field of vision. It lay on the linoleum, just under the kitchen table.

Around and around.

We both knew that one of us wouldn't leave the room alive. He'd made that choice before he came through the door.

What Jorin didn't know was that I'd made a decision, too: it wouldn't be me.

He howled in pain, a wild, unpredictable noise, and the force of it seemed to slow Isaiah for just long enough. Jorin's enormous boot caught him in the hip, and Isaiah was tossed into the wall. From there, he never regained his balance. Jorin's other leg flipped around, grabbing Isaiah in the ribs and throwing him to the ground. And then Jorin was on top of him, his fingers closing around his neck. They wrestled, moving too quickly for me to get a good shot off.

Blast.

I grabbed the stunner and braced myself to pull its trigger, but Jorin and Isaiah were locked together. If I stunned Jorin, the blast would hit Isaiah as well. Isaiah was freakishly silent, the pressure on his neck preventing him from making so much as a gasp.

Before I could think about it any further, I reached out

and grabbed the slender, slippery screen stem and used the bed to pull myself back up. Half the duvet came with me. I shoved it aside as though it were on fire and threw myself on top of Jorin. I plunged the screen stem into his neck, then pulled it back as hard as I could.

The entire action had taken less than five seconds, but I knew immediately what I had done.

Jorin reared back, releasing Isaiah's neck. The momentum carried through, and he tottered for a second on his knees before continuing to fall backward. I jumped out of the way just as his body hit the carpet. An awful gargling noise emerged from his throat and mouth.

His eye caught mine, and I stared, horrified, as dark blood covered his tongue and teeth and spilled from the wound in his neck onto the pale threads of the carpet.

Isaiah rolled to the side, gasping, and I jumped over Jorin to kneel next to him.

There was a sickening wheeze as Jorin struggled for air, and I looked from Eren's prone body to Jorin's face, then down at the tiny smear of blood on the side of my hand. I was afraid to watch Jorin, but more afraid not to.

It was all over in a matter of seconds. His head lolled to the side, and he never breathed again.

Isaiah stood beside me. "Shhh. It's okay. You're okay."

That's when I realized I was making a weird, moaning noise. I clamped my mouth shut.

"I—Ise. I killed him."

"Yeah. I'm not going to lose any sleep over that one. Neither should you." There was a strange pause, and a moment passed between us. Isaiah seemed to choose his next words carefully. "What do you want to do about Eren?"

"I—I'm not sure. I wish he were awake."

"I think we should leave him, Char."

I looked at Isaiah. He was probably right, but it felt all kinds of wrong. Eren was safe in Central Command. There was exactly zero chance that the Commander would hurt him physically. He would protect his son at all costs. On that count, I understood him well: so would I.

I could never be his wife. I was too broken for that.

But I could make him safe.

I had no doubt as to what I needed to do next in order to accomplish that. My hand tightened around the stunner.

"Can you get to my dad and stop Adam? We don't have much time."

Isaiah pressed his mouth together and nodded slowly.

"Good," I said. "I'm not coming with you, Ise."

He reached for my hand. "Char. Come on. You fulfilled your end of the deal. Heck, your dad is out there, about to fight my battle for me. It's time for you to come home."

Around and around.

I wanted off this insane merry-go-round.

My hand pulled back from his. "No. It's like you said. This is a war. And I'm putting an end to it. All of it. Right now."

I flicked Jorin's access card out of his pocket and forced Isaiah's hurt, confused face out of my mind. I was through the door and up the stairwell in about three seconds. I did not look back. My heart was pounding so fast that I needed to catch my breath, even though that was maybe the shortest sprint ever.

I'm coming for you, Commander. It's my game now.

Thirty-Five

At the entrance to the Command Level, my k-band began to blip. I paused in the stairwell, wondering what could possibly be so important that the Asian Ark needed to ping me *right then*.

I didn't wonder long.

"Charlotte? Ambassador? This is the Imperial. Can you hear me?" An's sweet, lilting voice filled the metal landing.

"An! Yes, I can hear you. I'm almost there. We just need a little more time."

She spoke as though she didn't hear me. "Ambassador Everest, I desire a word, if you please."

"This is Turner," I said quickly. "Everest is... uh, he's indisposed."

"Turner, then, if you haven't taken his name. Tell me something, Ambassador. I believed that we understood each other. Was I wrong to believe that?"

"No! I mean, of course not! I am doing the best I can. Look, I'm married and everything."

She laughed, and I felt myself freeze at the sound. There was nothing sweet or lilting about it. "That doesn't concern me anymore," she said, her voice like sharp silver. "I can hardly sit by and allow you to destroy another Ark. Our agreement is off."

"What? No, it can't be! We're going to stop Adam! We still have a few hours! You can't do this!"

"Your in-fighting no longer concerns me, either. Your Ark is armed, Ambassador."

"I know! I'm trying to end the battle. It's a little more complicated than we exp—"

"Not the people on the Ark, Charlotte. The Ark itself. My radar shows that a fully-equipped nuclear warhead has loaded into launch position." She paused, letting her meaning sink in. "I'm afraid we have reached an impasse. Our negotiations are over."

I was numb. A nuclear weapon? I braced myself on the cold steel door.

"The Commander," I whispered.

"It is possible," said An.

"An. Your Imperial—*please*, An. Please give me a little time. I'll stop him. Give me an hour."

"I'm afraid that is quite impossible, my dear friend. I am sorry it had to end this way."

"WAIT! An, no! Don't fire! Give me half an hour!"

"I cannot do that, Charlotte."

"Ten minutes! All I need is ten minutes to disarm it. Please, An! I know you don't want to kill us. Why else would you warn me? Ten minutes, I beg you."

There was a long pause while a girl a little older than I decided the fate of a hundred thousand souls from a universe away.

"Five."

Five minutes? Was she serious? I forced myself to maintain a composed tone of voice. Panic was my enemy. "You are seriously overestimating my abilities, An."

"You are underestimating mine."

The ice in her voice shocked me to my senses. An may have wanted peace, but her absolute priority was her people. In delaying her attack even an instant, she was already going against her better judgment.

"Okay, okay. I understand. Five minutes."

"Good luck, Charlotte Everest."

I shook my head again, forcing myself to stay in the game. I couldn't think about that name right now. "Thank you, An."

I swiped Jorin's card against the lock of the Command Level. Nothing happened. I harbored a fleeting moment of panic in spite of myself. What if the Commander had thought to deactivate Jorin's access card? But I shook it off quickly. He'd drugged the bed and sent an armed assassin to kill us in our sleep. At this point, deactivating the card wouldn't be the smart move; it'd be paranoid. I swiped again, willing my hand to move steadily.

The door to the Command Level sucked open before me, and I allowed myself a deep breath and a smile.

The smile was short-lived. Five minutes left to live.

Black carpet lined the gray hallway, leading to a series of identical black doors guarded by rows of complicated lights and buttons. The rooms were labeled with small dark plaques that said things like, "Gravity Management," "Water Distribution" and "O2 Generation."

My first problem would be figuring out which door led to the room that controlled the Ark's illicit weapons system. I couldn't think too far beyond that, or I'd probably panic. Again.

If I were the Commander, where would I put a room that shouldn't even exist?

I rushed down the hallway, reading every sign along the way. It turned at sharp angles, but thankfully, it did not fork. I couldn't get a feel for the layout of this level, but I knew I didn't have time to make the entire loop, what with the impending nuclear strike and all. Maybe twenty yards down the way, one of the plaques grabbed my attention, and I stopped.

The sign read "Negotiations."

Negotiating *what*, exactly? The Treaty was the last word on the relationships among the Arks, and the Tribune had the final say in its interpretation. And it's not like they needed a room. They never met in person, so that their identities could never be compromised.

This room held a secret. I was sure of it.

I removed Jorin's access card from my shirt and ran it over the scanner. A row of buttons lit up above it, and I pressed the green one. The door slid open, a cleaner sound than the doors on the level below.

The room was smaller than I expected. It featured a huge panel of controls on one wall, and a single metal chair. The fluorescent light was dimmer here than in the hallway, and the hum of the panel made me wonder whether it ran on its own generator. It would definitely be harder to detect that way.

Oh, yeah. And the Commander was standing in front of the controls. Pointing a gun at my chest.

"*You* again." He sighed, which struck me as odd. I'd expected more... cockiness. Gloating. Something. Instead, he just sounded tired.

"What is this place?"

"You know what it is. I've just had an unpleasant conversation with the Imperial." He looked at me frankly. "From the look on your face, so have you. It seems you've been one step behind me for some time now. It's impressive, actually."

"Commander, you can't fire on that Ark. Think of all the people who'll die."

The seconds were ticking by. He continued as though I hadn't spoken. "Even more impressive is the fact that you've taken my son along for the ride. I'm afraid things will never be the same between us, thanks to you." He uncurled a thumb from the handle of the gun to rub his forehead, pointing the gun toward the ceiling. I took a step forward, and the barrel instantly regained its former position. "No, no. None of that. Stay where you are."

I lifted my hands. "Don't do this. There will be consequences. The other Arks—"

"Will turn against us. Yes, I know. Do you think I hadn't thought of that?"

"So why are you preparing to fire on Asia?"

"It's complicated."

"I'm a smart girl."

"So I've noticed. That's why I can't let you leave this room. Of course, you've already worked that out for yourself by now."

"You don't have to kill me. You never did."

"Eh, I go back and forth. Keeps me up at night. Believe me, it hasn't been easy. I'll have to think of something to tell my son."

"It's too late for that. He knows the truth about you."

"I suppose you're expecting some kind of medal? What you've done, my dear… What you've done is ruin everything.

Without Eren, there will be no one qualified to lead once the Treaty is abolished and the government is consolidated."

That surprised me. I had always assumed he'd planned on leading himself. It must have shown on my face, because he gave a short laugh.

"No, it couldn't be me. The world needs someone... more idealistic. Younger. I can fight the wars, but Eren can keep them from starting up again. There won't be room for men like me in the new world. But Eren. He was always..." He trailed off, but I knew what he was getting at.

"Yeah."

He nodded. "Anyway. He'll never see reason, now that you've turned him against me. And the wars will never end, unless I finish this. You think the five governments were ever going to remain at peace? The only reason we had an armistice was because a meteor threatened to kill us all. Out here, there is no meteor. It's only a matter of time before the wars start up again."

"That's why the Treaty outlawed weapons. Especially nuclear warheads."

"Ah, yes. The Treaty. Look at where that's gotten us. You think those other Arks aren't armed? I'll tell you something. I didn't fire on Ark Five. That was someone else. And unless we end this, now and forever, it's never going to stop. More carnage. More destruction. Here's another secret, Miss Turner. *Ambassador* Turner. We didn't need a meteor to wipe us out. We were doing just fine on our own."

My head was spinning. If the Commander didn't attack Five, who did? It made no sense. But I had to focus. He was definitely about to attack Three. "Just disarm. Please. You can't possibly think that you'll solve everything by killing innocent—"

"People? My dear, they may be innocent now, but their loyalties will forever be adverse to our own. It could happen now, a year from now, or after the colonies are established on the new planet, but it is only a matter of time before they attack. The only solution is to centralize the government and increase its power. Only then will our loyalties be undivided. Only then do we have a chance at surviving. An understands this. You are a fool to believe otherwise."

"Just disarm for now. Buy us some time."

He ignored my plea. "I'll have to imprison my own son, yet again, because of your meddling. He will never forgive me for what I'm about to do. Now, give me back my wife's ring."

"No."

A flash of muscle across his jaw. "Turn around."

"No."

He sounded more tired than ever. And so old. "It's not going to stop me."

The hammer snapped back, and my breath caught in my throat, but I held his gaze, determined not to shut my eyes. "You're right, you know."

He paused, presumably to hear what he was right about.

"Eren will never forgive you."

"And whose fault is that? Now turn around."

"Seriously, no." My hands clenched into fists at my side. This was it.

"Suit your—"

And then the universe exploded.

The lights went black, and the shot from the gun was echoed by the loudest rumbling I had ever heard. It was like hearing the meteor hit Earth, except more immediate.

It was like a meteor hit *me*. My body was pulled backward in the darkness, and I slammed into the wall behind me.

Dying was nothing like I expected.

Thirty-Six

Every ounce of me pressed hard into the wall I'd hit, and the sensation increased steadily. An eternity passed, but I stayed pinned to the wall, as though the weight of my own body held me there. The Commander seemed to be sucked forward as well, toward me and the wall, but I thought it was a trick my mind was playing on me, sort of like the last of the neurons firing away without regard for making sense. So this was what it felt like when your body stops living.

Except, I was still breathing.

At least, I thought I was. If I concentrated really hard, I could feel my lungs expanding and the muscles in my chest struggling to make room for them, despite the enormous pull toward the back wall.

Okay. I think that means I'm not dead, right? Breathing means not dead.

I had to think, but nothing made sense. I felt no pain, which pointed toward death. But then, I was definitely breathing. And hearing. For example, right then, in addition to the general, Armageddon-type rumbling, I heard someone moaning.

Was I moaning?

Nope, I was just hanging out. Breathing, mostly.

So who was moaning?

Before I could figure out the answer to that, the moaning stopped, and another mystery presented itself.

Where was I?

There was a lit panel ahead of me, but no lights anywhere else in the room. And a humming noise I'd heard recently, kind of like a generator.

I struggled against the fog in my brain. *I am in weapons control. I need to stop the weapons.* But the Commander had stopped *me*. With a gun.

The Commander.

He was the one who had moaned. And though he was silent now, I knew he was still in the room. And the gun would be, too.

The pull lessened, and I peeled myself from the wall, but my feet didn't touch the ground. I shook my head. I was *floating*.

Was I a ghost?

No. I most certainly was *not* a ghost. *You're breathing, remember? Focus, Char. Gun. Commander. Missile. You can do this.*

I looked around in the dim light. The chair knocked against the ceiling, then lazily headed toward the wall with the door. A moment later, there was another sound, a lighter *clank*. It was the gun, which had hit the control panel and was now flying toward the ceiling in slow motion. I could barely see its outline against the pale green light the buttons gave off, but it was enough.

I pushed off the wall and launched myself in the direction of the gun. I misjudged its trajectory, though, and ended up slamming painfully into the ceiling. Now *I* was headed for the control panel. I grabbed its lip and tried to regroup. I had to find the gun.

That's about when my arm started hurting.

And by hurting, I mean a searing, white-hot pain shot through my entire right bicep, as though I'd been lit on fire. I pressed a hand into it, then moved my hand away to inspect. My palm and fingers were dark brown in the green light of the panel.

I was bleeding. A lot. And I no longer had use of my right arm.

On the other hand, I hadn't been shot in the chest or head. Silver lining.

At least, not *yet*. There were still a gun and a homicidal Commander somewhere in the room with me, and I needed to make sure the twain never met.

Another *thunk*, courtesy of the chair, followed by the *clank* of the gun. This time, the sound came from the wall, near the spot where I'd been pinned seconds earlier. But it was too dark to see the gun, so I waited. While I was waiting, I heard a third sound, a soft *thud* against the floor. That'd be the Commander. And I knew he wasn't knocked out, because I'd just heard him moaning. This was trouble.

If he got near enough to grab me, I'd never make it out of here. My only hope was to get to the gun before he did. Another *thud*, and I knew that the Commander was launching himself around the room, too, since he was traveling faster than the other objects. I took a deep breath, as silently as possible, and pulled myself under the panel, so I'd be hidden from the meager light.

I could do this. It was no different than trying to break

into a house in the middle of the night without a flashlight, other than the whole lack-of-gravity thing, and I knew a few tricks for doing that successfully. For example, I knew better than to stare directly at whatever I was trying to see. Instead, I let my eyes sweep back and forth across the room until my peripheral vision registered three moving shadows.

The smallest shadow was the gun, of course, and the largest would be the Commander. He must have also seen the gun, though, because he was pushing gently away from the door panel and toward the far corner of the room, heading for precisely the same spot as the gun, right before my eyes.

Not good.

I shoved away from the controls and kicked off toward the same corner as hard as I could. It was probably overkill. I went hurtling through space at roughly five hundred miles per hour and slammed straight into the corner an instant later. My arms flailed, trying to find something to keep me from flying backward, away from the wall, when I felt something small knock into my back.

The gun.

Hey, at least I had aimed correctly this time.

Now the gun was headed away from me, and the Commander was on his way over. I kicked out, trying to push harder off the wall than I'd otherwise have done.

It worked. I was now about two feet away from the gun, facing away from it, and gaining on it pretty steadily. When the gun clanked into its next mark, I was ready.

With my good arm, I reached behind my back, and when the gun ricocheted into my shoulder blade, its flight ended abruptly. My fingers closed around the handle, and I brought it to bear on the suspended form of the Commander, which was no easy feat, considering I was still floating uncontrollably around the room.

"Game over, Commander."

He sounded as weary as ever. "It certainly is, Miss Turner."

"Hey, that's Mrs. Everest to you. *Dad*."

I heard the door panel slide open, and light from the hallway illuminated the room. Using his arms, the Commander yanked himself through its frame and out of my sight.

And out of my range.

As much as I wanted him dead, I would just as soon not kill Eren's father myself. Ideally, he'd get arrested and go to trial for attempted crimes against humanity, or whatever they called it when you tried to blow up a quarter of the species with forbidden weaponry.

Except that no one would believe me. Around these parts, I was still little more than a fugitive and a traitor, and he was still High Commander. I put the thought out of my mind and tried to think of the next step.

I rubbed the band on my arm. "An? You there?"

"I am."

I took a breath, wincing at the pain. "So, are we all about to die?"

"I am sorry to report that preliminary readouts indicate that your Ark has sustained critical damage. It wasn't a nuclear weapon. More of a warning shot. Secondary life support should boot at any minute."

"Damage? Which sectors?"

She didn't answer.

"I'm in the weapons room. The control panel—" I gasped silently, willing my mind to ignore the pain in my arm, and continued. "The panel looks fairly complicated."

"Do not attempt to fire. You will not survive."

"Fire? An, I'm not going to fire on you. Tell me how to fix this. Let's just have peace. Please."

Another voice came on the line. "Press the following buttons in the sequence given."

"Okay," I said.

"Alpha, comma, direction left. Now type the word 'disarm.' That's Delta, India, Sierra—"

"Yes. Got it."

"Continuing. Alpha, comma, direction left. Now type 'command chute.'"

"Hang on." I pressed each letter carefully, using only my good hand. My forehead felt cold and wet at once. I could not afford to black out. "Okay. Got it."

"Continuing. Type 'evacuate chute.' That's Echo, Victor, Alpha—"

I hesitated before pressing the final command. It was one thing to stand down. It was another thing altogether to jettison our weapons into space. But An had checkmate. The game was over, and at this point, I was only playing for more time. Still, my hand shook as I pressed the button, permanently disarming the Ark.

Now, we were sitting ducks. No wonder humanity had a hard time laying down their weapons. This was terrifying. No wonder there had been no widespread panic, and virtually no protests, when the blatant violations of the Treaty of Phoenix had come to light. The memory of war was too vivid. It made us believe that it was inevitable, that it would always be a part of us, of who we are. It had made us afraid. So instead, when we found that the Arks were armed, we felt only relief. *Not us. We will not be the helpless ones.*

"What have I done?" I murmured to myself.

There was a pause on the line, and An answered. "You've saved your ship. I told you the truth, Charlotte. I am prepared to kill in order to preserve the long-term future of the human race." She lowered her voice, matching my tone, and spoke directly into the comm. "I have often wondered whether I am the only one who understands what's at stake." Another beat, and she resumed her usual volume. "If your ship has half your tenacity, you may yet survive."

"So we're square? No more bombs?"

"I have two final directives, Ambassador. This Commander. He is a problem for us. And your Adam, who deposed the King of the Remnant." The softness was gone from her voice. "You must kill them both."

I felt my face get hot. "You just fired on a hundred thousand people, most of them civilians, and forced me to jettison our warheads into space. I'm not really interested in taking orders from you at the moment."

"They are a threat to—"

"Yeah, yeah. A threat to the peace. Tell me something I don't know." I forced my voice back to neutral, but inside, I was fuming. All along, I'd wanted to work with An to achieve peace. All along, she'd done nothing but manipulate me—and our entire Ark—to further her own ends. As much as I respected her, I could hardly let her use me any further.

I had to face a truth of my own: we were not on the same side, no matter how much we wanted to be.

"I'll deal with them in my own time," I said finally. "You can rest assured about that. But at this point, the only Ark that's ever attacked another Ark is you, An. Justified or not, you're a pretty big part of this."

"I warn you not to test me, Ambassador."

"You just blew a hole in my ship! I'm done taking orders from you."

Infuriatingly, I couldn't hang up on her. The band remained locked around my wrist, *in* my wrist, taunting me. But I wouldn't let it control me.

I shook my head to clear my mind. First things first: I needed to deal with the gaping bullet wound on my arm. The blood coming off it was probably not as much as I'd assumed when I first saw it, but in my defense, getting shot is a bit traumatic. Kinda like losing gravity all of a sudden. It's disorienting.

I tore off a strip of my shirt and, holding one end between my teeth, wrapped it tightly around the hole in my arm, hoping the movies I'd seen hadn't lied to me. I couldn't figure anything else to do at the moment, so I tied it off, wiped my good hand on my pants, and forced myself to figure out my next move.

Eren. I should get to Eren. He was the only person I could think of who might know how to deal with the gaping hole in the ship's hull.

By now, I'd hit the wall across from the panel once again and had scraped my feet and my good arm against it in an attempt to aim myself at the open door. It was far from graceful, but I managed to hook an ankle around the edge of the frame.

I bent my knee sharply, which jolted me into the opposite side of the doorframe. Good enough. From there, I bounced myself into the hallway in the direction I'd come from. When I hit the floor, I squatted and pushed myself *forward* as hard as I could. My back scraped against the ceiling a moment later, but I was definitely making progress. I neared the floor again and repeated the squatting, pushing thing. I must have looked like a deranged frog.

In my defense, I had one good arm, plus a loaded gun to hang onto, and I was moving toward the end of the hallway in spite of the lack of gravity. So I wasn't too hard on myself.

If I hadn't had so much else to worry about, it might have been kind of fun.

Since the Commander had copped to locking him up again, I figured Eren was in the same mini-detention center I'd been in originally, which was on the Guardian Level, one floor down.

The staircase was at the end of the angled hallway, but it took forever to get to it. Once there, the railing made my trip down kind of awesome. I stuffed the gun into my shirt, making sure the safety was on, grabbed the rail with my good hand, and propelled myself straight down the center of the stairwell.

When I opened the door to the Guardian Level, I bit back a laugh. The carpet remained in place, and the chandeliers were still anchored to the ceiling. The people, however, had no such luxury, and most of them were clinging to the chandeliers like timid monkeys. The power appeared to be off on this level as well, with the main source of light coming from indirect fixtures along the wall. It was somewhat comforting to know that the emergency generators were in good working order, even after the second Apocalypse, or whatever it was that just happened.

I pushed myself toward the first chandelier. There was a light tinkling noise as its crystals collided. I shoved it away from me and went flying toward the next chandelier, which held a young man in a dark uniform.

His eyes opened wide, and I shoved him away, too, before he could say whether he recognized me, and continued to the next lavish light fixture. I Tarzaned like that all the way to the short cellblock, then used Jorin's access card to open every cell door, one after the other, until I found Eren.

"Hi," I said, clinging to the doorframe.

He, however, had nothing to cling to, and was floating back and forth through the small white room. "The minute I woke up in jail, I knew you'd come for me."

"Really."

"Yeah. I seemed to recall something about your intrinsic disregard for authority and figured it was only a matter of time before you stormed the gates to get me out of here. At least, that's what I've been telling myself."

I had to smile. "You know me too well."

He laughed, then knocked against the ceiling. "Somehow, I doubt anyone can say that about you."

I raised my eyebrows in mock surprise. "Not even my own husband?"

"I hear it's important to keep a little mystery in any relationship." He smiled, a mischievous look that crinkled the skin around his eyes, and it hit me that I was really glad I'd decided to rescue him, whether or not I wanted to be his wife.

"Grab my leg. Let's get out of here." Retaining my grip on the doorframe, I extended a leg toward him, and he grabbed my ankle just long enough to float toward me. His arms slid past my waist, and he wrapped them around my back, so that we were anchored against each other.

There was a lot to be said for zero gravity.

I tilted my head down to meet his gaze. Without thinking, I brushed his hair back with my fingers, and he moved up toward my face until his mouth found mine. We bumped into the bench inside the cell, and I realized I had let go of the doorframe.

"So much for your handhold," he observed, reaching over to grab the doorframe. We faced each other for a moment, just breathing, until he broke the silence again. "Char. We need to talk."

Before I could respond, a chugging, whirring sound filled the hallway, and the regular lights popped back on. There was a soft click, followed by the long, metallic beep of the intercom system.

"Citizens of the North American Ark. This is Commander Everest speaking. We have sustained damage from an unprovoked attack by a missile we believe to have originated from Ark Three. Please remain calm. Our emergency generators have now kick-started the Ark's power system, which was widely unaffected by the attack. While the blow stopped the Ark from spinning momentarily, the thrusters should re-engage within the next few minutes. Within an hour, we should be back to our regular level of gravity."

There was a long pause, and I pictured the Commander taking a deep breath before continuing.

"Unfortunately, the blast was enough to significantly weaken a major sector of the Ark, which is now beyond repair and causing a loss of oxygen throughout the ship." Another pause. "We have prepared for such an event and will proceed as follows: Citizens, you are to remain in your quarters. Guardians of the Peace have been dispatched to the blasted area and will begin sealing it immediately. You are safest in your rooms, and under no circumstances should you attempt to leave them. Thank you for your cooperation. Everest out."

Eren frowned at me. "We have to do something about my father."

"Wow," I said, deadpan. "Prison has really changed you."

"No, I mean it, Charlotte." Eren looked panicked. "They're sealing off the damaged sector."

"Right, to stop the oxygen from leaving. So that we will not all surely perish."

"Don't you see what that means? The ship is designed to close off the parts that sustain that much damage, so there's enough air for everything else. If he seals off an entire sector, everyone in it will die."

It hit me all at once that I knew exactly where An had aimed her missile. There was only one area she considered to be a serious threat, given everything I knew about her. And there was only one sector the Commander would seal off without a second thought: Seven.

The Remnant.

Thirty-Seven

I thought for a moment, shifting my hold around Eren's waist to grip his shirt instead. Once we were separated by a few inches, it was a lot easier to concentrate. "So, it doesn't just seal automatically?"

"No, it does, but the seal will only work automatically where it hasn't sustained a direct hit," Eren said quickly. "So whatever sector is affected, one side of it will close permanently and automatically, as part of the ship's emergency response system. Then the ship evaluates which levels have to be shut off from the other side, based on the damage report."

"It's gotta be the Remnant," I said.

"That was my first thought, too."

"Can we evacuate a damaged level?"

"If there's enough time. If we wait to seal it off and try to save everyone in the sector, then everyone on board could die. But if we seal off the damaged area, we can save whoever's left."

"So we let some people die in order to save the rest of us." It was like the meteor all over again. I gritted my teeth and tried to keep thinking. "So what if another Ark docked with ours? Couldn't we 'borrow' air from them? If both Arks' O2 generators were on full blast, and only one Ark had a deficit, then surely there would be enough air for everyone. No one would have to die."

"That depends on a few things. First, how long would it take to evacuate everyone from Sector Seven? There's a chance we could deplete the entire Ark before we clear everyone out. Second, once we seal off the part with the hole, there's no guarantee another Ark will come to our rescue, and we'll be too far behind on O2 production by then."

"We can't afford to lose any more people, Eren! We have to stop the dying." I felt dizzy, panicked, like I *had* to make him agree with me right away. I felt weak, too, but I couldn't remember why.

"Char, are you okay?"

"What?"

"You're as pale as a ghost, and the look on your face... You should sit down."

I was not so out of it that I missed the absurdity of that comment. "Sit down? On what? Eren, there's no gravity. We're stuck on a spaceship and there's no gravity and not enough oxygen and people are going to die unless we do. Something. Right. Now," I said.

"Okay, but you have to calm d—What the—what's with your arm?" He lifted my upper arm into the space between us and frowned at my do-it-yourself tourniquet.

"Oh, that. Your father shot me."

There was silence for a moment, then Eren cleared his throat. "With what?"

I bit back my initial response, which involved a good bit of sarcasm and a possible joke about a slingshot, and said simply, "With a gun, Eren."

He took another moment to process that. "I'm sorry. I'm really—Are you okay?"

"Not your fault. And hey. I got the gun. Turns out there are advantages to getting your ship torpedoed. Your father hit the wall and lost control of the weapon during the attack." I reached into my pants and pulled out the pistol.

Eren's eyes widened, and either it was my imagination, or he moved away from me, slightly.

"Look, Eren. The safety's on."

"Yeah. I just can't believe he would—I mean, I believed you, but seeing it is just…"

"I know. It sucks. But it's not over yet. And on the bright side," I said, leaning angrily into my k-band, "I totally stopped the attack on Asia."

"Bright side. Right."

"Here. You keep it." I handed him the gun. "I only have one good arm anyway."

"No, you're gonna need it more than I will. Just put it back. Let's head to IntraArk Comm. From there, we can confirm which part's sending a distress signal, and we can alert the citizens to head for the seal."

I bit my lip. My arm was killing me. "Do you really think we can get the entire Remnant to evacuate into Central Command? They hate the Commander, but they're also afraid of him."

"Instead of dying in the vacuum of space? I'd say we have a fair chance of obtaining their cooperation. And I'm done thinking about the Commander."

I nodded. He had a point.

"Here, grab this belt loop." He guided my good hand to the back of his jumpsuit, and I took hold of the small strip of fabric there. Then he pushed out the door and into the hallway.

The chandeliers were back on, but other than that, things hadn't changed much since my last trip down the corridor. We got a lot of attention, what with him being the Commander's newlywed son, but the look on Eren's face must have stopped anyone from questioning him. He swung from light to light so quickly that I had to remind myself not to loosen my grip. The looks I got were significantly more hostile. After several yards, I flipped over and faced the rug, hoping that would keep people from seeing my face. At least that way, I didn't have to look at their reactions.

Not that I hadn't seen it all before. I was used to being regarded as nothing but a criminal, a menace. That didn't make it any easier, though, so carpet it was.

Once we reached IntraArk Comm Con, I let go of Eren. A fraction of the gravity had returned, and I sort of floated toward the floor. He rushed to the command station and pulled up reports from the past hour. I watched in silence until he found what he was looking for.

He glanced back at me and took in the sick look on my face. "You okay?"

"Yeah. I just *really* hope we get there in time. Where exactly did the missile land?"

He frowned. "Looks like it was near Level Six, Sector Seven, and the seal is still open. Not for long. Everything below that's in trouble." He began fiddling with a set of nearby controls, and a comlink popped out from the panel. "We can bet that the Guardian Level of that sector is already cleared out, which just leaves the cargo level, where the Remnant is. The hangar and the docking level will already be evacuated, since they're in Command, and people were told to go to their quarters. There'll be a temporary patch across the hull, but it won't work for long. They'll want an internal seal to finish blocking off the entire sector."

"Good. Now tell them to go to the seal."

"On it."

"Then I'll go into the Remnant, and you can stay at the seal to stop people from, uh, sealing it." He looked back at me, and I raised my eyebrows. "Eren, there are only two of us. We have to split up."

He sighed again and turned back to the comlink, which was now glowing red. "Citizens of Sector Seven." He paused, rubbed his nose. "Citizens of the Remnant. This is Ambassador Eren Everest. Please proceed to the Level Six hallway as quickly as possible. Do not attempt to carry anything with you. Do not attempt to exit through the dark space between the sectors, also known as the Rift, which is sealed. This is not a drill. I repeat, you are to evacuate immediately to Sector Eight through Level Six. Everest out." He flicked another set of controls, his mouth set in a grim line.

I took a breath. "Good. Let's go."

Thirty-Eight

Not surprisingly, it was fairly difficult to get through the seal-in-progress, even though we were headed into the doomed sector, not out of it. But Eren pulled rank, relieving me of the need to pull my gun, and I slipped through the still-gaping crack without trouble.

"I'm going to organize whatever guardians are willing into search-and-rescue teams to hit each of the Common Quarters on every level," he said.

"Just be sure you get back before the seal gets all permanent-like."

"Right. And Char, I'll meet you *right here*. Come back as soon as you can."

"I will. Be safe, Eren."

He grinned crookedly. "You too."

I sprinted down the hallway, or as close to sprinting as I could manage with a gunshot wound and reduced gravity, until I got to the main hall in the Remnant. To my immeasurable relief, Eren's message appeared to have been effective. People flooded past me left and right, trying to get through the seal. Their feet brushed the floor. Gravity was slowly building back.

I descended as quickly as possible to the outer rim of the ship, where the Remnant had made its home.

When the bulk of the crowd was behind me, I looked around. Where to start? I threw open a door, and then another, checking for people. When I opened the entrance to the greenhouse, my stomach twisted into a knot. There was no one home, and whoever'd been here hadn't taken the time to save the plants before evacuating. That was as it should be. I forced myself to keep moving. I could mourn the potatoes later.

I came flying to a halt at the end of the row of doors. I was wasting precious seconds. This area had already been evacuated.

I needed to find the people who'd been left behind.

I needed to find the prison.

Two left turns later, I was standing in front of the locked detention hall, unable to figure out how to unlock it. A short, thin figure came flying up the hallway ahead of me, and I felt myself freeze against the white door panel just before she recognized me.

"You." Judge Hawthorne narrowed her eyes over a pair of cracked reading glasses.

"Yeah," I said flatly. "What are you doing here? You're supposed to evacuate."

She gave me a withering glare and turned to the panel. "Our passes are disabled."

"Adam?"

"He locked everything down until the missile hit. Now, every door above Clearance Two is still sealed. He wiped every access card in the Remnant." Her mouth was tense, lined with wrinkles, and pulled into a deep frown. Her eyes were watery. "I can't get to them." She held up a metal card. Her other hand made a fist against the door. "It's the third one I've found. They're all worthless. I'm the one who put those people in there, and now I can't get them out."

"Well." I pulled Jorin's card from my pocket. "Let's not panic."

The door sucked open, and the judge gave me a guarded look. "How did you do that?"

We started moving, both of us at a speed more like a hobble than a power sprint. "It's not a Remnant pass," I said. "I got it from—it's from Command. How do we open the cells?"

"I don't know!" she said, already winded.

Remnant jail was exactly as I remembered it, minus the soul-crushing boredom. Helen, my old cellmate, was pacing back and forth behind the locked cell door when I got to her.

"Hey. 'Bout time," Helen called. "Am I right? We're in the damaged sector? Are they going to seal us off?"

"Not if I can help it," I said. "Quick—where's the lock release?"

"End of the block, but you need an access card, and the Warden's gone."

"Not a problem." I fairly flew to the end of the cell, which was easier than you'd expect, due to the minimal gravity. Once I found the lock control panel, I breathed another little prayer that Jorin's access card was important enough to work even here. Surely Adam hadn't thought to change the internal locks within the Remnant during his short reign of terror.

It worked. The controls unlocked, and I threw literally every switch in the box.

"Let me know when you're out!" I shouted, frantically wondering whether I should try a combination of switches to get the right door open.

"We're out!" Helen called back. Four others stepped into the hall around her. "Where to?"

"Follow me," I said, heading back the way I'd come. "We have to get up to Level Six. Let's go, people."

Hawthorne shook her head. "I'm going to sickbay. I have to make sure they get out. You head on without me."

The seal, and safety, were so close. I thought of what my mother would do. I did not hesitate.

I waved Helen and the other prisoners on. "I'll help her. Besides, I need to clear this level out, if no one else has."

The others took off, but Helen looked back and forth from us to them. "One way or another, the two of you will be the death of me," she said finally. "All right, I'm coming, too."

Hawthorne gave us both an appraising glance, but said nothing.

She was right about the sickbay. Although the evacuation was underway, the area wasn't quite clear. People were grabbing at belongings and pulling their children.

"Alert. The oxygen level has fallen to critical level. Regenerative capabilities insufficient for recovery. Generators engaged at full capacity," said a monotonous female voice from the intercom.

"Well, no one panic," I muttered.

The judge took off down the hallway, and we followed as closely we could, swimming upstream against a mad rush of people and belongings. Someone knocked into me with a bulky suitcase, and I stopped long enough to give its owner a death-stare.

276

By this point, gravity was maybe halfway back to normal, partially because we were on one of the lower levels. I was wondering just how far down the corridor the Remnant kept its sickbay when I heard someone screaming for help.

A young man looked up from his position on the floor of the hallway. He was kneeling and struggling to pull a woman behind him on a bedsheet. Her belly was swollen out and her skin was nearly gray. The crowd and the abandoned belongings clogging the hallway greatly impeded his progress.

Helen knelt beside the woman and grabbed a corner of the bedsheet near her feet. "Gravity's only getting worse, and she's going to have to be up higher, or we'll never make it around these boxes."

I grabbed the other corner, and together, we lifted the woman. She lurched forward, and I realized that she'd lost consciousness.

"She has a pulse," her husband said, seeing the look on my face.

I returned his gaze without slowing down. "We won't leave you," I told him, trying to sound steady. The stairwell was twenty yards away, then ten.

We'd barely crowded onto the first platform of stairs when the ship lurched heavily, and gravity failed once again. The man at the other end of the bedsheet wrapped a protective arm around the woman. Nodding at us, he looped his other arm around her lower neck and armpit, like a lifeguard, and began "swimming" up the stairs with her.

Gravity swung us down again, and my stomach found its way to my chest. I gripped the nearest rail, white-knuckled, until it evened out. By the time I'd nearly recovered, I bumped into a solid figure at my feet. Judge

Hawthorne was crouched on the ground, arms tight across her chest, thin glasses slightly askew. "I can't. I can't do this," she said feebly.

Helen appeared at my side. "You don't have a choice, Judge. Get up. Let's go."

"One big jump and we're there," I said.

"No. I can't jump. Gravity could pick back up." Her voice had thinned out, like she was trying not to whine.

Another passenger stepped over Hawthorne. "If we're lucky, it will." She flipped herself over the banister and jump-floated up through the center of the stairwell. "Last one there's a rotten peach," she called back to us.

"You go on without me," Hawthorne said. "I did what I came to do."

I stared at her, trying to decide whether to force her or leave her. I took perhaps a second too long. Another inmate jumped, and Hawthorne stifled a scream.

"It's the Lightness," I muttered.

"Oh, brilliant diagnosis," said Helen. Her expression mirrored my own. I had the impression that neither of us was particularly fired up about staying behind to die with the judge who'd locked us up. "And so helpful. You get her other arm."

"No! Stop it. Just go," said Hawthorne, curling herself tighter.

Helen knelt next to Hawthorne and took hold of Hawthorne's wrist. She moved slowly, with surprising gentleness, in spite of the iron in her voice. "How about this. You put your arms around my neck. Just like that. You can keep your eyes closed." Helen put her foot over the rail and set her mouth in a line. "Ugh. Here goes."

She jumped, grabbing at the rail at Level Six. She was

hardly frail enough to miss on her own, but the weight of the judge must have made her miscalculate, and they swung up too far. The ship jerked again, disorienting me, but gravity remained near zero, as far as I could tell.

I jumped, slamming into the rail in mid-air, and scrambled over onto the platform. I'd misjudged the gravity. It was definitely stronger than I realized, or else it had begun to regenerate. I hooked my feet into the bars of the rail and leaned way over, grabbing frantically at Helen's shoulder and Hawthorne's drapey robes.

They tipped over the rail and landed in an unsteady heap. Hawthorne stood, regaining her balance, and spared a moment to straighten her clothes, a prim expression on her face.

"That wasn't so bad," she said. Then, clearing her throat, she looked at Helen. "Thank you."

They looked at me expectantly. "Uh, this way to the seal, everyone," I said.

Gravity built steadily as we made our way down the hall. We rounded a corner to find the man and the pregnant woman. As gravity returned, so did his struggle to move his wife. Helen and I ducked wordlessly as we reached them, grabbing the same corners of the sheet as before, and everyone kept moving.

We weren't nearly as fast as those around us, some of whom rushed by with heavy-looking boxes, but in time, we reached the seal.

"Oh, no," Helen breathed when she saw it. She set her end of the bedsheet on the ground and elbowed her way to the front of the small crowd that had gathered. I heard her curse from several feet back, and I couldn't blame her for it.

The seal was nearly shut.

Thirty-Nine

"Okay. Everyone stand back." I was surprised at how strong my voice sounded. A couple of people actually shuffled backward a couple inches. I pushed my way to the front of the crowd. "No, seriously. Stand *back*," I said.

"I recognize her," said a voice in the crowd. "She's that traitor. The one who took the judge hostage."

Several people started talking at once. "Should we arrest her?"

"I just saw her carrying a woman. Doesn't seem like a terrorist to me."

I rolled my eyes. "Oh, for Pete's sake, people. We can talk about this later. Stand back, or else." I pulled the gun from my pants.

They stood back.

"No need to get violent, there."

"There's enough of us here to take the gun from her," said a man I'd seen carrying a suitcase. "We're all goners anyway."

Before the crowd could decide whether I was a worthy target of their limited time and misplaced heroism, I turned my back to them and fired several rounds at the edge of the seal.

Nothing happened.

"Guns don't affect the ship," I said through clenched teeth to no one in particular. The sharp glow of the soldering torch on the other side of the seal blocked my view through the remaining hole.

So I shot the torch.

The soldering stopped. The seal was still cracked a few inches, and there was a hissing sound as oxygen sucked out of the healthy part of the ship and into Sector Eight. I put the gun under my bad arm and slid my good hand into the crack. I pulled as hard as I could, but the seal didn't budge. Some of the now-exposed wiring popped loudly, and I jumped back.

The faces of the people behind me were as angry as ever, but by now, their rage was directed toward the seal. I stepped aside, and a few of the stronger-looking crowd members shouldered their way to the front.

"Okay, *pull*, everyone. We can do this."

"On three," said one, and the others nodded. "One, two, three, *urgh*—"

Whoever was on the other side had resumed soldering.

"Fire again," someone said, and I was happy to oblige, aiming only at the equipment on the other side of the widening hole.

There was another round of pulling, and the seal slid to the side, revealing two soldiers with soldering torches and the Commander, who stood to one side.

"Charlotte Turner. You are an exceptionally stubborn young lady."

I leaped across the border and glared at him. I wasn't going anywhere until I knew everyone was safe, so I pressed myself into the side of the hallway as the crowd rushed past.

"Again, that's Mrs. Everest to you."

He paled slightly, and I saw him step aside, almost without thinking, as the pregnant woman's husband lowered her gently through the gap. But his scowl returned almost instantly once they had passed.

"People are going to die because of this," he growled at me, then turned to the soldiers. "Get out your stunners. Replace the seal immediately."

The guards moved to block the path out of Sector Seven.

"No!" I shouted. "Let them through!" I looked down at my gun, which I'd kept pointed at the floor, and raised it toward the nearest soldier. I felt stuck in a bad dream, unable to stop myself from doing what I dreaded most.

I aimed the gun squarely at the Commander's face. "Stand back," I shouted at the soldiers. "Let everyone pass, or he dies." I flicked my thumb past the hammer, allowing it to cock more loudly than necessary, and the soldiers took several steps away.

The crowd seemed to move in slow motion. I knew they were rushing, but every second the seal remained open raised our chances of dying to dizzying heights.

"Three hundred thousand," whispered the Commander. "That's how many human beings will be alive tomorrow, because of you. We have to seal the gap."

"I can't watch anyone else die. I'm sick of it."

"After tonight, you won't have to," he said, and a chill ran straight through my body.

I was so tired. I ran an arm over my brow, wiping my face on my sleeve. It was a stupid move.

It was all the Commander needed.

A second later, he slammed into me, knocking my wrist into the wall. The rest of my body followed, but not before he'd delivered a crippling blow to my stomach. The gun clattered to the ground, and I crumpled to my knees.

I couldn't move, but I knew without looking that the Commander had regained possession of the gun and was aiming it squarely at my head.

"Close the seal. Now."

This time, the soldiers leapt to comply. There were hysterical screams of protest from the other side, and I realized that people must still be arriving.

"You're making a mistake," I wheezed. I had to pull myself up, but it hurt to breathe. Gravity was increasing steadily, and the air was getting much thinner. I pressed a palm into the wall, then stood.

But the Commander was no longer looking at me. An emaciated arm shoved into his shoulder, moving him out of the way, and Judge Hawthorne slid into the middle of the seal. Turning her back on the Commander, she reached over to help the next person through the opening. She turned back only once the husband began pulling his wife out of the way of the next person.

They couldn't have guessed what the Commander was capable of.

As soon as Hawthorne was through the seal, the Commander fired a shot directly into the next person's chest.

Helen.

Behind us, Hawthorne's shriek reverberated through the dying sector and across the seal.

Helen slumped forward through the gap, and I realized that the judge was still trying to move her to safety.

"No! Judge Hawthorne! Stay back!"

The second shot was somehow worse than the first.

The judge slid to the ground in a heap, followed by Helen's lifeless body.

I gasped.

But the Commander's face showed nothing. "The seal. *Now*."

Again, the soldiers moved forward, soldering guns in hand. They were obliged to move the bodies out of their way, and I heard myself whimper. "Please. Please no."

The Commander pressed the gun into my forehead, and my mouth went dry. I knew he wouldn't waste another opportunity to kill me. He cocked the hammer, and I looked at his face. It was pure malice.

He pulled the trigger.

Nothing happened.

Well, nothing other than an impotent little *click*.

He pulled the trigger a few more times before swinging the gun at my head. I ducked, and he shoved me back into the wall. "The ring. Give me back the ring."

I grunted, finding it hard to breathe, and pulled the ring off my finger. No sooner had he snatched it away than his leathery hands found my throat, pressing me back into the wall with a thumb to my trachea. I played the only card I had left.

"He's out there! Eren's in the Remnant."

"You're lying. My son is in a safe place."

"You mean lockup? Not anymore, he's not."

The Commander looked back toward the seal. It was partly open and closing steadily. The only faces in the remaining crowd were strangers. The seal inched closer to the wall as the world faded to black. It was two feet away from the wall, then one. It was six inches away. I closed my eyes.

Then I heard the sweetest possible sound.

"Charlotte!" Eren shouted. "Charlotte, where are you?"

My eyes flew open, but I couldn't speak.

"Eren?" The Commander looked up. "Open the seal! Open it further!"

I hit the floor, but it was another moment before I could breathe.

"Come through, son."

"I can't. Not until everyone else gets through." Eren shoved the nearest person through the crack, then the next. A young girl flitted past, and I smiled dumbly, thinking of Amiel.

The Commander shouted over the heads of those escaping. "Can't do what, exactly? Survive? Lead your people? Which is it?"

I was gasping, sucking in air as hard as I could. Thanks to the broken seal, that was actually pretty hard to do. Oxygen was officially at a premium, and there were at least five more people still stuck in Sector Seven, Eren among them.

My view shifted abruptly, and I realized that the Commander was lifting me. He had one arm was around my chest, holding me up, and the other gripped me under the jaw.

When the Commander spoke again, his voice was tender, surprising me. "Please, son. Come through."

Eren took in my position, seeing his father's forearm pressing into my chin, and his face sank into utter disbelief. "Dad. What are you—?"

At his hesitation, the Commander changed tactics once again, bracing his grip with a forearm to the back of my neck. "I am done with these games, son. Come through the seal, or she dies."

That was checkmate. I could see it on Eren's face.

Reluctantly, he stepped through the seal. "Now let her go."

The Commander released me, and Eren turned back to the seal to help another person through the crack.

I saw the Commander's stunner move, but Eren never did. There was a loud crack, and Eren fell to one side. Two more people pushed their way through, leaving one, a smallish woman who had to be close to forty. The Commander lurched forward to push the seal into place, and she moved back, afraid of him.

Behind him, I climbed to my feet, and did the only thing I could: I shoved myself into the Commander's back. He fell forward into the gap, and his face hit the exposed wiring of the panel, where I'd blasted it apart.

There was a horrible, rapid thudding noise, and the Commander let out a sickening shriek. Frantic, I reached over him to help the last person through the seal. I was careful not to touch the Commander before I realized why.

"He's being electrocuted," I said numbly.

"What?" Eren looked up from the ground, where he was just regaining consciousness, and his jaw went slack. "Quick! Grab the other shoe. Don't touch his skin."

We each grabbed a combat boot and yanked the Commander back out of the seal, which slid into place. When his face hit the floor, it bounced up a little, as though his neck were made of rubber.

"Solder!" Eren shouted at the shell-shocked soldiers. "Now!"

We turned toward the Commander, who was face down and not moving.

"Oh," I said softly. "Eren."

Eren crouched, as though afraid to touch his father, then grabbed a limp shoulder and pulled the Commander onto his back.

I screamed. It would have been a lot louder, too, if I'd had any oxygen left.

His face was totally disfigured. The wires had burned deeply into his skin, leaving a grotesque map of tiny trails and burned blood.

"Dad? DAD!" Eren made an odd sound. "He's not breathing." He looked at me, stricken. "Help me."

I reached for the Commander's neck and tried to find a pulse. I shook my head, unsure of what to say.

"I don't... I can't..." Eren looked from me to his father in disbelief. "Dad," he said again, reaching for his father's hand. It went limp, relaxing the fist it held tightly only moments earlier.

His mother's ring dropped to the floor between us.

"Eren. I'm so..." The words sounded hollow, so I closed my lips. Eren stared at the ring, as though he didn't recognize it, or want to. Then he picked it up and shoved it deep into his pocket.

Then he held his father's hand again.

I couldn't think of what to do next. I couldn't think of anything, actually, so we just sat there, not touching, waiting for the air to come back.

Forty

I don't know how long we waited.

I barely felt afraid. I barely felt anything at all, except the pain in my arm and the exhaustion deep in my bones.

The comm crackled to life once again, but this time, the signal was so clear, I had to wonder if it was coming from a speaker at all. "CITIZENS OF THE NORTH AMERICAN ARK. This is your Captain speaking."

Eren looked up from his father's body. "Who is that?" he asked me. I shook my head, bewildered.

The voice continued. It was deep and strong. "The Ark has sustained critical damage, and we've lost all defensive nuclear support. And yet, all hope is not lost. I have assumed command of operations until such time as we arrive on Eirenea. I have obtained the assurance of the Asian Ark that they will forbear to fire on us again. Furthermore, I have installed a new life-support program on the Ark's mainframe. It will take effect shortly."

I swallowed, suppressing a rising feeling of panic. "There's only one person who could have accomplished all of that."

"*Adam*?" Eren's mouth hung slightly open in disbelief. "I thought you said he was a kid? He couldn't have."

"He could change his voice on the intercom. It would be nothing to him."

"We have to stop him!" Eren took my hand. "Get up! We have to find him." He turned back to the soldiers.

"To the citizens of the Remnant: there is no Remnant. Not anymore. You will be assimilated into the main levels of Central Command in accordance with your forgoing allegiance thereto.

"To the current subleadership of Central Command: there is no reason to fear for your life. Your cooperation will ensure your continued placement on board the Ark.

"To everyone else: the new system will take a moment to reboot. You should feel its effects shortly."

"Charlotte. We have to stop him."

"He's not the kind of guy you just waltz in and ask for his badge back."

"We have to try. He's got to be sending that signal from IntraArk Comm Con," Eren said. "Come on. We'll catch him"

If I'd had the strength to think, I'd have known we were making a mistake. But I didn't, so I followed Eren down the corridor, struggling with every step.

It was hard to run upright, and I didn't even know where we were going. I kept stumbling, and the hallway pitched off-center. We scrambled toward the stairs, and I made most of the climb up to the Command Level with my eyes closed. Whenever I opened them, the world seemed to pulse along with my heartbeat.

I wasn't going to make it much longer.

At some point, Eren jerked my good arm, and I opened my eyes.

"We're here. Guardian Level. Comm Con's just a few

doors away," he said, pulling me through the door and turning quickly to the right.

The lavish rug of the hallway was strewn with crystals that had broken off the chandeliers during the level's field trip through zero gravity land. Eren guided me around a full chandelier, which had popped off the ceiling and was now decorating the floor of the hallway, and I realized that I'd closed my eyes again.

I needed to wake up. Not that the terror was exactly sleep-inducing.

"Almost there, Charlotte. Stay with me."

Eren's voice was coming from somewhere to my right. I forced my eyes open in time for him to lead me through a familiar door and saw stars. The white lights of the holo danced before me.

This was the room where Eren first kissed me. This was the room where we'd gotten married.

Well, fake married.

Really, Char? That's what we're going to think about right now? I shoved the memory to the back of my mind and attempted to stand under my own power.

The room was empty.

There was no Adam. There weren't even any guardians.

"He knows where we are," I whispered. "Kuang bands."

"I have a weird feeling about this," said Eren.

Something tingled in my brain, but everything was fuzzy, all the way out to my skin, and I pushed it aside. "Let's just lie down for a minute."

"No, Charlotte. Get up," he said, pulling me into his arms. "We should get out of here. Maybe find Isaiah. Or your father."

"Dad? I don't know. Something doesn't fit. I can't—"

"Come on," he said, punching the doorpad.

Nothing happened.

Eren tried again, and again, but the door didn't move.

"Here," I said, pulling Jorin's card out. I dropped it, and it fell to the ground in front of us. "Use that one."

It was no use. The door wouldn't budge.

"It's a trap," I said. "We're trapped."

"Very good, Char," said a voice. "You certainly are."

"Adam? Is that you?"

"Maybe you should have listened to me. Maybe you should have paid a little more attention. Bet you'll listen now. When I let you out of here, everything will be different. The Remnant will assimilate with Central Command, and you're going to help them. You will recognize no leader but me."

"Adam!" I stumbled, hit a chair. "Wh—*why*? Why have you done all of this? Isaiah was good to you. You were loyal to the Remnant."

There was a pause. "You really don't get it, do you? It was only a matter of time before he kicked me out. I had too many weapons. I got too strong. I could see it coming already. They always want their soldiers smart, but not too smart. If I learned one thing at the Academy, that's it. The Remnant is no different."

"You were in the Academy?" I asked, hoping to stall him long enough for Eren to get us out of there. But in the back of my mind, I knew that wasn't happening. Adam had been two steps ahead all along. He wasn't likely to fall back now.

"Too smart means bad soldiers. And I was a very bad soldier," he said.

"What are you doing?" I whispered. "What's the plan, Adam?"

291

"I'm taking over the world." I heard a smile in his tone. "That's my line, right?"

"He's insane," said Eren.

I couldn't manage a response just yet. My arm hurt so much that I sat down heavily on top of the nearest desk.

"That's a matter of opinion, sir. But don't worry, Char. I'll take good care of you. As long as you cooperate, you'll be safe."

"Safe?" I wondered what he meant by that. "I've been thinking, Adam. There's no way you outpaced Asia's technology single-handedly. So tell me. How long have you been allied with the Imperial?"

There was a long pause, then a snort of laughter. "I guess you got me there! Oh, An and I. We go way back."

"She's not a good ally. She'll betray you, too."

"I like to think we respect each other. I can handle her, Char. Just like I can handle you." There was a hissing sound, and I felt myself begin to suffocate. "Don't worry," he said gently. "I'm just going to knock you out a little. Shouldn't be too permanent. I hope."

"Adam!" I gasped. "Your sister is dead. Did you know that? Guess how she died, Adam. Take a guess." Amiel's face flashed before mine, her brown eyes huge, thin shoulders weighted with sorrow.

The oxygen returned.

"Speak."

"A bolt of lightning," I coughed. "You killed her, Adam. She's dead because of you."

"You're lying."

"Am I? Something tells me you've figured out how to hack my k-band by now. Is it green, or what?"

There was a long silence, then the oxygen began to drain

from the room in earnest. "You're going to regret that, Char. You really, really will. So remember this when you wake up: there will be consequences for your insurrection. Fall in line, and remember what I'm capable of. *Remember who controls the air*."

There was a sharp *click*, and the transmission ended. I held my band close to my lips. If they were anything like Eren's, they'd been blue for several minutes. "An, are you there?" I muttered feebly, but there was no answer. "How could you. How could you."

Eren was staring at the holo. "The hoppers are leaving the Ark. Look at that."

I wondered if my family were on them. Eren continued. "And something else, too."

"Another Ark?"

"No, it's much bigger. A planetoid, maybe. Doesn't matter. The war is over. We lost."

The room slammed sideways, and I realized that I'd fallen out of the chair. I wondered whether the tingling in my cheeks was because of the rough carpet pressed into my head. Eren's face came into view, and I watched as he settled himself next to me on the ground. Our faces were inches apart, and his fingers found mine.

"Charlotte," he whispered. He smiled, a real smile. "I wish I could have saved you." His grip tightened on my hand, and I felt my heart break as he struggled to speak through blue-tinged lips. His smile was, somehow, unaffected.

"I wish I could have been your wife."

He laughed, gasping. "You are."

"It wasn't real. I'm sorry about that."

"It was, Charlotte. The lights were green. On the kuang bands."

I looked at him. "Both of them? Both our bands?"

He nodded with visible effort. "Whatever it was, we meant it."

I laughed, a gasping, raspy sound. "I think that means we're married."

"I think you're right, Mrs. Everest."

I had reached my last breath, and it was a struggle. I tried hard not to think about dying. "What makes you think I'm not going to keep my name?" I said.

Then I couldn't see anymore, and I lost all sense of feeling, except for the weight of his hand.

And then there was nothing.

Forty-One

Dark dreams hunted me.

Meghan. Helen. Judge Hawthorne, whose face was too close, and whose glasses were cracked. Amiel. My mother.

My mother.

Nameless soldiers and a pale pregnant woman. Each haunted my sleep in their turn. The greediest among them took more than their fair share of my sanity, pulling apart the delicate threads of my consciousness until I had no choice but to scream, even as my mouth refused to obey.

In those moments, only my mind could react, and its screaming was all I had.

There was no peace, although the strongest dreams I suffered were not nightmares. Not exactly.

A flash of red hair.

A warm, familiar hand against my own, and the low tones of Isaiah's softest whispers, mouthing reassurances I couldn't hear. It was just as well, on that account.

I would not be reassured.

Something cold touched my face, and a muted sound made its way into my consciousness. Now Eren's hand was heavy against mine, and I told my hand to squeeze it. My hand obeyed.

The deep, melodic noise continued, encouraged. It was a familiar sound, one I was glad to hear. But it was not Eren, and I couldn't place it.

I strained my ears. In response, it increased in intensity.

"Doctor! She's waking up. Alert the Commander."

No, not the Commander.

Another voice came onto the scene. "Mrs. Everest, can you hear me?"

I could. I just didn't know how to tell her so. I moved my mouth. *Not the Commander.*

I opened my eyes, and a face came into view.

"That's good! It's about time, isn't it?"

I frowned at her. She was entirely too bright, just like the rest of the room.

I was lying on a white sheet, several feet off the ground. Around me, everything was white: white beds, white uniforms, white walls. The room went on and on, punctuated every few feet by a bright overhead light.

"Where am I?"

The nurse smiled. White teeth. "You're on the sickbay."

"The Remnant?"

She made a face, then disappeared.

A moment later, Eren hovered over me.

I breathed him in, relieved. "What's going on?" my voice was hoarse, dry. But it worked. I could speak. It was enough, for now. "Where is everyone? How long have I been asleep?"

"Charlotte." His face was drawn, his eyes rimmed with red. He hadn't been crying, but he definitely hadn't been sleeping, either.

"You look awful," I croaked.

He laughed, a real laugh, and I tried to smile. Nothing happened.

"Three weeks. That's how long you've been out."

"My family. Where is—?"

Eren made a noise like a grunt, like someone had bumped into him unexpectedly, throwing him off-balance. "We can't find them. No one knows. Adam found out about your father's Arkhopper. He destroyed it. He destroyed all the hoppers except his."

"West," I said voicelessly.

He wet his lips. "Adam was ruthless about the refugees. He wanted cooperation. I'm pretty sure I'd know if he'd found them."

I considered that. My father was far from helpless. If he didn't want to be found, Adam was out of luck. "What else has he done? Tell me everything."

"Just *shh*. I will. He held an election. I think he must be working with An somehow. He promised absolute stability. He won by a low margin and forced the Remnant to assimilate."

"How's that going?"

Eren shook his head, and I thought I saw a hint of a smile cross his face. But his features were shaded by some other emotion. Something worse than exhaustion. "Not so great."

"Good," I coughed.

"He's... he's put me in charge of things. Sort of like a lieutenant. I think he's expecting me to give him some extra legitimacy."

"*You said yes?*"

"It's the reason you're alive, Charlotte." He looked like he wanted to say more, but he stopped there.

I considered that. "Not worth it."

"He monitors everything. He's listening to us right now."

"The k-bands? Surely we can—"

"On me. Not you. Charlotte. There's something else. This will be hard to hear."

I nodded, telling him to continue, but he took a long time before speaking again. His eyes were so blue, untinged by his lack of sleep.

"The doctors weren't able to save your arm," he said at last. His tone cut short, as though he were going to tell me something else, but changed his mind.

I stared at him. My arm? I fought the urge to look down at it. Not able to save my arm?

"Charlotte, I'm so sorry."

So many people had lost so much more than an arm.

Surely, I could at least look at it. I turned my eyes downward, but stopped at the last second. Inside, my head was screaming, *screaming* that I couldn't have heard him. *My arm?*

Somewhere, an alarm went off.

"It's okay! It's okay," Eren was saying, but strong hands pulled him away.

"Heart rate's up. Blood pressure too elevated." A nurse pressed a needle into my IV, and I began to plead with her.

"No, no, not that. I don't want to go back to sleep."

Eren was shouting from across the room. "It's okay, Charlotte! I'll be back here as soon as I can. You're not alone!"

I awoke again to an empty room.

No, not empty. My younger brother had come to see me. I'd long suspected he was afraid of me, but that wasn't it, exactly, the thing that had grown thick and gnarled between us.

I didn't know how he'd gotten there, and I wasn't able to ask. But it didn't matter. I looked at him, and my heart was so full that I could only press blue-tipped fingers into the rail of the bed. Eren was wrong, of course. My family hadn't gone.

West had come to see me.

The years lay heavy between us, but West was young and clean and so tall he'd nearly had to duck to enter the room. He had the same short haircut he'd sported since he was eight, but his once-wide eyes were strained with cynicism. In the time since I had seen him, he'd gained a lifetime's understanding of the things I'd done, the things we'd both been a part of.

Still, he wasn't angry.

He simply watched as I spoke at him. "West, they took my arm. The Commander took my arm away. But there's always a silver lining. No k-band. See?"

No response.

"I know you can't talk. I know the room is bugged."

He looked at me in careful silence.

"West, are you real?" I whispered finally.

But instead of answering, he glanced over his shoulder and fled from the sickbay, and I was alone again.

I awoke again in the half-light of the twilight program. Or the dawn.

A dark, familiar figure hovered barely out of sight. I craned my head and saw Isaiah. One hand held a syringe, which he slipped out of the IV tube. The other hand lifted a finger to his lips. "Shh. We don't have much time."

"What is that?" I squinted at the syringe.

"Wake you up a little. You'll be asleep again soon. Sorry, little bird. Couldn't do it any other way."

"Fair enough."

Isaiah leaned in close, then looked back toward the door. Black hair. No gray. "You made it."

"Well. Most of me."

He slid into a chair and pulled it so close it was touching the cot. "They're gonna have to try a little harder than that." He tapped the bed rail, the blanket. My arm. Long fingers slid down to the silver cuff around my wrist. It was like seeing a friend in a crowd, then realizing you've got the wrong person. Isaiah never fidgeted.

"So," I said. "You've come to tell me something."

"I have," he said, and there was a long silence. He pursed his lips, took a breath. Laced his perfect hands together, then separated them.

"And I'm not going to like it," I said.

"No."

"I'm a big girl, Ise."

He smiled.

"I know about the Remnant," I said quietly. "I'm sorry."

He looked down. "It was all for nothing. Everything I did. Everything *we* did."

"You can't think like that. Adam and An didn't kill them all. They're assimilating."

"The ones who keep quiet. The ones who behave. He's taken everything."

"No!" I tried to sit up, but my back hit the bed a second later. "Now they're everywhere. They're legitimate. They won't forget what's possible. This is bigger than you, Ise. It always was. We won't give up."

"Not me, little bird."

I blinked. "What are you saying?"

"I'm out. I need a break."

"That—what? You can't."

"You're not hearing me. *He took everything*. What more can I do?"

"This isn't you! Look. Fine. You take a break. We lost, and it hurts. I get that. But we're not done yet, surely. We can still find a way to—"

"That's not what I came to tell you," he cut me off, and his dark frown deepened. His hand found mine. I squeezed back, and he enclosed both his hands around it, pulling it toward his lips. "I kept my end of the agreement, Char," he said, sounding suddenly out of breath. "And I'm sorry."

"What do you mean?"

"I mean, I made your family safe."

I stared at him. "That wasn't the agreement."

"Citizenship. I know. But Marcela is a target. She went to the Academy. Adam knows she knows too much. And she and West—"

"Are *children*."

Isaiah raised an eyebrow. "Now that doesn't sound like you, Char. You know better."

"Isaiah. What have you done?"

He set his jaw. "I evacuated them. West, Mars, your father. That new kid. I got them out. That's what I owed you. Your family, right?"

"My family is gone? *You took my family?*"

"I made them *safe*. I didn't have a choice. You and I—I don't know, Char. But I know what they mean to you. And I know that I owed you that. So I saved them." I looked from Isaiah to my severed arm. I flinched, and he gripped my hand more tightly, lowering his voice. "But I'm not giving up on everything. Come with me."

"I'm being watched. We wouldn't make it past the door. Adam probably already knows you're here."

"Oh, we'll make it out." He took a deep breath. "I set a bomb."

"A—*Isaiah*. No. No." My hand moved in his, and he released me. I pulled away, but the motion was stopped short by the cuff. Isaiah sat back in his chair. A *bomb*?

"Not where people are. But a big one, Char. Big enough that they won't exactly be scrambling to secure a crippled prisoner. One last trick, and I'm out."

I breathed. In and out, in and out. If Adam were listening, if he were planning to grab Isaiah, or to try to shut me up, he hadn't made up his mind yet. Maybe, for once, I could beat him to it.

In and out.

I'd lost an arm.

I'd lost my mother.

But *why?* For what?

I turned back to Isaiah. "I'm not going."

He let out a breath, frustrated. "I can't tell you where we'll be. If you know, then he can find us. It will be years before we reach Eirenea. Who knows what will happen by then. We may never make it."

"I know."

He wrapped a hand around the rail of the cot. "Charlotte, we may never see each other again."

"I *know*," I said quietly.

"Look at me."

I took in all of his face at once, like drinking too much

water too quickly, so that I had to stop for air. The smooth-
ness of his mouth, the dark glasses. The set of his head on
his neck. Strong, or just stubborn. Earnest.

Somehow, he saw me too. "This really is goodbye," he
said at last.

"I'm sorry, Ise. I'm not done yet." I shifted on the bed.
"Take care of them. It's a good family. It will be."

He leaned in close and kissed my forehead. "Always,
little bird."

He stood to leave, stopping to look back when he reached
the doorway. Then he rapped once on the frame and was
gone. Whatever he'd spiked my drip with wore thin, and
the tendrils of nothingness pulled me back into the pillow.
I slept again.

At last, I awoke for good, and Eren was at my side, just
like he promised.

"Eren." I spoke urgently. "I'm letting you go."

"What?"

"I'm letting you go. We're not meant to be married."

"But we—"

I lifted what was left of my arm barely off the stark white
bed in an open gesture. "*I* was never meant to be married.
We never made any sense, anyway. You don't know what
I'm like. What I'm really like. But more importantly," I
touched his arm with my remaining hand, "my life was
never meant to be so precious. I can see that now." I gestured
at my forearm, which ended before my wrist. "Look at me.
Everyone can see that now."

"Charlotte, that makes no—"

"I'm not done. You said once that Isaiah is a criminal.
Well, so am I." I waited, but Eren was, at last, silent. "You

don't understand the Remnant, but I do. And I'll never stop fighting for it, for what it stands for. And I don't deserve your mother's ring, not that you were planning to give it back to me. I feel like I've been riding this split. Between my family and the rest of the world. The Remnant and Central Command. Me and everyone else. But I can't do that anymore. Believe me, it's better this way."

"Speak for yourself." Eren didn't look hurt. He leaned back, slightly, his eyes wide. As far as I could see, the only indication that he didn't like what he was hearing was the slightest push of his jaw. It was barely forward. Everything else was, as ever, solid.

"You don't know about the crimes I've committed. The people I've hurt. Everyone's in pain. So you made me into something in your mind. Something you needed at the time. But it's not real."

"Of course I was in pain. Of course I needed you! I'm not stupid, Charlotte. I know you've been to prison."

"I know you're not. But the kind of person who does the things I did—it's someone who doesn't care about the people she hurts. I have so much to make up for. I can't be divided like this. I can't keep doing everything backwards." A wracking cough shook my body, and I realized that my throat was sore. I continued, rasping. "Think about this, Eren. Think about what we're up against. An was prepared to kill a hundred thousand people just to save her Ark. Her loyalties are not divided. She could have been with Shan, but she's not. She's strong."

"Being with me doesn't make you weak, Charlotte."

"I'm not trying to copy her. I'm trying to defeat her. But *that's* what we're up against. She's single-minded. Like a machine. So that's what I have to be. Isaiah always understood this. I should have listened to him. I lost my arm for the cause, Eren. Stopping that nuke from firing. And I understand something now: *it was worth it*." I paused to cough again. "Everything makes sense now. My mother died for me, but she never wanted me to hide. I can feel her with me, Eren. All the time. And she wants me to fight."

He looked at me sadly. "The fight is over, Charlotte. All that's left is to survive until we reach Eirenea."

I had to make him understand. "This isn't over."

He held his face in his hands. "It is, Charlotte. It is over."

I reached up and took his wrist between clumsy fingers. My lips were so dry they cracked. But he let me pull his k-band to my mouth.

An Zhao was listening to us. I could feel it. So was Adam.

"It's not. Over." I took a deep breath. "The Remnant isn't over. *This isn't over*."

"Charlotte!" Eren jerked his band away. "You're going to get us killed!" He stood as though electrocuted and gave me a final, angry look before stalking out of the room.

He didn't get it. He never had.

Our race had all but died in an inferno, and those few of us who remained were falling through space toward the dream of a planet we might never see.

But my family was safe, and so was Isaiah. It was enough.

I had been asleep for too long, but I was awake now. Adam hadn't killed me. That was his first mistake.

In time, he'd make another.

"You can't keep me here forever," I whispered into the empty room. "This isn't over."

An army of the dead waged war on my mind, and I did not sleep again.

Acknowledgements

Thanks to God for loving me.

I owe debts of gratitude to Will Nolen, Morris Liddell, and Jenna Wolf I'm pretty sure I can never repay. Except to you, Will. I figure carrying your children should about cover it.

Major thanks to Natasha Bardon, Lily Cooper, Rachel Winterbottom, and all the fantastic minds at HarperVoyager UK. I am honored to work with you. Thanks to Richenda Todd for your editorial support and to my book brothers and sisters at HVUK and HVI.

My sincere thanks to Eleanor Ashfield for your brilliant comments and support, and for pointing out that dictatorial regimes don't just casually lend spaceships to rebel fighters. I loved working with you!

Thanks to Benjamin Morris for your friendship and extraordinary insight into storytelling.

I'm deeply grateful to those who have been so tremendously supportive of me during the release of The Ark, including the Book Aunts and Uncles (Alex, Courtney, Sammy, Elizabeth, Holly, Jennifer, Julie, Lauren, and Jordana.) Thanks to Lesha Grant and to my family, especially my mom and dad (HI!)

Thanks to my sweetheart and companion of many years Miley, who was a very good girl. To Taylor, my new puppy, who shows enormous promise in her housetraining efforts: welcome to the family. We're going to love each other for a very long time.

Love, love to my William, my Ava, and my Liam, and to the child I've yet to meet.

– Laura

Printed by RR Donnelley at Glasgow, UK